Maggie –
From one book
to another!
Enjoy!
Anastasia

Emerald Fire
The Winds of Fate

By

Anastasia Conklin

PublishAmerica
Baltimore

Hardcover 978-1-4560-2693-6
Softcover 978-1-4560-2694-3
PUBLISHED BY PUBLISHAMERICA, LLLP
www.publishamerica.com
Baltimore

Printed in the United States of America

Mom, dad and Nic—
Thank you for always supporting me with my writing. I know I can be a pain sometimes. Someday mom, I'll get you the flannel board so you can keep up.

Lisa and Brandy—
Thank you for being the best "sisters" I could have asked for and for putting up with my endless "does this make sense" questions.

Vixen—
You were my ears and eyes throughout this whole process. Thank you for always letting me come to you when I needed some input.

Nicole—
You are one of the greatest friends in the whole world. I love ya! There are no words for how much you have influenced me. You rock!

Also a special thanks to Steve Badgley for the most beautiful cover art I could have ever dreamed up. You are awesome!!!

"Fate is nothing but the deeds committed in a prior state of existence."
—Ralph Waldo Emerson

Prologue
Vivienne's Recollection

I was born seven hundred ninety nine years ago.

It was January the first, just after midnight in a small village out-side of Paris, France. I was truly a new baby. The world was fresh and clean, untouched by the hazards of the year previous. Nothing mattered within those few moments of the New Year, only that I was healthy and safe and eager for the warmth of my mother's nurturing bosom.

The night I was born, my mother told me, was cold and the wind was wild as it beat against the shutters of the small hovel we lived in. She told me my lusty baby wails were just as wild, as if when I was brought into this world, I was torn from another. I don't remember a lot of my childhood. How I do remember it though was it felt as if I just existed. I felt as if I never belonged in that small hovel, covered in mud with a shabby thatched roof that was replaced every spring. I knew I was meant for something more, something beyond the small village and small life I was born into.

I wasn't necessarily a terrible child, but I did give my mother a fair share of grief. I was always getting into trouble and seeking that wind that I was born into, but never able to catch. My mother used to tell me that the color of my hair reflected the wildness in my heart —red and gold, the color of flame in a hearth, when caught by the sun the licking flame seeming to ignite the air around me. She said even my green eyes were like licks of the flame. My temper seemed to match the color of my hair and I remember the children in the village teasing me relentlessly that I was a witch. Even as I grew older, they still teased me, though instead of ignoring them, I would sneer or bare my teeth and hiss. It was my way of embracing the witch inside me. That was when I began to look into what is now known as the old ways. Back then they were just, the Ways.

It was a common custom when I was a child for a young girl, between the ages of eleven and fourteen to be fostered to a different family in the next village to learn a trade or to learn the old ways of magic. In our little village, my mother was the mid-wife, though I remember some villagers calling her a seer and a priestess —such old terms for being a witch. So I couldn't be fostered to my own mother. Back then the new religion had spread up into our village rather quickly. The older members of our village, my mother included, still clung to our "old ways." But because of who my mother was, many of the villagers followed my mother blindly, even though the new priests said not to. I look back now on the dying custom and I am glad that I was able to partake and learn something more about the world around me; and those "old" ways seemed to compliment what Fate had in store for me.

The "old" ways, as many of the older members of the village called them, were forgotten long ago, or so I was told. As the new religion spread up from Rome and through Europe, our ways seemed to fall to the wayside —just as the priests said that they would. But I remember finding them rather easily as if somehow, they were just waiting for me. It didn't take my mother long to find someone to teach me what I yearned to know either, or more importantly, what I was destined to know. It was as if Fate were once again holding her hand out and giving me what I needed in order to fulfill her plan of my life.

I met André when I was twelve.

André was a powerful man. Some called him a sorcerer; some even called him an ancient elder of knowledge. But to me he was just my savior, my confidant. He took me away from a world that was unkind and cold and showed me warmth and gratitude. He started each lesson every morning as the sun came up over the trees in the valley where his cottage rested. He would conjure potions and showed me how to change my appearance by simply waving my hand in front of the person I was with. He formed my mind and my skills as if they were clay, so that after a few short years, I had become a rather powerful woman. Each lesson was dedicated to a different element —earth, air, fire and water. André always told me that my power would lie with my temper, so it was easy enough to become the element of fire. As I got older, simply walking into the room would cause candles to ignite or dance higher than they normally would.

André taught me many things while I was his student. While most of what he taught me related to magic, he taught me of what it meant to be a strong and powerful woman and to use that simple fact to my advantage. Looking back, that is one lesson I have kept close to my heart. I remember him telling me about a world that was behind our own, an Otherworld. Within this world, magic was more potent and more widely used than in our realm. He always told me that whenever I needed to escape from this realm, even from the everyday trials and tribulations, I could enter the Otherworld and be safe. Though I now have the knowledge to enter The Otherworld, I never have.

André was a beautiful man, old enough to be my father, but a beautiful man nonetheless. He stood tall with broad shoulders on a lean frame. He was always clad in long dark robes and buckskin breeches. I never saw him without one of his robes on; it was as if they were his skin. Just below his chin on the left side where the robe clasped, was an emerald broach encased in an old iron setting with a Fleur de Lis at the top. The emerald was large and flawless and I admired it greatly over the years I was with him. It was held in place by a rope of gold that was attached to the other side of the dark robe. His honey brown eyes showed bright beneath heavy eyebrows and held wisdom beyond his physical age. His brown hair was shaggy, only coming to brush his shoulders. Sometimes, when he was being playful during our studies, his graying hair would fall into his eyes, causing him to look like a young man again, though I never saw him as a young man.

"Vivienne, pay attention!"

He would yell at me his thick, heavy voice with an accent that seemed to be older than he. When I would stare at him, mesmerized by his mere presence I would blush and he would laugh and hug me and tell me that someday my daydreaming would get me into trouble. But I was always getting into trouble, regardless of my constant daydreaming.

Looking back on my lifetimes, I miss André. I miss him beyond all recognition and comprehension. He was my everything for the four short years I was with him. I miss his laughter and I miss the way he could make the most complex spell into something that was extraordinarily simple —something in my almost eight hundred years that I have yet to accomplish. André always made it look so easy.

I studied with André until I was seventeen. That year, on my birthday, my mother gave me an ultimatum and told me it was time to find a husband, a daunting task that I rebelled against at every chance and with every fiber of my being. All I wanted was to hone my magic and become a powerful priestess. More importantly, I didn't want to have to leave André. With him I felt safe and could remain as the ever-watchful student that studied his every move. I didn't want to become a wife or mother yet. I didn't want to take off the student robes unless it was to put on the robes of priestess. I didn't want to face the fact that I had grown up —without André around.

As I got older, I was told that I had become beautiful, though I didn't see how. My hair was bone straight, falling almost past my hips, always braided away from my face —as was custom for a student. My eyes had not lost their wild look and I still sought after that wind I was born into. André told me that my eyes were my best feature and even if I lost my beauty when I grew old, I would always have the vibrancy of my eyes. I had grown tall, taller than most boys in the village, standing almost to the shoulder of my white mare. My body had blossomed into what I was told was not suitable for a proper woman. Good thing I wasn't a proper woman.

My breasts were too large in my opinion and I always kept them hidden beneath a bodice that crushed them to my chest. My stomach was flat, though I had wide hips that made dresses cling to the curve of my waist and fall off my hips. My long legs were kept hidden beneath yards of fabric and my delicate feet were hidden in boots that laced up to my knees. In the winter I would wear a pair of buckskin breeches and fur lined boots that I had made my first winter with André.

Remembering those dresses is difficult after almost eight hundred years and sometimes, I wish for those simple frocks, instead of the modern clothes designed for women much thinner and younger than I. But still, we tend to cling to the ways of our youth, no matter how long ago they truly were, even if it is just for a simple dress.

The year my mother told me I needed to find a husband was the same year André was taken from me. I don't quite remember how or why, I just remember that one day he was there and the next he wasn't. It was as if he had left the realm, riding away on the wind that I was never able to catch. I remember that I cried for him for days after he vanished. He had taught me what I needed to know and I guess he thought it was enough. I wanted to hate him for leaving me like that, but my mother told me it was better that I just remember him as a good man and a good teacher. Looking back on it, I wonder why my mother ever gave me any advice at all when it came to André. I don't remember her ever liking him.

I remember going to the cottage after a day at the market with him, only to find it burned to the ground. We had argued at the market and I ran off without him in a huff of teenage annoyance. When I went to look for him later, he was nowhere to be found. Where the cottage once stood, there was nothing left to acknowledge the existence of the man that meant more to me than the air I breathed or even the fire I wielded.

It was that day, while I was lost at the market, that I met Vincent.

Vincent was a striking man and so much different than André. His features were dark with perfectly manicured black hair and piercing blue eyes that were almost black when he turned his head a certain way. There was something about Vincent that made me shiver with pleasure and fear. He looked at me and held my gaze as if he had forever to do so, and that thought, scared me to death. His skin was sun kissed and through innocent eyes and having a naïve brain, I wondered if it were warm to the touch. He was tall with broad shoulders and a solid muscular frame, yet he was elegant. When my mother approved of him from merely glancing at him, I remember blushing and he grinned, knowing he had caught my eye. And I am sure; looking back on it, that it didn't hurt that he was Duke. My future was set and my mother was beyond proud.

We were wed that fall, just as the trees turned the forest ablaze with color. I remember being very nervous that morning. Having not slept the night before, I was sure I looked horrid. My mother told me it was normal to be nervous, especially because I was marrying such a handsome man. But in my head, I was nervous because I wasn't with André and I didn't know where he was. The ceremony was small in an elegant church just outside of Paris. I wore a simple white dress with long sleeves and a scoop neck that revealed the rounded top of my breasts. The dress clung to my hips and fell to pool around my feet. For one day, I promised I wouldn't wear my boots. My mother made me white slippers; I still have them tucked away in a box beneath my bed.

Vincent was handsome, but he always was. Whenever I looked at him, even after years of marriage, he seemed to wake up looking beautiful. Perhaps that's why I felt inadequate beside him; I was his simple country girl, but somehow he wanted me and I decided to just let fate have her way with this one. I would owe her one later.

After the brief ceremony a kiss that left me breathless, Vincent and I climbed into his carriage and rode to his estate. For the entire ride my eyes wouldn't leave my finger and the Fleur de Lis ring with diamonds and sapphires that adorned it. Coming to the grand palace I realized, or more so felt as if I had traded in one prison for another. Yes, the hovel was simple, but it was familiar —even in André's cottage I didn't feel trapped. To me that was more my home that my mother's hovel ever was. But this new place was large and cold and made of stone, nothing like the warmth of André's home. It frightened me more than the inevitable pain that the marriage night was about to bring me. I remember feeling as if I were floating when we entered the château. Dozens of staff members greeted me with smiles and light voices of "welcome milady." To this day I never liked that term. I was no one's lady but my own.

Vincent led me up the grand staircase and down several hallways before coming to the grand bedchamber. I remember holding my breath as he scooped me into his arms and carried me into the large room. The room was decorated with pieces of hard oak furniture and heavy burgundy curtains hung at the full-length windows, blocking out the sunset. It was that evening that I became a different woman. I was seventeen and naïve and thought that I had married the most wonderfully uncomplicated man in the world. That was until he told me how old he truly was. And at seventeen the number of three hundred forty two scared the hell out of me.

"You are how old?!" I roared at him, staring at him with huge green eyes, pulsing with anger, confusion and fear.

Vincent sat beside me, calm and collected as usual and he again told me that he was three hundred forty two years old. Again, I roared at him, demanding he tell me how. He told me it was magic and if I wanted to, I could become immortal as well. Millions of thoughts flew through my head. I was trying to remember if André ever told me about immortals, but suddenly my brain was ceasing to work.

Vincent smiled at me, melting my anger away, as he always did. He told me the story of how he became immortal. It wasn't through some kind of biting, no; it was through a special brand of magic that was his own. In those days, vampires were the furthest things from our minds. And now knowing some vampires, I laugh at the fact I thought Vincent was one. Vampires were cold and colorless and Vincent was warm and inviting. Though vampires were seductive and sensual like Vincent, vampires didn't have feelings like humans. They only wanted what was right in front of them and didn't want to pursue anything. Vincent pursued everything he wanted, including me. The thought that Vincent was immortal through a simple kind of magic just drove me crazy.

So he showed me the potion that he took every day with his meals. A small vile filled with a sweet smelling tincture that he mixed with his tea. He was happy to look thirty forever, I just didn't want to stay seventeen, and it seemed too childish and selfish to remain that young. I wanted more wisdom, more knowledge before I committed myself to a certain age for all eternity. I just wanted to wait until I was a bit older. So on the day of my twenty-fifth year, I took the potion and to this day, I remain twenty-five.

Still, that's not where my life got interesting; Vincent and I were happily married and remained so for a few hundred years. Even our children became immortal when they decided they were old enough. My twin girls, Adrienne, with her raven black hair and Audrey, with her strawberry blonde locks, became immortal when they were twenty-nine. And my son, the strapping boy with hair as dark as midnight and whom I named after my mentor, André, became immortal when he was eighteen. Even now it makes me laugh to think my son will forever be a teenager.

My life became most interesting on the eve of my six hundredth birthday. I had just kissed Vincent and wished him a happy New Year when he handed me a small black velvet box. Over the years I had received many gifts from my husband, all wonderful and precious, but this gift was different. For when I opened the box, shining brilliantly against the velvet interior was a single emerald pendant attached to a silver chain. The emerald was the same color as my eyes and was just as big. I stared at the shimmering jewel, somehow drawn to the beauty of it. He fastened the necklace around my neck, the pendant resting at the swell of my breasts. The stone was cool against my skin, yet warmed instantly to my presence. It was as if it were meant to be around my neck.

From the moment the pendant was hung around the thin, graceful column of my neck, I felt powerful. I had always had magic in me, but with that jewel resting upon my chest, more importantly, upon my heart, I felt as if I could take on the world. I felt empowered and strong. Vincent and I had moved through the ages with our children, always a step ahead of the world, but now I felt as if I could become part of the world, not just someone that looked on from the sidelines.

As the years went on, I rarely took the necklace off or even let it out of my sight. With Vincent in my life I felt as though I had caught my wind and the necklace was my fire. It was the one thing other than my family that kept me warm. I needed that feeling in my life and no matter what I would keep it. I would make sure that I would remain powerful for all my days, no matter how much it changed me.

I guess Vincent felt the change in me and knew that one day the power from the necklace would consume me. So one night, as I slept, he slipped from my embrace and stole the precious stone from me. That was the day he slipped from my life as well. He left me with a note that said he would return someday when he felt it was safe to give me back my wind. I remember waking up and feeling empty and angry. Who did he think he was to take something that was rightfully mine?

Sure, I had my children and I had my fire, but the world seemed less bright without Vincent. Since that day almost one hundred seventy five years ago, I have felt like a flightless bird, unable to glide on the wind. The love of my life had stolen into the night, leaving me to fend for myself.

Now, my eight hundredth birthday looms near and I feel a tugging on my heart that not only Vincent is coming to me again, but also an unspeakable force that I dare not think about. Vincent will not just to return my keepsake, but also to return my heart. I thought I saw him once in 1955. He watched me from the shadows as I entered the town-house in Paris. But as I turned to grin at him and welcome him home, he had ridden the wind away from me again.

I have traveled the world over, searching and waiting for him to return to me. Now I have come to New York City, my children close by as always; Audrey and Adrienne in Long Island and André in the city. I sit in the apartment above my bookstore and gaze out at the busy streets of the city, longing for the day when I have Vincent beside me watching the world turn. I remember living in the castle in France, sitting in the parlor room in matching wingback chairs, staring at each other as if there were something new to discover about each other even after centuries of marriage. We loved passionately with and without words, facing the challenges the world threw at us and we threw them right back.

I again feel Vincent searching for me and I feel the urging to return to Paris. But for now, I remain in America, the young country that has not seen the wonder I have in my lifetimes. Vincent was the one thing that kept me going for so long; I wonder when I do see him again what I shall do to him. Run to him and love him as if he had just been gone but a day, or make him pay in some way for what he's done to me. I guess I'll just have to wait and find out. Let fate work her magic yet again.

I'm good at waiting; what else is there for me to do?

Chapter One
Mourning

"Come on Vinny! We're going to be late and I really don't want to miss the start of the game. It's the World Series."

Vincent ducked his head out of the cab and sighed at Steve. Steve was a tall, young man, young to Vincent, no older than thirty-two. His lean frame was clad in jeans, a t-shirt with a fat Buddha on it that read, "I have the body of a god" and a brown leather jacket that had seen better days. Steve's brown hair was short, shaved close to his skin and his honey brown eyes held wisdom beyond his youth. Steve stared at Vincent, asking him silently if he was going to get out of the cab or just sit there for the rest of the afternoon and stare off into space. With a roll of his dark eyes and an annoyed huff, Vincent handed the cab driver the money and stepped out into the cool October rain that chilled him to his bones.

"I'm coming, hold your horses," Vincent replied, his French accent almost gone after decades of travel and years living in America. He opened the umbrella to ward off the cold Boston rain and shook his head at his friend, "The beer can wait you know."

"Yeah, yeah," Steve replied, "but the game won't. So get a move on."

Vincent nodded, "I will be right in; I'm going to have a smoke first."

Vincent stepped under the awning of the bar and closed his umbrella, clasping the button and hanging the hook on his arm. Lighting up his cigarette, he inhaled deeply and grinned. Though he complained out loud of the cold rain, he secretly loved it. It reminded him of long ago when he was in France.

Over the years Vincent hadn't really changed his appearance, though as the fashions changed, he did cut and mold his raven black hair to the current styles. In recent years he cut it short and V'd at the back of his neck, disappearing into the folded collar of his white button down shirt. Slicking it back away from his onyx colored eyes, a few stray stands would sometimes fall to make him appear to be hiding a secret from the world. With a smirk, Vincent took another puff at the cigarette; he was hiding a secret —a big one too.

Vincent hung around outside for a few minutes, finishing up his cigarette and flinging the butt toward the street. Breathing in a deep encouraging breath, he tugged at the lapel of his long black trench coat, adjusting it on his frame. He slowly walked into the dimly lit bar and found Steve already watching the game. Vincent rolled his eyes, wondering why every Sunday he let Steve talk him into coming down to O'Malley's Pub with him. He supposed it was because every other day of the week he stayed hidden in his enormous apartment painting and writing songs.

"Vinny, you are seriously bumming me out with looks like that," Steve replied, sliding him the beer he had already ordered. "Are you still mad at me for dragging you out today?"

"A little," Vincent replied, "I was in the middle of a new song, you know. I had a rhythm going."

Steve shook his head and sipped at his beer. With a roll of his eyes, he huffed, "No, you've been working on the same damn song since the day I met you five years ago. There are only so many ways you can say you're lonely buddy. What I need to do is get you a girl."

Vincent shook his head and held up his hands in gesture, "No. I told you, no more set-ups. The last girl you set me up with turned out to be a stalker."

"Not my fault she thought you were pretty," Steve replied with a laugh and punched Vincent playfully on the upper arm, "and it's also not my fault that you slept with her after two dates."

"Three," Vincent replied hastily showing him his hand with three fingers up, "it was three dates and I didn't sleep with her. She wished that we had, but I told her the connection between us was strong, just not strong enough. I just didn't realize that she wouldn't take no for an answer."

Steve laughed and sipped at his beer, "You just need to stop giving off that vibe that says you're lonely and heartbroken. It's been how long since that girl left you?"

Vincent brought the beer mug up to his mouth and muttered, "One hundred and seventy five years."

"What?" Steve asked, not really paying attention and staring at the television.

"Nothing," Vincent replied and finished off the beer. He handed Steve a ten and stood up, "I'm going to head back to the apartment. Call me this week okay?"

"Dude, you're leaving now?" Steve asked, pocketing the money.

Vincent rolled his eyes when Steve called him a "dude". He hated being called "dude." With a sigh, he nodded his head toward his friend, "Yes, I'm going now. I told you, I have a song to work on."

"Whatever," Steve replied and nodded to the bar tender for a second drink, "I will call you this week. Just make sure that your phone's turned on okay?"

Vincent nodded and waved goodbye to Steve and the bartender. Once again, he stepped out into the rain and smiled, breathing in deep the cool autumn air. Vincent always thought that the air in Boston wasn't much different than the air in France. He just had to remember sometimes that he wasn't in France anymore; he wasn't in the place that was more familiar to him than anywhere he had ever traveled.

As he started walking down the sidewalk away from the bar, he began to think of why he had come to Boston. It had been 1955 and he had just left France and decided that America was his next journey. Leaving his home was the most painful thing he had ever done, but he had really left his home years before that. Thinking of that reason always gave him a headache, probably why he could never finish her song. It was too difficult to think about.

Boston in the 1950's was wonderful. It was alive and full of youthful rebellion. He first decided to try banking, working as a teller close to where he lived. He never needed to have a job, he was more than set for the rest of his lifetimes, but he decided to blend into the world by working a job and not looking as if he was some hermit all alone living in the big city. When time was no longer on his side and because he never aged, he moved on, working at various places throughout his time in Boston until he had found the perfect apartment and decided to live in seclusion with his paintings and music. He seemed to fade into the culture of the big city and that was more than fine with Vincent.

Vincent met Steve five years ago on one of his rare outings at the bar. Steve was eager to have a new friend for he was fresh out of graduate school and looking to start his career in broadcasting. Vincent didn't know why he hung out with Steve, but it was refreshing for a time. To actually have someone to talk to other than the walls was something he longed for and searched for. Vincent was an old man, and all he truly wanted was the warmth of his home, but he couldn't go back just yet. He didn't even know if there was a home for him to go back to. All that was back in France was a castle filled with furniture covered by dusty white sheets, forgotten long ago from what seemed like another lifetime.

What Steve didn't understand was Vincent's need for privacy. Vincent would one day have to leave and any attachments to the mortal realm were messy. Attachments meant that a life had been established, and that was the worst mistake that Vincent could make until he was once again at home in France with Vivienne and his children.

Turning another corner, Vincent eyed his high rise. He dropped the umbrella and folded it up, clasping the piece of fabric and fastening the button just in time for the sun to peek out from behind ominous clouds.

"Good afternoon, Mr. LaTorche," the doorman said softly when he saw Vincent. Stepping out of the shelter of the doorway, he tilted his head, lifted the black hat off his head and smiled, "Seems as if the rain has stopped."

Vincent nodded and returned the doorman's smile, "It would seem so, Carlos. How are you today?"

Carlos shrugged, his coal black hair falling into his youthful eyes, "I'm doing all right today Mr. LaTorc. I don't have anything to complain about."

"Well that's good," Vincent replied and headed through the doors, his back to Carlos. Tossing a look over his shoulder, Vincent smirked, "Plus, who would listen, Carlos?"

"Very true, sir," Carlos laughed in reply, "Have a good evening sir."

Vincent entered the posh apartment building and silently walked through the lobby, decorated in red and gold and ignored the passersby whose gaze seemed to follow him wherever he went. Not paying attention to any of the details, he made his way to the elevator and rode it to the top floor. As the doors opened to his immaculately neat apartment, he pulled his cell phone out of his pocket and turned it on vibrate, making sure to not ignore Steve's statement of making sure that it was turned on.

"It's still on buddy," Vincent said to himself, tossing the phone onto the table near the door, "Just not near me."

Taking off his coat, he hung it on the standing coat rack by the door and scanned the room. It was sparsely decorated with simple yet necessary items including a couch, glass coffee table and a few lamps. By the window near the kitchen were his easel and art supplies. The most elaborate piece in his entire apartment, apart from his plush bed, was the grand piano by large, floor to ceiling balcony doors. Atop the piano was a single silver three-pronged candelabra with three white candles melted almost to the holders.

Along with the candelabra were various picture frames from the past one hundred years. The picture frames were photographs of the various places he had traveled, including Rome, The Grand Canyon, Tibet, Russia and China. Of all the pictures he had, he longed for those of his children and his wife the most. The only portrait he had of Vivienne was one he had commissioned when they were still married, just before he stole away from her. With a huff, he shook his head, remembering that it was a lifetime ago since he'd seen her last.

Sitting at the piano his long elegant fingers began to play a melody that was all too familiar to his ears. It was Vivienne's song, a hauntingly sweet melody that flowed out of his body as if it was meant to be heard. As he continued to play, he closed his eyes, remembering the last night he had held Vivienne in his arms.

Without giving it a second thought, he starting putting words to the melody, words that he recalled from a distant memory. Softly, his voice floated above the smooth sound of his fingers playing along the ivory keys, *"Visions of delight revealing, breathes a pure and wondrous feeling, from dusk till morning light."*

That night haunted him and to this day he still regretted that he had left her, but it was necessary if he wanted to save her from the harm that the emerald would have caused. He never believed the nonsense that the emerald was cursed and was only waiting to find the chosen woman —the chosen witch —that would bring forth the power again. Vincent was so frightened that the emerald's power would consume Vivienne that he stole away from her. He didn't want the emerald's power to taint the beauty that was Vivienne.

Even now, after one hundred seventy five years, he could still see her face as vividly as the last night he had last gazed upon her. Her skin was like porcelain and milky white against the dark sheets of their bed; she looked like an angel, a goddess disguised in human form just for him. He wasn't sure if he deserved a beauty such as Vivienne.

He had pursued her since she was sixteen, but knew that if he interrupted her teachings that he would regret it. Even though he hadn't believed in much magic before he knew Vivienne, he knew now that the world needed her magic. He realized, being apart from her, that *he* needed her magic. So now, he only regretted not having her in his life, for leaving her alone to wonder if he would ever return to her.

But he never truly left her alone. He was always there in some way, watching her, making sure she was safe from harm. Over the years, he had learned to be a part of her life without being in her life, even if he were but a shadow in her doorway. But he hadn't shadowed her doorway since that day in 1955. Seeing her there, alone but safe, made him want to keep her that way. Even though she looked as if she were sad, she was safe from the harm of the emerald and that was all he had ever wanted. So that day, he decided to leave France. Leaving the castle in the hills, he boarded it up, paid the family that took care of it and left for America, knowing that one-day he would have to come back and find her again. He just didn't know how long that would be, or how to find her when he needed to. But now, he felt the day when he would have to return to her was looming closer. And more than anything he wanted to finish her song in time.

***

Vincent slowly opened his eyes. It was dark in his apartment; the only light was that of the moon casting silvery shadows into his bedroom. He turned his gaze toward the balcony doors and folded his arms behind his head, stretching his torso and causing the lines of muscle in his abdomen to tighten. A playful smile tugged at his lips as he laid on his king sized bed, shirtless and motionless, silently watching the moon.

He remembered nights like this when he was younger. A laugh escaped his full lips at that thought. He hadn't been younger in more than a millennia. He was now 1,142 years old; no, he wasn't young anymore. But nonetheless, he remembered nights where the soft glow of the moon was the only light needed or wanted. The moonlight caressed him like a lover's hot passionate touch on sated skin, keeping him in her embrace and warming him. He missed those nights when he held Vivienne, where the moon was their only guide, as they loved each other.

With a sigh, he unfolded his arms from behind his head and reached over to the bedside table. Opening the drawer, he pulled out the small black velvet box that contained the emerald he had taken from Vivienne. He always kept the emerald close to him, not ever letting it out of his sight for one hundred seventy five years. He opened the box and gazed at the jewel, instantly remembering the color and the vibrancy of Vivienne's eyes. That's why Vincent had chosen the emerald to begin with. It was the same color as her eyes.

There was an old story about the emerald; one that Vincent didn't put much stock into believing. The story told that the emerald's power sat dormant until the day it found the chosen woman, the chosen witch. The emerald's power, though, was a mystery; no one really knew if the power was light or dark. He remembered Vivienne telling him of the emerald her teacher, André, had worn. The day he met Vivienne, when they had gone back to the cottage to see it burned to the ground, he pocketed the precious stone.

Perhaps, because André had worn it was the reason he had given it to her. Even though he loathed the man, he knew that Vivienne had a place in her heart for him. So he gave her the stone, hoping that the gesture would make her smile. And it had, making her even more beautiful that he had ever seen her. Most people only told of the beauty the stone possessed. And the witch that wielded that power would match it in beauty; and in Vincent's opinion, Vivienne's beauty out shined the stone.

As the moonlight glistened off the jewel, he saw something shimmer from inside the gem. From deep within, the dark outline of a woman began to take form. Focusing his keen eyesight, he sat up and watched as the image began to blossom into something more familiar. At first, the woman in the stone was just a black profile, and then as it began to move and take shape within the stone, he saw that the woman's hair started to flow down her back and blow in some invisible wind. He couldn't make out an eye color, but his gaze was drawn to the clothes that had sprouted from nothingness. Her skin began to take on a peach-pink shade beneath the modern clothes. She wore a black waist length leather jacket with jeans and a red top. Upon her small delicate feet were black flats and upon her shoulder was a bright purple bag that looked as if it were filled to the brim with books, a datebook and at least two aluminum water bottles.

Vincent watched this woman inside the emerald. She was familiar, yet distant. She was someone special, yet he knew it couldn't be Vivienne; her hair wasn't the same flame red that he remembered. This woman's hair was dark and brushed back away from her porcelain face. Yet her features were very much like his memory of Vivienne; she was just different. Her face was cold and emotionless as if she had been carrying a great burden with her. And then, all of a sudden, the image changed and he saw her walking along a busy sidewalk. The purple purse hung on her left shoulder and she walked at a slow pace, as if she had all the time in the world. This was when he saw her hair, peeking out from beneath a brunette wig. He knew that it was Vivienne in the stone.

Vincent quickly got out of bed, his black boxer-briefs hugging his slim hips and walked to the balcony doors to look at the emerald in the moonlight. He felt his lips tug up into a genuine smile, something he hadn't felt in years. He laughed and let his gaze fall upon the full moon hanging in the velvet black sky.

"Thank you," he whispered.

Turning his gaze back to the stone, he saw that Vivienne's image was gone and the stone was once again empty. Vincent felt a tug of sadness in his heart, knowing that he had been able to see her and she was taken away from him. Closing the black box, he placed it once again in the bedside table drawer. He would have to be content with the mere fact he was able to gaze upon her, even if it were through magic. Vincent sat on the edge of the bed, his long bare legs hanging over the edge and held his head in his hands, once again feeling the melancholy he'd felt for more than a century.

"Someday I will see you again," he whispered to himself. He lifted his head and gazed at the moon. With a soft smile of acceptance, he asked the moon a simple question; "Will you watch over her and keep her safe for me?"

He waited for a moment, his gaze never falling from the large silver sphere in the sky, as if he were going to get a response. When a cloud covered the moon, hiding her from his dark gaze, he sighed and fell back against the plush mattress of his king sized bed. As his eyes drifted closed, he didn't hear the sound of his cell phone buzzing on the table in the other room. And it wasn't until the next morning, when he checked the cryptic voicemail that he knew it was time to find her.

It was time to start the journey that would take him to hell and back, but it needed to be done, for his sake and for hers.

***

"I need to get on the train," Vincent demanded to the clerk behind the window.

The woman, plain brown hair tied back away from her round face, eyed Vincent from behind thick black-rimmed glasses and shook her head, "I told you already sir. The train to New York is already booked. If you wish to wait for the next available train, one leaves in the morning at ten o'clock."

Vincent growled and picked up his suitcase, "No, thank you."

Turning quickly, he brushed shoulders with the man behind him. Sighing, he apologized to the man and quickly made his way out of the station. Standing outside in the cold October rain, he once again growled, remembering the voicemail he had received not two hours before. He glanced at his watch, something he had not been in the habit of doing. He only started keeping a watch upon his wrist after pocket watches fell out of fashion. When you had forever, what was time? But now, when he needed to get to New York, time was everything and unfortunately he was losing it quickly.

Pulling out his cell phone, he opened it and dialed the voicemail number, needing to hear the message one more time. After entering his PIN, a soft musical voice filled his ears.

"I hope I have the right number," the girl on the message said. Her voice was delicate, yet a bit frantic, with a slight French accent that made him long for his home, *"I'm looking for Vincent LaTorche. I have information about Vivienne and her whereabouts. I hope this is something you are interested in, and that you come looking for her soon. She is not in danger yet, but if you delay even a day, then I fear that I cannot promise that she will be safe for long. I have kept watch over her for a very long time, but I am afraid that I do not have the*

26

power to keep her safe any longer." The voice paused and Vincent could hear heavy breathing on the other end, *"She is in New York City. I can only tell you to start looking in the Village. She would kill me if I told you exactly where to find her. Come quickly...Father."*

Father, that word he had not heard in a very long time. He wondered which of his daughters it was that had left him that message. Audrey? Adrienne? He couldn't tell; he hadn't heard their voices in over a century. Suddenly he longed to see his children's faces and longed to hear their voices as much as he longed to hear Vivienne's, which made him all the more anxious to get to New York and figure out what was wrong and get to the bottom of the mystery he was suddenly thrust into.

Wrestling with his conscience, he pulled out his cell phone again and dialed the number he really didn't want to dial, but at the moment he didn't have a choice.

"Steve?"

"Hey buddy," Steve replied on the other end, "where are you? I just stopped by your building and the doorman said you were gone for a while."

Vincent sighed, "Well I haven't left yet. That's why I'm calling; I was wondering if you could do me a favor."

"Anything," Steve replied, "Just name it."

"Well," Vincent began, "I need to get to New York City and all the trains are booked and you know my fear of flying. I was wondering if you'd let me borrow your car."

Steve laughed; "You want to borrow my car? Why don't you just rent one?"

"I thought of it, but I really don't want to take more time to get one," he replied, "If you don't want me to borrow it then let me know. I'll figure something else out. I just really need to get to New York."

Steve sighed, "What is in New York and why do you have to get there in such a damn hurry?"

"Steve, this really isn't any of your business," Vincent replied starting to get a bit annoyed, "Look, never mind. I'll figure something else out."

Vincent closed his phone then, stopping the conversation with his friend. As he placed the phone back in his pocket, the phone rang. Vincent picked it up and saw the text message Steve had sent. *"Where r u? I'll pick u up."*

Vincent smiled and replied quickly to the message, telling him where he was. An hour later, Steve pulled up in his classic black GTO. Vincent always thought this car was a bit too flashy for a guy like Steve, but in some cases it suited him very well.

"Thanks again, Steve," Vincent said softly, placing his suitcase in the backseat.

Steve grinned, "No problem. But just remember, I'm your road trip buddy right now. Two bachelors on their way to the city in search of what are we in search of?"

Vincent sighed and looked out the window, "You know that girl I told you about, the woman that I write all those songs for, the one that has my heart?"

"Yeah," Steve replied, pulling out into traffic, "The girl that left you heartbroken and sappy."

Vincent rolled his eyes and nodded, "Sure, if you want to think of it that way. You know," he said after a few moments pause, "I was the one that left her."

Steve turned onto the highway that led out of the city and laughed, "Really? You're always moping about; I just assumed she was the one that took off."

"I know," he replied, "there are a lot of things that you don't know about me Steve. And I thank you for just getting up and going with me, and not asking a lot of questions."

"Oh I will ask questions," Steve said with a laugh. When Vincent quickly turned his head toward him and glared, Steve shook his head and held up one hand in defense, "but don't worry. I'll respect your privacy and refrain for now. Just remember, if you want to talk about it, just let me know. It is a long ride after all."

Vincent sighed again and turned his head to gaze out the window, "I know. Thank you. But just step on it, I don't have much time to waste."

Steve flashed a grin and stepped on the gas. Hearing the engine roar, he laughed and took the exit toward New York City.

Chapter Two
Ghosts

"Mom?"

I look up to see my daughter, Adrienne, standing in the doorway to my small new-age bookstore. I grin and set down the book I am looking at and brush back the plain short brown hair that hides the vibrancy of my long red tresses. I hold out my arms to my beautiful daughter with raven black hair and sparkling blue eyes and I hug her tightly to me, "Hello my dear. What brings you down here?"

In Adrienne's arms is a box with a couple loaves of baguette bread sticking out of the top. Shrugging her shoulders, she smiles, "I decided that it was time to come see you again. I haven't been to the city in almost a decade Mom. So I brought some lunch."

A smile crosses my lips at the thought of her bringing me lunch. She hasn't brought me lunch since we lived in the town house in Paris. I watch my daughter as she speaks to me; her long arms and torso are covered in a blue cashmere sweater, a black vest buttoned across her flat stomach, skinny jeans on her long, lean legs and a pair of black flats on her delicate feet. Shaking my head, I smile at her and turn back to my pile of books, "I know you haven't been here in a decade. The only one of you I see any more is André, and even that is only once a month. Even Audrey is too busy to come see me anymore."

"No," Adrienne replies to me, shaking her head and following me through the forest green curtain to the back of the store. She sets down the box and pulls out the bread, condiments and lunch meat, "Audrey just doesn't know how to be around you when you're sad. And from what she tells me, you've been pretty sad lately."

I look up at her then; feeling my green eyes pulsing a bit with annoyance. Lowering my gaze, I pick up a loaf of bread and rip off a piece, "What makes you think I've been sad?"

Adrienne cocks a sleek dark eyebrow at me and laughs, "C'mon mom, you know better than any of us that you've been sad. We all know what's coming up. You get like this every year before your birthday. You are anticipating Dad coming back so badly, that we really don't know how to be around you. We know it, but you don't know if he is or not."

"Adrienne." All I can do is say her name I am so mad at her. I can't believe she would even bring it up, and so close to the time when I knew that he would come back for me. I toss the bread back onto the table and walk back to the front of the bookstore.

"Mom," Adrienne says softly, her eyes soft and apologetic. She follows me, quick on my heels and places her right hand in mine, her long slender fingers with unpainted nails and adorned only with a single ring —its twin on Audrey —silver Fleur de Lis on her middle finger that was given to her by her father centuries ago, "I'm sorry. I, I know you're sensitive about Dad, but…"

"Stop," I tell her, holding up my other hand and shake my head. Placing my hand atop hers, I sigh, "Don't talk about your father. It's not that I don't want to hear about it, I just don't want to talk about him. Okay?"

Adrienne slips her hand from mine, and for a moment I feel emptier than I have been for the last one hundred seventy five years. She chews on her bottom lip for a moment before turning her gaze to the window and I wonder what she is thinking.

Turning back to me, Adrienne adjusts the purse on her shoulder, "Okay, fine. Look I have to go. I'll stop by again sometime soon, I promise."

I am confused for a moment and point behind me towards the curtain, "What about lunch? I thought you were going to stay with me for awhile."

"I just can't right now mom," she says, her eyes cold, "I don't want to fight with you right now and if I stay that's all we'll do. I'm staying with André, so if you need to get a hold of either of us just call him."

I nod to her and with a slightly annoyed voice I answer her, "All right. You two kids be good."

Adrienne grins at me, a sly smile that reminds me of when she and her brother and sister were children. She places her hand on the door and winks at me, a gesture that makes me smile back at her. With a nod of her head, she speaks softly, "We're always good, mother."

"Uh huh, sure you are." I laugh at my daughter and blow her a kiss.

With those words spoken, she slips from my bookstore and once again out into the cool October air. The door remains open slightly after she leaves, the noise of the city filtering into the store. Annoyed, I roll my eyes. Though I love the city and the little piece that I have here, I still can't stand the noise. So I shut myself once again into my bookstore, *Books de Magique*, hidden between the concrete and the bricks that make up the city.

It is almost Halloween, a time of year that I love. It is also the time of year when Vincent and I were married. Though I miss the smell of autumn in the country, the city is interesting and always changing. That means I can stay in one place longer. I hate having to move around as much as I do. It has been more than fifty years since I have last called a place home, and that home was France. Oh, how I long for France in the fall.

Though I have come to love my little slice of the city, I still long for the vast expanse of land we had in France. It was the pull of a different place that brought me to America, more importantly to New York. I could fade into the culture here, open my own bookshop and live my life. All I ever do is work, sleep and long for the day that Vincent walks back into my life. Over the years, I have continued to work with my magic and what André had taught me all those years ago. I continue to look for that part of me that is missing, that piece that Vincent took with him. I have feared for so long that I can only get it back when Vincent returns for me, but I have searched and searched to find that part of me without the love of my life. I need to know that I am just as strong without him, as I was with him.

Here I sit, in the bookstore that I have owned for fifteen years and I still don't look a day over twenty-five. This sometimes makes it difficult when people ask me whom the owner is. When people ask, I have to hold back my laughter, and then I tell them that I am the owner. But it's been a while since someone has asked. Perhaps that is because I've received a little reputation in our neighborhood. It is a reputation that I have received since I was a child. Witch; I roll my eyes at the word anymore. I've come to embrace the whole notion that I am something that this modern world has come up with. In my day, a witch, a woman, was respected and revered. We were not something to be trifled with and if someone dared do so, heaven help him or her when our wrath was brought down upon them.

I can't stand when I get lost within my own thoughts. The sounds of the city are still coming in through the open door and I am disgusted by the noise I hear on a daily basis. To shut myself back into my silence, I wave my hand and shut the door from where I sit behind the counter.

It's as soon as the door shuts that it opens again. The bell at the top of the old oak door jingles and immediately I let a smile tug at the corners of my lips. The sun shines through the windows just as the customer walks in the door. It's a young girl, dark hair striped with pink and blue and tied back away from her oval face. The make-up around her eyes is black and upon her lips is a red that reminds me of blood. She doesn't look much older than my son and seems to dress like many of the girls in this modern city, trying to be gothic and menacing as if the world owes them something more than the black clothes upon their back.

"Hello," I say to her, "May I help you?"

Her eyes focus on me for a moment; they're green which surprises me. With the fierce look in her eyes, she reminds me of someone I met long ago. Someone I saw once before André left me.

She mutters something inaudible, and turns toward a section of books on crystals. I laugh to myself and sit back on the stool behind the counter, adjusting the green skirt about my knees and crossing my legs. When she looks back up at me, I smile again and look at her questioningly, "Did you find something?"

She shakes her head at me, "I just needed to come in and see you."

"See me?" I laugh slightly, my French accent coming out a bit; something that has not happened in almost forty years, "Why do you want to see me?"

"Well aren't you a witch?"

Again, I laugh at the word and nod, "I guess in a way I am. What makes you ask?"

She looks at me oddly. Coming slowly toward me, she stops every few feet to look at what books lay out on the shelves. Her soft voice barely meets my ears as she speaks and walks, "Well, I wanted to know if you could teach me."

"Teach you?" I am dumbfounded by her admission. Here is this girl, no older than my son, who I don't know, asking me to teach her magic. "Well my dear, I have nothing to teach."

By now, she is close to the counter where I still sit, cool and collected. It's when I tell her that I have nothing to teach that a sudden pain of guilt hits my gut and her eyes blaze with a sudden annoyance that can only be held within the eyes of a teenager. At that moment, I almost hoped that I never gave my mother that look. If I had, it must have destroyed her, for that was what this girl's look is going to me.

"I just want to know what you know," she admitted to me.

I can't help but roll my eyes at this girl, which I'm sure doesn't help the annoyance she is exuding, "You don't know me, nor do I know you. Why did you come to me?"

She stops walking when I ask the question and her eyes are soft again. She now stands on the other side of the glass counter and her black tipped fingernails tap the clean, clear glass, "Well I met this guy a few weeks ago and we had a really awesome conversation. We talked about life and magic and he told me all these wonderful stories as if he had actually been there."

I hear the wonder in her voice and laugh to myself. I am going to kill my son.

"Well, he told me so much that it sparked my interest and this is the only magic-type bookshop that's in this neighborhood," she adds after a few moments. She is now leaning her elbows on my clean glass, but I don't stop her. Instead, I let her continue with her story, "So I figured, since this shop has been here forever and you never seem to age or look anything less than perfect, I figured you are a witch."

This time I don't control my laughter, "Perfect? What was the name of this gentleman you met?"

"Gentleman? You even speak like him," she says to me, her voice still full of wonder. "Well anyway his name is André. It even sounds exotic."

I am really going to kill him. He used his real name.

"What is your name?" I ask her, my fingers itching to get to my son.

"Gabriella. Gabby," she adds after a moment's pause.

I smile softly; it was a pretty name for such a harsh looking girl. I would never have guessed she would have such a sweet sounding name.

"I'm Vi," I don't have the heart to give her my real name.

She grins at me oddly. I don't know why and for a moment, I really wish I knew how to read minds.

"So Vi, are you going to teach me or not?"

I shake my head at her, "I told you, I have nothing to teach. I am simply the owner of a bookshop. I am not a witch, my dear."

The light in her eyes fade and she pulls herself up from the counter, no longer leaning on my clean glass. Her head drops and she nods, "Oh, well I'm sorry that I wasted your time."

A sudden pain of guilt hits my gut again and I shake my head, "Wait."

She turns and grins at me, a slight rise of the corners of her lips, "Yes?"

"If you really want to learn, I can show you some good books to get you started." I get up from my stool and smooth out the green skirt that hangs just past my knees. I skirt the counter and smile at her, watching as she nods.

"I have to know something," she asks me after she has paid for her books.

I sigh and nod, "What is it?"

"Just tell me how old you are," she replies, her eyes piercing into mine, "and don't say that you are in your twenties. You have to be far older."

I can't help but smile at her innocence. It really is quite heartbreaking, but I can't tell her my real age. I don't even want to know my real age. So, with a smile I bag up her books and answer her, "I am twenty five, but I've been told that I'm an old soul."

She laughs at me and adjusts the bag on her shoulder, "Well, Vi, I'm glad that I came in here today. Maybe I'll come back again soon."

"I'd like that," I say to her and watch her walk out of my store just as quickly as she had walked in.

After she is gone I can't help but wonder why she was sent to me in the first place, other than for me to find out that my son is going to get the beating of his life. With that thought, I pick up my cell phone and dial his number.

"Mom?"

"André, you have some explaining to do." I don't even say hello to him, I just roar out my anger.

"What are you talking about?" He asks me, though I can tell in his voice that he knows.

"Don't give me that bullshit, André," I am beyond mad at him now. I never curse at my children. "You've been telling people about us."

I hear the defensiveness in his voice, "I have not, Mother. I met one girl and we were talking about life. I never said how old I was."

I roll my eyes at his excuse, "Then how did she know to come to me?"

"The girl came to see you?" He asks me, his voice full of awe. "What did she say?"

I sigh, "She is convinced that I am a witch."

"But mom, you are a witch," he says to me, his voice light with a hint of laughter.

I growl, "Not the point, André! Did you tell her to come to me?"

André sighs, I can almost picture him shaking his head at me, his dark hair falling into his green eyes, making him look more like his father than I care to think about, "No, mother. I told her about a book-shop on the other side of town. I didn't know she would come to you."

I roll my eyes at his statement and growl again at him, "André you are in so much trouble for even thinking of telling a mortal of what you know. I don't care that this child came to me; it's the fact that she came to me because of you. You need to learn a thing or two about what exactly it is we are capable of. I have magic in me and so do you. Your power of persuasion is far better than mine ever was. So keep your mouth shut. Or at least learn to lie better."

I hear him breathing heavily into the phone. After a moment or two, he sighs and his soft voice catches my ear, "I'm sorry mother. I didn't think. I'll be more careful, I promise."

"Your sister came to see me today," I say to him, changing the subject, "she says she's staying with you."

I hear him let out an annoying huff this time, "Yes she is. Just for a few days though, then she's going to Boston, I think."

"She didn't tell me anything about Boston." I replay the conversation in my head, but I can't recall her saying anything about Boston. Perhaps she was going to, but she had upset me so much that I didn't want to hear anything. "What's in Boston?"

He is silent for a moment, something I've always hated, "Hey, mom. I have to go, I think Adrienne is here and she has some stuff for me."

"Why aren't you answering me André?" I am a bit annoyed when he changes the subject.

"It isn't my place to say anything mother." I can tell that he is getting annoyed with my questions.

I roll my eyes at this; he was always the one to tell on his sisters. "Fine, but you have to promise me something, André."

"Anything mother," he says to me and I can hear his voice is a bit anxious.

I don't quite know how to put my thoughts into words. I want to tell him to be careful and to stay out of trouble, but I know him too well to say such things and believe them to be true. I also want to tell him not to listen to his sister about Vincent, I don't quite trust my daughters when it comes to their father; life is just too complicated when it comes to him.

"Mom?"

I shake my head to clear it and answer him, "I'm here. Just promise me that you'll come by to see me soon. I miss you."

"I will mother," he says to me, but I hear that he isn't paying attention, "I'll call you this week."

"Goodbye."

I am quite disgusted with myself for not getting as mad at my son as I had wanted to. There is just something about André that makes me want to hold him and keep him safe instead of yelling and scolding him.

Over the years, being apart from my family has hurt my heart. I can't help but remember the day when seeing them was refreshing and an escape from my own mind. But I know that with my nearing birthday, everyone, including me, is holding onto a breath held for far too long while waiting for Vincent to return.

I have to get away. I know that. What I really want to do is get on a plane and fly to Paris; to find our home, the castle in the hills that was a part of our lives for almost six hundred years. For a moment, the thought crosses my mind to take the money in the cash register, gather my belongings and lock the door. But I know that isn't possible. I have this urge to stay in New York and wait.

When I first came to New York, it was a city that was flourishing. It was growing in leaps and bounds into what I now know as the "big apple." New York City was already large and bustling, but as selfish as it sounds, I feel as if being here helped the city a bit. I don't know how, but having my little bookshop and having my little place in the city, it seems as if it is complete now.

I shake my head to clear it and let my mind come out of the little trance I was in. I look down to my counter top and see the mess of books that I had been scanning before Gabby came in and sent my morning into a whirl wind. Needing to clear my mind and my counter, I pick up a few books and in midair, let them go, watching them float in front of me. With a flick of my wrist, I send the books across the room, watching as they find their homes on the freshly dusted shelves. I dust my hands off and smile; I've always loved using my powers, even if it was for a small chore that I loathe doing. And shelving books is one of those chores, especially when I have to climb the ladder to get to the top shelves.

Behind the desk, my large grandfather clock chimes noon and my stomach growls in a loud response. With my hand on my stomach, I walk over to the door to pull the blinds shut and turn around the sign that says I am out to lunch. I had almost forgotten Adrienne had brought me lunch. There is a place across the street from my bookstore where I usually go. They have a great roast beef sandwich and for some reason it reminds me of warm sandwiches Vincent and I would share on lazy Sunday afternoons. My hand is on the string that closes the blinds when I see something that I don't expect. A car drives by, a very good-looking old muscle car, but it's not the car that turns my head. No, it's the man in the passenger seat that makes me look twice.

"A ghost; it can't be him." My voice doesn't sound like me; it's soft and scared. I don't recognize the scared girl that I have suddenly become.

I shake my head, and open the door. I quickly step out into the autumn air, pulling my coral colored jacket about my body, shielding it from the chilly air. As the car passes, almost in slow motion, I blink.

Sitting in the passenger seat is Vincent. My Vincent.

Chapter Three
Fate's Knowledge

"I don't understand the reason why you toy with the mortals so much."

Renée turned slightly to settle her piercing green gaze upon her brother and shifted her perfect form on the stone where she sat before the gazing pool. A sly smile formed on her perfect crimson lips, "Well Aeron, I am Fate after all."

Aeron laughed, "You may be, but to me you are just my sister Renée. And whether you toy with mortals in this form or another, it is still cruel."

Renée laughed again and stood, her green robes falling about her slender form. She patted her brother on the shoulder and winked at him, "I never said I wasn't cruel, Aeron. Fate can be both cruel and kind. And the one I was watching isn't mortal remember? Perhaps you should be more sensitive to my work, instead of sensitive to the mortals."

"Sensitive? Ha!" Aeron followed his sister down the path leading away from the gazing pool. He had to pick up his pace to keep up with her long stride so he pulled up his blue robes around his ankles. "Perhaps you should let this obsession of yours ebb for awhile. Leave the Otherworld for awhile and live amongst the people you love to torture."

Renée stopped at her brother's suggestion, her raven black hair, braided away from her sun kissed skin and fierce green eyes, whipped to lie on her left shoulder, "I don't know Aeron. I did just get back from there."

"Ah yes, the journey that will bring the emerald back," Aeron responded with a sarcastic snicker. He ran his hands through his short black hair and paced around his sister, "Do you really think that this witch will be able to handle the emerald's power?"

Renée rolled her eyes at her brother's question and started to walk down the path again, "Really Aeron, must you ask such silly questions? You know the answer already; of course she will be able to handle the emerald's power. She was made for it after all."

Renée and Aeron walked the path that led around the Otherworld. All around them all four seasons bloomed and died at once, separated on individual islands and were connected with elaborate oak bridges. Spring and summer blossomed all the while autumn and winter slowly made the earth go to sleep, waiting once again for the renewal of spring. While following his sister, Aeron thought of what she had said about the witch handling the most powerful stone in both realms. He knew her a long time ago, in a different lifetime, but this woman he gazed upon in the pool was different than she used to be.

"Aeron, she's not that different," Renée stated, "She just needs to find her path again."

Aeron sighed, rolled his eyes and pointed to his head, "Will you please get out of my head? You know I hate it when you start poking around like that."

Renée laughed and winked at him, "Sorry Aeron, I can't help it sometimes." She paused for a moment as they walked across the bridge that led from summer to autumn and then autumn to winter. Once they were over, she pulled her shawl about her bare shoulders, "She has to be able to find her path again. It's the only way to fulfill her destiny."

"I know," Aeron replied, "But she looks so sad. She's looked this way for more than a century. She hardly even uses her powers anymore."

Renée nodded and opened the door to her small stone cottage, "She may not use them how we want her to, but I plan on changing that."

"You can't just put on that guise and trick her into becoming the powerful witch she was when she was André's student," Aeron stated.

"André taught her well," she said, moving to the hearth to place the teakettle over the smoldering coals, "She will be able to bring that power once again to the surface. What I need to do, is find a way of bringing her here to help her find it again."

Aeron shook his head and folded his arms across his lean chest, "It's a good idea sister, but what of her obsession with that love of hers? She will not be easily taken away from that world."

Anger blazed in Renée's eyes for a moment at the mere mention of him, "He wasn't even supposed to come into the picture. But that mother of hers just had to push and push. She was supposed to stay with André until…"

"I know," Aeron interrupted and sat beside her, "But it happened, and then you had to stir the pot and come up with a different way of her getting to her ultimate goal. Or André's ultimate goal that is."

Renée laughed loudly, the ripe sound causing the birds outside to whistle in response, "André will be pleased with the outcome of this. We just need to find him and I have a feeling that Vincent can help us."

Aeron shook his head and gazed at his sister with confused eyes, "André is alive." It was a statement, not a question, "We just need to find him."

Renée replied with a snicker, "He's hiding and has been so since Vivienne was taken from him. You should know that Aeron."

Aeron shook his head again and grinned, "André truly saw something in her that no one else saw."

"Oh yes," Renée replied. She stood and poured two mugs of tea and returned to the table, "So now, we must keep Vincent and Vivienne from seeing each other for just a while longer. I may need you to go to the other realm with me as well."

Aeron sipped at his tea and laughed, "I've never been to that realm."

Renée let a sly grin form on her perfect crimson lips and she patted her brother's hand, "Don't worry brother. We'll find you the perfect disguise."

"You know, for the Goddess of Fate, you truly are wicked," Aeron stated with a snicker.

"And for the God of Knowledge, you go along with me too easily without question," Renée countered.

***

The Otherworld, no matter the time of day, was always perfect, but at night, when the moon cast its silvery gaze down upon the realm, it seemed beyond perfect, especially in the spring where Aeron lived. It was that thought that had kept Aeron awake that night. He was a god; he was perfect, yet the perfection around him always astonished his keen mind. He had a tall, lean frame wrapped in corded muscle and skin colored to a light bronze from the hot sun. His black hair, with hints of blue in the moonlight, lay just above his wide shoulders in large wild curls. During the day he wore blue robes, tied with silver sashes. But this night, as he leaned against the doorframe of his stone cottage, he was shirtless. Wearing only breeches that clung to his muscled legs and reached the top of his calves, he crossed his left leg in front of his right and tried to relax as his thoughts got the better of him.

If anyone would happen to come by him this night, it would be a normal sight to see him gazing at the moon with a look of pensive wonder in his blue eyes. But with the knowledge of what lay ahead of him and his sister, he was not at ease with his own mind. Knowledge and Fate, two things people, mortals, strive to obtain, he and his sister had in spades. And sometimes, it was the most annoying thing to have.

For a moment, Aeron couldn't wait to put on his mortal guise and step into that world; but only for a moment.

This world, his Otherworld, was the only thing he had ever known. Renée was the one that always ventured back and forth between the realms. It was never something that Aeron desired and he had his own reasons. The mortal realm was messy and loud. The people there rushed around and never took pride in the wonders around them.

"Aeron!"

He lifted his head, the distressed voice bringing him out of his trance. Rounding the cobblestone curve of the road, he saw his sister, normally calm and collected, running up the path toward him. He pulled himself from his place on the railing and stepped down onto the path to join Renée, "What is it?"

Renée's aura was erratic and panicked. She dragged her hands through her hair, her fingers tangling the ends into knots, "Aeron, we might be too late."

He shook his head and guided her up the two steps onto the stone porch, "What are you talking about?"

"She's already seen him," Renée stated, staring at the moon, "I can feel her need to follow him. She's trying to guide her fate herself."

Aeron nodded, suddenly feeling the knowledge of the outcome if that came to pass, "I don't want to put an even bigger damper on this sister, but you do owe her one."

"I what?!" Renée turned quickly to face her brother and glared at him, her eyes ablaze with fury, "I owe her nothing but the fate already laid out before her. She's the one that shouts to the heavens that I owe her something. You know for certain, brother that she needs to let this take its own course!"

At that statement, Aeron couldn't help but laugh. He shook his head and leaned against the stone wall behind him, "Are you serious? You want her to let this fate run its course?"

Instantly Renée realized her mistake and dropped her strong shoulders in defeat, "You know what I mean, brother."

"Yes, I do know what you mean, but that's not what you said," Aeron replied. Under his breath, he made a tsk tsk sound and shook his head, "You want to let this fate run its course as long as you are the one in control. You put on your mortal guise, trick her with an innocent persona that makes her want to befriend you and expect her to follow your every whim. And without knowing who you truly are!

Renée, this witch is nothing more than the carrier of the Emerald's magic. The love she has for this man is merely a background note for her story."

Renée shook her head, "No. She's so much more than just a carrier of magic. She can bring him back."

Aeron rolled his eyes, "Yes, so you keep telling me. But Renée, I know for certain, that André is gone."

"Have some faith, Aeron," Renée replied and placed her hands over her heart, "Trust *me* for once, instead of your logic."

Aeron sighed, knowing that Vivienne could bring him back from wherever André had gone after he disappeared almost eight hundred years before. "You want me to have faith in something that I know for certain won't happen unless this fate comes to pass?"

"Yes," Renée replied softly with a nod of her head, "I will admit that I want to control the situations that surround me, especially Vivienne's, but I have faith in our quest for André. We need him back Aeron, you know that."

"No, Renée," Aeron replied, moving away from his sister and sitting on the railing of the stone porch, "You need him back. We will be fine if we never find him again. You just have this insatiable need to find him."

Renée dropped her head and closed her eyes, trying very hard to control the anger building inside her. Fisting her hands at her sides, she lifted her hooded gaze to her brother and glared, "You do not understand my need for him. His magic is something that this realm has needed for almost a millennium! And you stand there with your knowledge and tell me that we don't need him. Well I will tell you this once, brother, you are either with me in this fate or you are against me. And I pray that you are not against me, because the outcome of that decision is far greater than letting Vivienne follow Vincent now before we have time to prepare her."

He watched his sister, anger resonating from her normally cool and collected aura, stalk away from him back down the cobblestone path. He sometimes couldn't get over how dramatic his sister was. One minute she was overreacting and the next, plotting again. But it was her prophetic words that kept him from going after her. For now, he'd let her plot and set her plan into a course that he could do nothing about except know the end result. And that result was bloodier than any other he had seen yet.

It was the next day, when Aeron woke to find Renée gone that the realization came to him that she had decided to do whatever she wanted to work in her own way. Cursing the day itself, he dressed and headed straight for the silver gate and the gilded boat that would take him to the other realm. With his mortal guise in the bag strapped over his shoulder, he let the boat carry him along the River of Time.

The river was filled with time itself. If one reached into the cold, crystal-clear water, they could pick a time and place, anywhere, and be there in an instant. Not many immortals, gods or spirits, dared cross the river of time for fear of being tempted of changing the course of time itself. Aeron was a strong god and with the knowledge of what could happen, he sat up straight in the boat and let it guide him to the point where he would be able to cross the line and find himself in the "real world," as Renée called it.

Aeron reached the other realm's shore in no time, watching as he approached the sandy coast with its dull hue and bright sun. He stepped onto the sand and quickly changed into his mortal guise. He pulled out the black t-shirt and faded jeans and groaned, hating the feeling of the itchy fabric against his sensitive skin. Not wanting to take the time, he snapped his fingers and the flimsy materials appeared on his skin, covering his lean muscled body from view. Upon his feet, he put on a pair of combat boots and across his lean torso he placed his over-the-shoulder messenger bag. With a sigh of encouragement, he passed through the wooden door that would lead him to the busy streets of the other realm.

He came out on the other side through a plain door in an alley. Looking up and down the alley to make sure he wasn't seen, he quickly closed the door to the River of Time and made his way down the cold, damp alley to the busy and noisy world his sister loved. It wasn't difficult for Aeron to find his sister. She was in the one place he knew she'd be, watching Vivienne.

"I knew I'd find you here."

Renée turned around quickly and Aeron was disgusted at what he saw. The mortal guise his sister had chosen was of a young punk teenager with pitch black hair streaked with pink and blue, tied back from a flawless oval face, clad in a dark purple mini-skirt, black leggings, combat boots, a black tank top and a leather jacket. Renée grinned, the crimson color upon her lips pulling back to reveal perfect white teeth.

"Of course I'm here," she replied with a sneer, "where else would I be?"

Aeron laughed, "Oh I don't know; in front of a mirror, perhaps?"

"Don't even start," Renée replied and gave him a look of pure teenage defiance, "there's nothing wrong with what I am wearing."

He shook his head and moved to stand beside her, rolling his eyes in disgust and annoyance, "Oh no, nothing wrong at all." With a sigh, Aeron folded his arms across his chest and stared across the busy street to the small bookshop that Vivienne owned, "Is she in there?"

Renée nodded, "Yes. I watched her open up this morning and she seemed different. Her thoughts are scattered."

"Of course they are," Aeron replied, moving to lean against the brick wall beside him in the alleyway, "She just saw a glimpse of her true love and as quickly as he appeared, he vanished again."

Renée rolled her eyes, a move that Aeron thought was a bit too mortal and she sighed, "I hate it when you can so easily fall into mortal emotions. Love and longing, the drama of it all, yuck! Mortals can keep it."

"Did you just say, yuck?" Aeron asked with a laugh. "Renée, you've taken to being mortal too easily."

She shook her head, "It's not Renée here. In this realm I am Gabby. Gabriella."

Aeron let out another laugh that shook the brick at his back, "Gabby? Where did you come up with that?"

Renée rolled her eyes at her brother, "I like the name. What's wrong with liking the name?"

"Nothing's wrong with liking the name," Aeron replied running his hand lazily through his raven black hair, "it just doesn't sound like something you'd pick. That's all."

Renée rolled her eyes again and turned her gaze to the bookstore. There, she saw Vivienne let down the blinds slightly as the sun beamed into the store. Renée tilted her head as she watched Vivienne, as if doing so would help her get into her mind better. She always enjoyed the trips she took into Vivienne's head, it was a way for her to get close to the woman and her memories; to find a way back to a time when André was still alive and the world was at peace.

"The world is at peace now, Renée," Aeron replied, moving away from the wall and standing closer to the edge of the alley, "You just don't want to see it that way."

Renée placed her hand on his shoulder, her black painted fingernails digging into the leather coat on his broad shoulders and pulled him back, "Don't go too far out, she'll see you."

Aeron sighed and took a step back, standing once again beside his conniving sister in the dark alley, "Oh, let's not let her see me now. You've only been standing here all day."

"Don't start with me Aeron," she replied with a short snip, "This is a delicate situation and must be handled with care."

Aeron laughed at her statement. Out of the corner of his eye, he saw someone walking down the sidewalk, heading straight for the bookshop door. A smile tugged at the corner of his lips and he nudged his sister with his elbow, "Handled with care right?"

Renée turned to him and nodded, her eyes on her black painted nails, "This sort of thing, her fate, must not be taken lightly. You know that, Aeron."

"Yes," he replied with a nod and pointed across the street, "But you may want to look now, All-Knowing One, because things are getting complicated."

Renée whipped her head quickly at Aeron's statement and then got her vision. As the vision clouded her mind, the sight in front of her was that of Vincent, clad in a tailor made suit and long black coat, moving into the doorway of the bookstore.

"Shit!"

Just then, Aeron lunged from his hiding place in the alley and dodged traffic to get to the door before Vincent could open it. He knew that Vivienne was not at the counter inside, so there was no chance of her seeing what he was about to do.

"Excuse me, sir."

Vincent lifted his head to see Aeron running toward him. With a look of confusion on his usually cool and collected face, he answered, "Yes? Can I help you?"

Aeron nodded and acted as if he were out of breath, "You seemed like the most trustworthy character on the street. My daughter and I," he pointed to Renée and motioned for her to wave, "are lost and can't seem to find our way back to the hotel. It should be around here somewhere. Do you know anything about the area?" He carefully placed his hand on Vincent's shoulder, guiding him away from the bookstore doorway and out of view of the window, knowing that Vivienne was moving toward the front of the store.

Vincent, obviously annoyed by the interruption, sighed and shook his head, "Unfortunately I do not. I'm just here looking for a book."

Aeron laughed and shook his head, "How ignorant of me to think that everyone in this area is a New Yorker."

Vincent nodded and patted Aeron on the shoulder, "Sorry I couldn't help you."

"No, that's fine," he looked up to see Renée waving him over just as Vivienne was turning the sign in the window saying that she was closing early for the day. Aeron nodded and extended his hand to Vincent, "Well it looks like my daughter has figured something out. Thank you anyway."

Vincent nodded and shook his hand, "No problem. Now I'm off to see if I can find this book." He turned and growled, kicking the brick wall, "Great! They closed already."

Aeron held back a smile of relief and shook his head, "Sorry dude. That's life I guess."

Renée watched her brother run back across the street and into the alley where she once again hid and punched him in the shoulder, "Are you insane?! I can't believe you just went out there and talked to him like that."

"You should be thanking me," Aeron replied, rubbing his shoulder, "I just saved your precious fate. Your visions don't come as quickly as they do in our realm. Vincent almost made it in the door, Renée."

Renée growled and held his gaze, "I know, Aeron! You don't have to state the obvious. I can't help it that my power of sight isn't as strong in this realm as it is in ours. I don't know how André stayed here for so long without feeling the effects."

Aeron shrugged his shoulders, the worn leather of his jacket rising with his slow even breaths, "Who knows, Renée. But that was too close for comfort and I don't want to have that happen again. Okay?"

"Yeah, whatever," Renée replied with an annoyed huff, "I just don't know what I would have done if he had gotten to her first."

"We would have dealt with it," Aeron stated coldly. With a sigh, he leaned against the dirty brick building again, "Everything happens for a reason, remember?"

Renée growled and punched his shoulder again; "Don't use my own line on me! I know what I am doing and you shouldn't have run off like that."

"Fine," Aeron said, holding his hands up in defeat, "I won't help again. I'll let you make a complete mess of the whole thing and André will be that more pleased when he is found."

He started walking down the alley toward the door between the realms when he heard Renée call him back. He stopped and turned his head, so only one eye was visible in the dark alley, "Have something to say?"

She nodded, "I'm sorry. Look, I'm just mad because I wasn't the one to jump. You acted first and it pissed me off."

"I know," Aeron stated and turned fully to face her, "but Vivienne has seen you in this... 'outfit'... and it wasn't a good idea to have you running after the love of her life. I'm a bit more convincing as a human being."

Renée rolled her eyes again, making her look even more like the defiant teenager she was dressed as, "Fine, you're right."

Aeron nodded, "At least you know I'm right. Can we go now? This place is starting to get into my skin."

"Yes, we can go. But not too far," she replied, tossing him a set of keys, "we have a room at a hotel around the corner."

He caught the keys and shook his head, "Oh no. We can go between the realms and you want to stay here?"

"Yes," she replied with a nod and started walking back down the alley toward the street, "Don't worry. It won't be for long; just a day or two."

Aeron rolled his eyes and followed his sister, "This better be worth it Renée."

With a sly smile, she turned slowly and held his gaze, "You know it will."

Chapter Four
Magic

"Did you find the book store you were looking for?"

Vincent looked up to see Steve leaning against his car and smoking a cigarette. With a sigh, Vincent shook his head, "By the time I got there they were closed. I guess they close early on Wednesdays."

Steve finished the cigarette and tossed it onto the sidewalk, "We can try again in the morning."

Vincent nodded and moved to lean against the car beside him, "I know we can. Just bugs me because I want that book tonight."

"What book are you looking for?" Steve asked glancing over at him, "And why is it so important that you go to a magic store for it?"

Vincent rolled his eyes, "It's not a magic store. It's a pagan book store. And to answer your other question, it's a book on emeralds; one emerald in particular."

"Oh," Steve replied with a soft laugh, "what's so special about emeralds?'

Vincent pulled himself away from the car and started to pace, "You know, you're very curious. Can't you just go with me blindly?"

"No," he said with a snort and pulled out another cigarette, "I told you the minute you got in the car that I wanted answers. So are you gonna tell me what this wild goose chase is about?"

Vincent sighed and stopped pacing the sidewalk. With a breath of encouragement, he opened his eyes and let his piercing gaze fall upon

Steve, "You really want to know? Because if you say yes, then there is no going back, there'll be no turning back from what I'll tell you."

Steve eyed him cautiously, flinging the butt of the second cigarette, "Dude, you're scaring me. Are you a spy or something?"

"If it were only that simple," Vincent replied under his breath. He looked up to see Steve staring at him with a perplexed look upon his face, "All right, I'll tell you. Are you sure you want to know this?"

"Yes," Steve replied impatiently.

"All right, are you ready?"

Steve nodded and moved closer to him as if Vincent were going to whisper to him, "Of course."

With a sigh of encouragement, Vincent said the words slowly, "I am an immortal."

"You're a what?"

"I am an immortal."

Steve stared at him blankly for several moments and then burst into a raucous laughter, "Yeah, okay buddy, me too."

"I'm serious," Vincent replied, shoving Steve's hand away when he pats him on the shoulder, "I'm an immortal man."

Steve shook his head and smirked, "Like 'Highlander'?"

Vincent rolled his eyes and groaned, "No, not like 'Highlander'."

"Well then how?" Steve asked, moving again to lean against the side of his GTO, "Because that's the only thing I can think of."

Vincent put his hand into his pocket and pulled out a small vile with a blue colored liquid inside it, "You've seen me drink this before right?" Steve nodded and Vincent continued, "Well, it's a tincture that I take every day to stay young."

"You always told me it was liquid vitamins." Steve laughed at himself and eyed Vincent curiously as he held his hand out. Vincent placed the vile in Steve's hand, "This little bit of liquid, keeps you young? Impossible."

"Quite possible," Vincent replied with a smile and took the vile back. "Just think of it as my own personal fountain of youth."

Steve eyed the small vile cautiously and sniffed it, "What's in it? It smells like really bad alcohol."

Vincent laughed and snatched the vile back, "There are some magical herbs in here that are infused in alcohol. The alcohol releases magical properties in the herbs to make the tincture work."

Steve was blown away and overwhelmed with all the information Vincent was giving him. With a sigh, he spoke, "Then how old are you?"

Vincent grinned, the corners of his lips lifting up into a smirk that caused the tiny wrinkles around his eyes to deepen, "I am 1,142 years old."

Steve's eyes widened and he suppressed a choking cough. Placing his hand on his chest, he shook his head, staring at Vincent in disbelief, "You're...you're... what?"

"You heard me," Vincent replied with a laugh. When Steve didn't reply or even move, Vincent lightly tapped Steve on the cheek, "You all right?"

Steve shook his head, as if doing so would clear it, "Um...yeah. Sure. I just don't get it."

"What's to get?" Vincent asked with a snicker, "Look, you can ask me anything you want now, all right?"

Steve shook his head, "What's to get? Are you kidding me? Vinny, you just told me that you're immortal and you expect me to brush it off like I hear this kind of thing every day? I don't believe it, you have to prove it."

"Prove it?" Vincent rolled his eyes and let out a low growl deep in his throat. Holding out his hand, Vincent held Steve's gaze, "Give me your lighter."

Steve pulled out his Zippo and placed it in Vincent's wide palm, "What are you doing?"

"You want proof?" He asked his voice a bit manic as he flipped open the top and ignited the flint, "Then here you go."

Vincent held his hand, palm down, over the orange flame, grimacing as the heat peeled away the first layer of skin. Groaning in pain, he looked up to Steve who was watching him with a wide, frightened gaze.

"Dude, what are you doing?!" Steve pulled Vincent's hand away from the Zippo, flipping it closed and pocketed it once again. Steve turned over Vincent's hand, inspecting it thoroughly. With a shocked gaze, he looked up at Vincent who was just grinning at him, "What is so damn funny? You just lit yourself on fire and you're laughing? That's sick Vinny!"

Laughing, Vincent pulled his hand away from Steve's grip and shook it out, watching as the red burn shrunk quickly, his skin turning back to normal, "You wanted proof, I gave it to you."

"That was bullshit, Vinny!" Steve growled and stalked away from him. He turned around quickly at the bumper of his car and faced Vincent once again, "What the hell do you expect from me? It's not like this is a normal thing; I don't hear that one of my best friends is immortal every day. Bullshit, Vinny, bullshit!"

"I expect a friend to still take me as I am," he replied softly, rubbing the palm of his hand with the pad of this thumb, "There are things in this world that are beyond what you've been told or even taught. Magic exists, even though I may not like most of it, but it's out there. Witches exist, vampires exist, there are even fairies and sprites out in the world that help keep the earth plentiful and beautiful. You may think what I just did was bullshit, Steve, but it needed to be done. You know the truth; you can't go back now, no matter how much you want to. So are we cool?"

"Sure, whatever; so, where are you from?" Steve asked quickly, changing the subject. His voice wavered some as he spoke, "Where were you born? I know nothing about you now."

Vincent smirked softly, "I'm still the same person, Steve. I never lied to you about where I was from; you know I grew up in France. Only now you know that it was almost twelve hundred years ago."

Steve's jaw dropped again at what Vincent had told him, "Wow, I-I don't even know what to say. How did you find the tincture?"

"I was nineteen when I learned of the potion," Vincent began with a smirk at Steve's question, "I was the squire for a French Lord, Grand Duke Jacques LaTorche. He took me in when I was eight and taught me the highs and lows of working in a castle."

Steve raised one sleek eyebrow, "The duke's name was LaTorche? Isn't that your last name? Wait, you grew up in a castle?"

Vincent laughed at the bombardment of questions Steve had strung along and ignored him when it came to the name, "Yes, but it wasn't as glamorous as you may think. Think about it. There weren't any of the luxuries that we have today. Castles were cold, dark, damp and very poorly maintained. I was lucky to have survived as long as I had. The bigger cities in France weren't pretty places. The countryside however was amazing; the colors back then weren't anything like we see today."

"Okay, so if this duke guy had the tincture, how did you get it?" Steve asked, folding his arms across his chest as he leaned against the car and listened to Vincent speak.

Vincent moved to stand beside Steve and continued, "One day, I was lurking around the back stairwell with one of the duchess' hand-maids and to find a more private place, I opened this old wooden door hoping to find an empty room."

"What did you find?" Steve asked, interrupting Vincent, his voice soft as if he were listening to a horror story.

Vincent continued as if he hadn't been interrupted, "I found a room that I had never been in before. I had lived in that castle for eleven years and I had never seen that door before. What I found in that room changed my life and my future. The room was lined with old wooden shelves that were filled with bottles of herbs and colored liquids. But in the center of the room, on a glass pedestal was the tincture that keeps me young."

Steve nodded and lit another cigarette, "Did the duke find you there?"

"Yes," Vincent continued, "In those days, anything that was different or not given to us by the priests was considered evil. Unfortunately, I fell into that category where anything that had to do with witchcraft I believed was evil. So when Jacques told me that he was two hundred years old, I wanted to run to the monastery and turn him in to the priests."

"But he stopped you?" Steve asked, exhaling smoke.

Vincent nodded again, "Yes and he told me about the potion, tincture, telling me that it wasn't evil and neither was he. Both he and the duchess were growing weary of the immortal life and wanted to stop taking the mixture. They didn't have any children and had no one to leave the land and title to. So he told me that if I wanted to, I could start taking the tincture then he and the duchess would stop and when they died, I could have the title, the land and the castle. So I took the tincture, only aging when it was too difficult to get the supplies needed to make the mixture and waited until the duke and duchess passed. When they did, I took the duke's place and took his name."

"You've never had any problem with living as long as you have?" Steve asked, flinging the cigarette towards the building they faced. "What if someone recognized you, what would you do then?"

Vincent sighed and shrugged, "Well, I only spend about twenty or thirty years in one place. When Vivienne and I lived in France, we had a bit of a legend attached to our names. Some said that the castle we lived in was cursed and all that entered would have to live all eternity as our slaves."

Steve laughed loudly, his movements slightly awkward as they spoke, "So how long did you stay in France?"

"For six hundred years," Vincent replied bluntly.

Steve nearly choked, "Six hundred years?! How did you get away with that? How is it possible?"

"It's possible because Vivienne and I embraced the legend that surrounded us," Vincent said sternly. With a sigh, he softened his features and his eyes, "Look, Vivienne and I have lived a life that both of us wanted. We loved each other fiercely everyday and lived with our children the only way we knew how. I don't regret a single moment of my life or how we have managed to get around anyone really figuring out what we are. Though I do sometimes regret not being able to make connections with people, especially since I left Vivienne, I don't regret a single moment."

Steve nodded, his perplexed gaze wavering as Vincent's voice softened, "So what was so special about making that connection with me? If you came to Boston in the 50s, why did you stay so long?"

For a moment, Vincent didn't have an answer. He hadn't thought about why he had stayed in Boston, hadn't tried to come up with a reason to leave. Starting to pace, he shook his head and answered Steve, "Well, I honestly don't know. Boston was new and exciting for me. I hadn't been to America since the 1840s and I suppose I wanted something new and different than the old history of Europe." He stopped pacing and faced Steve, "And as far as making friends with you, there's something about you that just made me better."

Steve laughed loudly at Vincent's admission and holds up his hands, "Dude! Why did you have to play the mushy part? Why can't you just be normal?"

"I am normal Steve," Vincent replied with a laugh, "I'm my kind of normal. I don't know how to be any other way." With a sigh, he shook his head and moved back towards the car, "Look, you're my best friend okay? Can we just leave it at that?"

"Yeah, sure," Steve replied and pulled out the car keys and changed the subject as quickly as he could, "So you haven't regretted a single moment of being immortal?"

Vincent hesitated for a moment before answering. He really hadn't thought of regretting his life and with a smirk, he answered very matter-of-factly, "No. If I hadn't taken the tincture then I wouldn't have found the love of my life."

"So, this girl that we're after, is she an immortal too?" Steve asked, moving to get into the car.

Vincent nodded, "Yes. She's also a witch and a very powerful one at that," he added after a moment. Vincent moved to get into the GTO and sat back, placing his hand in his pocket, his fingers gently playing over the smooth velvet of the emerald's case.

"What's her name again?"

Vincent smiled and looked over to Steve once he turned on the engine of the car, "Her name is Vivienne and she is the most beautiful woman you will ever gaze upon."

"I'll get to meet her then?" Steve asked, pulling out into traffic.

Vincent sighed and shrugged, "Only if we find her first."

"Do you have any idea where she is?" Steve asked. "And speaking of which, where are we going?"

Vincent let out a soft laugh, "I have a small flat here in New York. I haven't used it in almost thirty years, but it's been well taken care of. If you want me to drive, I can. Trying to get to the flat can be a bit tricky; it's in a very old part of town."

"All right, sure," Steve answered and pulled over. Quickly switching spots, Steve smirked, "It would probably be easier if you drove anyway. I always get lost in this city. "

Vincent, who hadn't been behind the wheel of a vehicle in about ten years, felt a bit strange driving Steve's GTO. But he quickly got over it when he revved the engine, "I miss that sound," he said with a smirk and took off down the street toward Manhattan, Steve laughing as they swerved down the busy street.

"So are you going to answer my question?" Steve asked after a few moments of silence.

"What question?" Vincent asked, forgetting what Steve had asked him.

Steve grabbed the side of the door as Vincent took a sharp turn and let out a frightened noise, "Do you know where to find Vivienne?"

Vincent glanced over at Steve and smiled, laughing at his startled expression. With a nod, he answered him, "No, I don't know where Vivienne is, nor do I know where to start. My only clue is to start looking in the village. But I do have something that could possibly help."

Steve laughed, "What is it, a magical map?"

"That's going to get old before long," Vincent replied and shook his head, "No, it's not a magical map, but it has led me to her before."

Steve eyed him curiously, "Are you going to tell me or just sit there and let me guess? If I keep guessing, then it's just going to piss you off."

Vincent shook his head, knowing Steve was right about his endless questions, "It's something that has led me to her before. I just hope that it works." He paused for a moment and continued, "Just trust me and know that I have a plan."

Steve sighed again and shook his head, "Well I guess I have to go with you blindly after all. Just know that I don't like it."

Vincent nodded, "I know you don't like it, but as I said before. A true friend would take me as I am and that includes withholding information."

"Well I can't really do anything about it, but you're right," Steve replied and glanced out the window, watching as the hustle and bustle of New York City passed them by. After a few silent moments, he turned his gaze back to Vincent, "I'm behind you, Vinny, no matter what."

"Thank you," Vincent replied, "that means a lot."

It was later that night, after they had settled into his Manhattan flat, decorated much like his apartment in Boston, when Vincent finally started to relax. Most of the drive was spent in silence, giving both of them time to process the afternoon. Vincent sat at his piano, this one smaller than the one in his Boston apartment, and played softly Vivienne's song. His thoughts raced as he played, images of his life with Vivienne flashing in his mind. Her smile haunted him, her scent was always with him and he could feel her power even as he sat there not knowing where she was. In front of him, on the piano, was the emerald in its velvet box. His cobalt gaze held onto the stone as he played her song and a tear threatened to spill from his eye.

"Is that the emerald you were talking about earlier?"

Vincent stopped playing, wiped the tear away and turned to see Steve standing behind him leaning against the doorframe. Turning away from him, Vincent nodded, "Yes. It's her stone."

"All right, then why do you have it?" he asked, not moving from his spot.

Vincent rolled his eyes, "You ask a lot of questions, Steve. I know this is all a lot to take in, but you really need to get off my back and just let me do what I came here to do."

"Then you shouldn't have let me tag along," Steve replied sharply. He pulled himself away from the doorframe and moved to stand beside the piano, "And what exactly did you come here to do? From here, all I see you doing is the exact same thing you were doing in Boston."

"You don't understand," Vincent stated, getting slightly annoyed at Steve's insight.

Steve laughed, "No, not at all. I suppose you enjoy being miserable and lonely. It helps you get through the day knowing that you don't do anything at all to better your mood, let alone your life. You want to find Vivienne? Then do it."

"It's not that simple, Steve." Vincent stood and moved to stand by the window, "Vivienne and the emerald have a storied past and it's not my job to give that power back to her. Granted, it's her power to have, regardless of whether or not I think she should have it. The stone will find its way back to her when she's ready for it and I suppose in some way, it's almost ready for her."

Steve rolled his eyes, "You aren't making any sense, Vinny. You talk of all this power, but you don't believe in it. That's what gets me. You act as if it's an inconvenience for you to have the stone. So why do you have it?"

"Because I took it from her," Vincent whispered softly. He turned to face Steve and sighed, "I was afraid of what it was doing to her, so I took it from her and left."

"Sounds a bit selfish to me," Steve replied bluntly. "What was it doing to her?"

"It gave her such power; it was beyond her control, or even my control. She was becoming someone other than the woman I loved and I didn't like it." Vincent's voice wavered at the memory and he ignored the selfish statement.

Vincent thought about that night, the night she first gazed upon the stone when he gave it to her. Her green eyes, always vibrant and full of life, lit up at the sight of it, as if seeing an old friend. Vincent's mind was so clouded with her happiness that he didn't see what was right in front of him; a woman gaining her full power and it scared the hell out of him once he figured out what he had done.

"I remember seeing her one night," Vincent began, his gaze on the moon's reflection in the building's window, "She was sitting at her vanity in our room, the mirror poised in front of her. She wore the stone as a pendant, always hung around her neck and placed on her chest, close to her heart. Her eyes, usually green and lovely were clouded with the power possessed within that emerald. I never liked the way she looked at the stone; she never looked at me like that. And it broke my heart.

"Vivienne was powerful from the start; she was born with fire inside her. The emerald seemed to enhance that fire. For a hundred years I sat idle with her, not saying a word at the change I was seeing. Not even our children dared to say anything against her for fear that they might be burnt on sight."

"You have children?" Steve asked.

Vincent nodded, "Yes, three of them. Twin girls, Adrienne and Audrey and a boy, André." Vincent laughed and shook his head; "I didn't even have a say in my children's names. Vivienne had to name them after her mentor, an obsession I have never been able to take her mind from."

"Seems to me that Vivienne was meant for something more than this world," Steve stated softly, his gaze following Vincent's, "I don't mean that disrespectfully either, Vinny, but you stole from her what was hers because you didn't like it."

Vincent growled low in his chest, "I know what I did, Steve. It eats away at me every day and has for one hundred seventy five years." Vincent lifted his gaze from the moon's reflection and settled on Steve, "All I have ever wanted was Vivienne and this emerald has kept us apart for too long."

"Then what do you propose to do?" Steve asked, leaning against the wall beside the window, "Because I'm getting quite weary of all this talk of prophecy and power. Just do what you came here to do, no questions asked. Fate be damned."

Vincent whipped his head at Steve at that statement and shook his head, "Never speak ill of Fate. She is a cruel mistress and you never know what she'll do to you."

Steve rolled his eyes, "You believe in fate too?"

"Yes," Vincent replied sternly.

At that, Steve sighed and pulled himself away from the wall. He grumbled something under his breath and sat on the arm of the black leather couch, "I get the broody moods, I do, but this talk of fate and power, it's all a bit much. A few hours ago I didn't even know that this stuff existed."

"I told you that you wouldn't want to know," Vincent replied. He turned his back on the moon, pulled the white blinds across the floor-to-ceiling windows and faced his friend, "I'm sorry I brought you into this. Tomorrow I promise to find that bookshop and get that book I need. This will all be over soon enough."

Steve shook his head, "I don't believe you, but all right."

Vincent nodded his head and walked into his bedroom. Again, this room was decorated much like his bedroom in Boston. The only difference here was there weren't as many pictures. There was only one painting hung on the wall in the bedroom, and that was of Vivienne.

A thought crossed his mind as he lay on his large bed, naked from the waist up, and he let his eyes fall to the painting of Vivienne. Steve had said to him that he didn't believe this would be over soon enough, and for some reason, Vincent agreed with Steve. He knew that this was going to be a long up-hill battle that would not end well. A power, beyond anyone's comprehension was resting silently in a small black velvet box on his nightstand, ready and willing to go back to Vivienne. But what Vincent couldn't bring himself to admit was there was a part of him that wanted to see Vivienne in all her powerful glory. Part of him wanted her to have the stone so badly, just so that he wouldn't have the burden of keeping it from her anymore.

In that one single thought, Vincent sat up, the muscles in his abdomen rippling as he did so. He swung his legs over the side of the bed and laughed at himself, "Of course I want to see her powerful." Vincent stood and began pacing back and forth in front of the balcony doors wearing only his boxer briefs and talking to himself. "Vivienne deserves to have this power; she was built for it after all. Who am I to keep it from her? Who was I to take it from her?"

Vincent laughed again and stopped pacing. His gaze fell onto the black box on the nightstand and for the first time in one hundred seventy five years, he was finally ready to face Vivienne and the wrath that he knew would come down upon him.

Chapter Five
Sacrifice

I remember the morning of my seventeenth birthday vividly, as if it had only happened yesterday.

André woke me up early, shaking me awake with the gentle touch of his strong hand. I opened my eyes, still innocent and seeking the wisdom that André had to offer me. I could have stared at him forever, but unfortunately the real world called from beyond the safe haven of slumber. Sitting up, he took my hand and silently asked me to follow him into the other room. I don't know what I expected to find in that room; a grand breakfast perhaps, maybe a dozen presents. With the anticipation of a child, I followed André, hoping that what he surprised me with was something to truly look forward to.

Instead, I found my mother. It wasn't even sun up and she had already traveled from across France to see me there in André's cottage. My heart sank when I saw her, knowing that, on this day, this first day of the New Year, she would burden me with bad news.

"Mother, what are you doing here?"

Her face, slightly wrinkled and sour from years of frowning, should have told me what she was about to say. But even with all the magic I had acquired, my gift of foresight was lame to say the least. My eyes fell on her thin lips as she opened them to begin speaking at me.

"My darling daughter," she began and my stomach churned in anticipation, "you have grown so much since last I saw you."

I laughed at her, "Mother, it has been three years since you've seen me."

She nodded, still seated at the small wooden table where I had learned to sort herbs every day, "Well yes, it has been a few years. But I only stayed away from you so that I would not hinder your teachings."

I wanted to start pacing the room as she spoke to me, but my feet felt heavy as if I had been dragging them through mud and muck, "Why have you come now, mother? It is my birthday, so if you have bad news just say it."

"Why would you think that my visit is to bring you bad news?" she asked me, her eyes piercing into mine, "Can I not just come here to see my daughter on the day of her birth?"

I just shook my head at her, not believing that she would have the gall to even ask that of me, "No, mother. Last time you came here to just say 'hello' was the day you told me my father died —a man I've never met may I add. So, no, I do not believe you came here to simply wish me happy birthday." At the time, I thought nothing of it, but when I said 'father' my mother's eyes darted to André.

"Vivienne!" she roared at me, having shifted her gaze back to me and stood up, her blue priestess robes falling around her aging form and pooling at her feet, "You spoiled, selfish child!"

I didn't back down from her, I couldn't. Instead, I held my ground, "Spoiled? You only remember the girl you left and threw to the wilderness, not the woman in front of you now. How dare you call me a spoiled child!"

At this point, André intervened and stood between us. He shook his head at me and turned toward my mother, "Celeste! Please stop yelling at your daughter." Then André turned to me, his eyes soft, "And Vivienne, please stop yelling at your mother. Yes, she did come here to tell you something, so please sit down and speak with her as the young woman you are, not the rebellious girl you've suddenly turned into."

Hearing André's voice always calmed me, so I nodded and slowly moved to sit beside him and across the table from my mother. I remember the room was deafeningly silent as we sat there. Outside, the sun was dawning and the world was starting to come to life, even with the ground covered in snow. I heard an owl howl for the last time as the morning sun tried to shine through the window covered in dust and dirt.

"Vivienne, will you stop daydreaming!" My mother always shouted at me when my mind started to wander.

With a shake of my head, I sighed and apologized, "Sorry, mother. Now please tell me why you've come."

My mother looked to André and shook her head, "Always daydreaming and impatient, is she like this now?"

André shook his head and placed his hand atop mine, almost lovingly, "No, quite the opposite really. Vivienne is a very good student and very patient with her studies. I am very privileged to have had her here."

"To have had me here, what does that mean?" I turned quickly toward him, my eyes full of worry and I tugged my hand from beneath his.

André didn't answer me and for a split second I hated him. But that feeling quickly left and went towards my mother as she told me why she had come to visit me.

"Well my dear, as you know, it is your birthday," she began. When I nodded and rolled my eyes, she continued, "I have come to tell you that by the end of the spring, you are to return back home with me and find a husband."

At once I was infuriated and stood, toppling over the chair behind me, "What?! I will do no such thing!"

"You will and you'll do it willingly," she said to me, her voice calm and that annoyed me. "You have no choice Vivienne. Your time with André is up and you must take off the robes of priestess."

"Why? You didn't!"

My mother, cold as a stone statue just shook her head, "It was my path to be a priestess and I have done so without complaint. If my mother had given me the choice I would have chosen marriage."

I just groaned at her statement, "But you did get me, regardless of whether you had a husband or not. Please, tell me why being a priestess, something I am truly talented at, is not my path."

"Yes I did get you and I would not trade it for anything in the world," she began, her eyes shifting from me to André. I suddenly felt a slight pain of guilt, but it quickly left when she continued, her eyes moving back to mine, "What you need to do is realize that what I chose is not for you. You need to come home, find someone to marry and live a normal life. You also need to realize that the world is changing out there, Vivienne. You must realize that what you have learned is not welcome out in the open."

"Then why would you have me study with André if you knew that this was the outcome?" I began pacing at that point, my anger seeping from every pore of my body. "Why would you let me have something so wonderful and great if all you wanted was for me to live a 'normal life' as you put it?"

My mother shook her head, "I have no answer for you Vivienne. This is what you must do. You must obey me."

I didn't want to obey her, she was turning my world upside down and I hated her for it. I couldn't believe my mother was saying this to me and on my birthday nonetheless. My anger poured out of me like lava. I could feel the earth shake beneath my bare feet and behind me, under the cauldron that held the boiling water, the smoldering embers burst to life. I knew that if I didn't calm down, I would burn the cottage down to the ground, but part of me didn't care as long as she went with it. It was André that calmed me, as always. He placed his strong hand on my shoulder, brushing away the ends of my red hair that had burst into flame. My green eyes, pulsing with anger, dulled and turned to normal and I turned my head towards him.

In my mind I heard his voice, *"Vivienne, you must calm your anger. Tell your mother that you will think about what she has offered and send her on her way. I will not have you burn down this place with your anger."*

I nodded toward him and turned back to my mother. Her eyes were wide with a mixture of horror and astonishment, "Did, did you do that, Vivienne?"

"Yes," I replied to her softly. I lowered my head so my eyes were hooded from her gaze and sighed, "Mother, I will think about what you have said, but for now I must ask you to leave. André and I have much to do today."

She stood, her robes falling around her aging form. With a nod of her head, her once red hair, now dulled with age and littered with gray, fell into her eyes, "All right. I will see you in the spring."

Once she was gone from the house, I stormed out of the room and slammed the door to my bedchamber behind me. I threw myself on the bed and roared with anger into my old beaten up pillow. It was sometime later when I heard André again. He must have gone out to speak to my mother. I heard the door open behind me and knew that André stood there, watching me throw a fit because my mother had upset me.

"You truly scared her with your show of power Vivienne," he said to me. Coming closer, he sat at the foot of the bed and placed his hand on my shoulder, "Vivienne, please look at me."

I turned my head toward him and tried to smile, but failed miserably. I sat up and wiped my eyes with the back of my hand, "I'm sorry André; I didn't mean to let the fire go that easily. I thought I had a better anchor on it."

André shook his head at me, "It's all right."

"No it's not all right, André," I roared and stood. I paced around the room, trying to let my anger lessen again. With a sigh, I stopped and faced him, "Take my mind off of my mother. Tell me what the lesson is for the day."

André smiled at me and stood. He took my hand and squeezed gently, a silent command for me to follow him. My fingers entwined with his and I felt as if he truly did love me and want to keep me safe. I followed him, still in my nightdress, out the door and into the cold morning. We stood on the wood porch and watched as the sun tried to warm the cool valley. I turned to him, rubbing my shoulders and shivering with cold.

"My lesson for you today," he began, seemingly untouched by the cool morning, "is for you to let your fire warm you, wherever you might be. Even in the snow. You might be forced someday, when you are alone and away from me, to warm yourself without the aid of a fireplace."

I shook my head at him, "I'm not going to let that day come André. My mother can't take me from my home."

André ignored me and that infuriated me further. I suddenly started to feel warm standing on the cold porch in nothing but a nightdress. I got even madder when he only grinned at me. I glanced down to my bare feet to see that the snow and ice that had formed on the porch ran away from the heat of my feet.

"See," he said to me, "your temper can help you heat yourself and perhaps even heal yourself."

I smiled and suddenly felt cold again. I jumped back to the doorway and laughed, "I guess it only works when I'm mad."

André just shook his head at me and silently told me to go back into the house. With a sigh, he shut the door behind us. I could tell that he was annoyed and it was evident in his voice when he spoke to me, "That's why you have to focus on it, Vivienne. Yes, you're temper can help you more than you are aware of, but you cannot rely on it."

I just stared at him, my eyes wide and curious with his sudden change in mood, "Why are you mad at me all of a sudden?"

"I'm not mad at you, Vivienne," he replied and stalked off into the kitchen area, "I am frustrated with how the morning has gone."

I just shook my head at him and followed, "Because of my mother? André, you shouldn't worry. You know I don't want to go with her. I want to stay here with you."

I watched as he hung his head, his back still to me. I heard him sigh and grip the side of the table, as if what he was about to do took all his strength. In that moment of silence, I felt as if I were a child again, meeting him for the first time. He towered over me and intimidated me by his sheer size and brilliance. Quickly, my mind came back to reality as he turned to me and asked me the question that to this day I have regretted not answering right away.

"Vivienne, are you sure you want to stay here?" When I nodded he continued, "What if I told you I could offer you so much more beyond what I have taught you? What if I told you that I am more than what I have said?"

I swallowed hard, a lump forming in my throat. I stared at him with a mixture of confusion and wonder, "What are you talking about André?"

He smiled at me, a smile that I loved to see every day. He placed his hands on my shoulders, the only way I could remain standing as he spoke to me and told me what he could offer, "Vivienne, I am not mortal. I am a spiritual being that is transcended above the earthly plane of existence."

"You…you're a god?"

Again, he smiled and nodded, "I can offer you the gift of becoming one of us. I can give you more than just the ability to mold fire to your will. To become heat and life and passion; it's all in you Vivienne, if you would just let me help you mold it into something so much more. I can make you the flame itself."

I heard the urging in his voice, the encouragement for me to take him up on his offer, but what he was offering scared me half to death. I knew I didn't want the life my mother wanted for me, but to become an immortal —a god; that was something I couldn't even compre-hend.

"Vivienne, did you hear me?"

When I nodded my head, it felt heavy, as if a weight had been placed there. My eyes were fixated ahead of me and for some reason I couldn't get them to shift at André. It wasn't until he gripped my shoulders tighter and shook me gently that I moved my gaze to look at him.

"I…yes I heard you," I replied softly. I pulled away from his grasp, something I never did and placed my back against the wall, "I don't know what to say."

André's lips rose slightly at the corners in a smirk, "You don't have to answer me now. I'll give you the same amount of time your mother gave you. You have until spring to make your choice; choose me and become a goddess or choose your mother and live a normal life. The choice is yours to make, I can't do it for you."

I nodded and smiled, "Thank you André. I just need some time to think this over. I don't know how to understand all of this."

"I understand, Vivienne," he said to me, staying away from me as I slowly moved backwards toward my bedroom. "You can have the rest of the day off from your studies. Do whatever pleases you. Happy birthday."

I slipped into my bedroom after I thanked André and fell back onto the plush bed. With a sigh, I glanced out the window, watching as fresh white, fluffy snow covered the French countryside, "Happy birthday to me. What a way to start the New Year."

***

The last couple months of winter passed quickly and soon the time was upon me to make my choice. I had spent every day working harder than I had before on my studies, trying to make the choice to stay with André easier. But there was a part of me that didn't know if staying with André was the right decision.

I loved André and even though the life my mother wanted for me wasn't what I saw for me, becoming a goddess, the flame, was just hard to wrap my mind around.

Spring came slowly to the valley. Snow had long since been gone, but the cold had remained with a slight frost that kept us from being outdoors. One morning, I woke up before André to find the frost gone and a smell of freshness that had settled in the valley. I pulled on one of my blue student priestess robes and sat out on the wooden porch to watch the sun rise over the crest. Outside, by myself, I let my thoughts run away. I was always thinking, one of my downfalls, at least according to André. It was out on the porch, as the sun rose to greet me that I thought of a world without André. That world terrified me. It was cold and predictable, where I would rise only to do the daily duties of a wife and mother. In a world without André I had no power, no respect; I was merely a pawn in my mother's game.

"Vivienne, what are you doing out here?"

I looked up to see André, standing there in his brown robes and smiling at me, "Good morning, André."

He moved to sit beside me on the stair, pulling the robe about his knees, "Are you all right? You're never up before I am."

"I know," I replied, "I just felt the urge to watch the sun come up this morning. Something told me to treasure it."

With a grin, André glanced at me, "You should treasure each sun rise and set. You never know when it could be the last one."

He was always saying things like that, even more after the unwelcome visit of my mother. I shifted my eyes away from him; I didn't want to remember this sunrise if he was going to talk cryptically. After long silent moments, I turned to face him; the soft fabric of my priestess robes moving with me like water lapped the shore, "You're right, I should treasure each one."

André smiled and stood up, "After breakfast would you like to go for a walk through town? I believe the market is opening today."

"That sounds wonderful." I smiled at him and stood, following him into the cottage. I always loved the first day of spring when the market opened. The winter blues were gone and everyone that hibernated for the cold winter months came out to replenish supplies and visit with each other.

Breakfast was quiet. Neither of us spoke as we sat eating porridge and day old bread. I didn't know what to say to him, especially seeing as the day for me to make my choice was looming ever closer. More and more often our days were starting and ending like this; in silence. It was deafening and most days I wanted to scream out my frustration and tell him and the world that I wanted nothing more than to stay with him and accept his offer. Day after day, my thoughts always fell to my decision and it had made my focus slack in my studies. I know André had seen the change in my attitude, but I don't know what to do.

"Vivienne, are you ready to go?"

I heard André call for me from beyond my chamber door. With a sigh, I finished lacing up the side of my blue dress and placed the dark blue robes of priestess over the plain frock. I slipped my feet into faded brown boots that came up to my knees and laced them. More often than not, I braided my long red, flame-like hair away from my eyes, but today, I decided to let my hair fall over my shoulder in a ponytail. With an encouraging smile, I opened the door to see André waiting for me, in his brown robes as always, but there was something missing that day. Usually, on his left shoulder, was an emerald broach that he wore to clasp his robes together. But that day, upon his shoulder was a silver arrow pointing upwards towards the heavens.

I smiled at him, trying not to let him know I noticed the lack of glistening stone upon his chest and nodded, "I'm ready André."

He handed me a deep woven basket, one that I had made the first year I was with him. It was worn and well used and I loved using it to go to the market.

As we walked down the worn dirt path leading away from the cottage, we were once again silent. I loathed this silence all of a sudden. Usually André spoke to me every minute of every day, always teaching and always wanting me to learn about the world around me —and the magic within.

I was daydreaming again, I knew it because André had stopped walking and I was still going on ahead. I bumped into someone and blushed. Apologizing to the woman, I turned around to see André behind me laughing.

"I've always told you that your daydreaming would get you into trouble," he said to me with a snicker. He placed his hand on the small of my back to guide me away from the crowd and down the market place, "What do we need at the cottage? I don't remember."

I sighed and shook my head. I thought I was the forgetful one, "We need wheat so I can make flour and we need more thread so I can patch up the dresses I've ripped."

André nodded and pointed to a small covered gypsy wagon, "Try there for the thread and pick out some new fabric too."

I grinned from ear to ear, "Really? Thank you André." He just nodded and pushed me away, letting me run off to find what I wanted.

When I got to the wagon, a plump middle-aged woman stepped out and smiled at me. I had to cringe because her teeth were all but gone. The ones that were left were either yellow or so dark brown that they were about to rot right out of her head. Her dark brown hair was pulled back into a tight braid, making her look much older than she was. I know I made a face at her appearance, because she growled at me and stared, her gaze piercing into mine. She started to speak to me in Romanian and I just shook my head.

"Do you speak French?" I asked her. When she nodded I smiled, "I am looking for thread and some fabric to make myself a new dress."

The woman, in a rather annoyed huff, turned around and grabbed a spool of thread. Tossing it at me, she pointed to the table of fabric, "Ladies' choice."

I rolled me eyes at her. I couldn't believe this woman was being so rude. But with a smile, I nodded and started to rifle through the pile of cloth set out before me. I must have been at the table for a while, because a line was starting to form behind me. I looked up to the gypsy woman and she rolled her dark brown eyes at me, her way of silently telling me to move on my merry way.

"All right, all right," I said to her. I grabbed a cloth in a deep green that I knew would match my eyes. I gave the woman the money and she shooed me away as if my presence there was upsetting her.

"I'm glad I could make your day," I muttered to myself as I walked up the middle pathway. I folded the fabric and placed it neatly in my basket and began to search for André.

I soon found him, wandering as he always did and not speaking to a soul. Sometimes, especially after he told me he was a god, I wondered if people even saw him. André always seemed to move about like the mists moved on a lake after the rain; he was there, but did anyone even notice?

He lifted his head, but I don't think he saw me, because his eyes widened as if he saw something that annoyed him. Quickly, he moved towards a vendor and started talking to a young woman with raven black hair and milky white skin. She wore a dark hooded robe that hid her form from view, but her piercing gaze peeked out from beneath the silver embroidered hood.

I watched silently from a distance as André spoke with this woman, almost enamored with every word she was saying. They held each other's gaze intently, never letting it waver. I felt a sudden pain of jealousy as I watched them together and an urge to hear everything they were saying to each other came over me.

I didn't notice I was moving until I was almost within earshot of André and the woman he was intently speaking to. To this day I still don't know what they were speaking about, but I did catch a few words, *fate, emerald,* and *power.* My gaze was fixated upon André as I approached him and suddenly, I felt as if I were a child cast away from the one person I held above all else.

"André?"

He turned to face me and his usual calm eyes, now filled with an anger and annoyance I had never seen, flashed black at me. He growled and roared at me in a voice I had never heard before, "What?!"

My eyes must have instantly filled with tears at the sound of his voice, because his eyes immediately softened and his hands fell to my shoulders, gripping me in place, "Vivienne, what are you doing? I thought you were at the gypsy wagon."

I nodded, still stunned by his outburst and stammered when I spoke, "I, I was. I, I'm done now."

Though I didn't want to shift my gaze from André, I couldn't help but let it slip to the woman he had been talking to. Her head had lowered and she gazed at her hands, as if doing so would keep her from hearing us. I felt André's hands slip from my shoulders and my gaze fell back upon him, "I am busy here. Go find another wagon to look at."

His voice was harsh as he spoke to me, a harshness I had never heard before. Looking back on the event, I know that he must have been annoyed by what he and the woman were talking about, but then, at seventeen, my world revolved around André; no one else existed but him.

I nodded to him and held back my tears, "All right André."

"I'll find you when I am finished here," he snapped at me and I nodded again.

As I stalked away, feeling a mixture of jealousy, rage and sadness, I heard him say to the woman, "She's just not ready yet. I don't think she will be for some time now."

After I heard that, having the dreadful feeling that he was talking about me, I ran down the center of the marketplace. I remember pushing past the crowds of people that had started to gather as the morning changed into afternoon. At one point I must have dropped the basket with my new fabric, because as I rounded the corner, I fell and landed at the feet of a very tall man.

"Are you all right?"

The voice I heard was deep and resonant and I knew that I would remember that voice for the rest of my life. When I lifted my head, I couldn't see his features right away, for the sun was directly behind his head. My eyes focused on him and as he moved to help me up, I realized that he had eyes the color of midnight.

"Did you hear me?" he asked. He reached for my arm to help me up and I suddenly felt as if my body had turned to putty.

I nodded and smiled, "Yes, sorry." I laughed and let him help me up, "I am all right. I was just startled."

His grin widened at me, revealing perfectly formed white teeth, something I rarely saw while at the market. What was even more rare was how this man was dressed. I was used to André's robes and the patched garments of the gypsies and vendors in the marketplace, but this man wore black breeches, a white tunic threaded in red and black and a black knee length vest that buttoned across his abdomen. His boots were polished to a shine; I could see my disheveled reflection in them.

"Startled and daydreaming I see," he smiled at me again and kissed my dirty knuckles. "What is your name, chérie?"

For a moment, I couldn't remember who I was. Only that from this moment on, no matter what I did, I would only know him. When his lips lingered at my knuckles I blushed and tried to take my hand away, but to no avail. Again, he encouraged me to tell him my name.

"Vivienne."

He smiled again, a slow lazy tug of full lips, "Vivienne, what a lovely name. I am Vincent LaTorche."

I blinked my eyes in awe and pulled my hand away, "LaTorche, as in, Duke LaTorc?"

"Oui, I am one and the same."

My eyes widened in amazement at his admission. I had heard some people say that the duke was a conjurer of magic and a man of impeccable looks. But as I stood there and stared at him, he was beyond anything that any of the local girls had said. And he answered me as if this were a normal question for me to ask him. Suddenly, arrogance I didn't see right away crept up and struck me between the eyes. I felt the sudden urge to bow or curtsey to this magnificently beautiful man and before I knew it I was doing just that.

"What are you doing?" he asked shaking his head and quickly pulled on my arm to help me stand once again, "You do not have to bow to me."

I blushed again and looked around, trying to focus on something other than the mesmerizing look of his midnight blue eyes, "I am sorry Monsieur."

"Vincent," he interrupted and corrected.

"Vincent," I replied and smiled, "May I ask you a question?"

He nodded, still standing so close to me I could smell the soap on his skin. It smelled of roses and mint, similar to the soap André used. When I didn't immediately speak, he encouraged me with a rise of one sleek black eyebrow.

"Oh, sorry," I began. I hate it when I daydream. "Why are you out walking the marketplace on a Monday morning by yourself? Don't you have escorts?"

I looked around for a servant or guard that would be following him, but I saw no one. Vincent smiled at me and shook his head, pieces of his raven black hair falling into his dark eyes, "No. Today I roam the marketplace alone and for that fact I am grateful—especially today," he adds with a sly grin.

"What's so special about today?" I asked him, my naïve brain not comprehending at the time that he was flirting with me.

He grinned at me and said the words that I will remember always, "Why is today special? Well, because I was on my way out when Fate chose to smile upon me and send you to me."

I blushed. Looking back on the event I should have flirted back, I should have enjoyed the moment, but instead I felt the urge to flee. I picked up my basket from the dirt road and smiled at him, thanked him for his kind words and turned on my heel.

I didn't get far. Of course I didn't. I rolled my eyes because fate just had to intervene. I felt Vincent's hand on my shoulder and he pulled me around to face him, "Why are you leaving? Have I offended you in some way?"

My eyes were wide when he turned me around and I shook my head, "No, not at all. I just have to go."

He shook his head at me again, "I don't believe you. I think you're running away from me. Is it because I am royalty?"

"Heavens no," I snapped and moved so I could walk around him, "I must find my teacher. I am sure he is looking for me."

I heard Vincent laugh behind me as I started walking away from him, "Well I doubt anyone would be able to let you out of his or her sight, even for a moment."

I rolled my eyes and continued to walk away, "Stop following me please. I have to find André."

"André? Is that your teacher?" he asked, moving quickly to stand in front of me again.

I nodded, "Yes and I am sure he is worried about me."

Vincent tilted his head when I said that and gave me a look that told me he didn't believe a word I was saying, "Well from what I witnessed before you bumped into me, I doubt that. He treated you like a child just then. I'm sure, Chérie, you are no child."

"You saw that?" I asked and suddenly felt intruded. "Have you been watching me?"

Vincent grinned, a slow tug of pink lips to reveal perfectly straight, white teeth. He nodded, "Oui, for several years now, Vivienne. I have grown quite enamored with you."

I was taken aback by his admission. No one, in my entire life, had ever told me that he was enamored with me. I wasn't anything special, but I guess to Vincent I was. Even while my mind reeled with reasons why I should run from him and never see him again, I smiled at him. My eyes never wavered from the sincerity in his eyes.

"You are speaking the truth." It was a statement, not a question. From that moment on, I knew that Vincent would never lie to me. And the next moment I realized that I wanted Vincent in my life. My world had turned upside down in the matter of moments and I didn't care. A weight was lifted off my shoulders, a weight that was more than just my mother and her stupid ultimatum for me to return to her. This was a weight that had been resting there since I was a child and it was gone in a matter of moments following my meeting of Vincent.

"I will never lie to you Vivienne," he softly replied. Again, he took my hand and grazed his lips against my dirty knuckles. When I blushed, he grinned, showing off his pearly white teeth that should have been more menacing than seductive.

"Will you walk with me and help me locate André?"

I waited only a moment before he took my arm in his and nodded, "I would love to Vivienne. And when we find him I shall tell him that you are the most beautiful girl I have ever met."

Again I blushed and he squeezed my hand. I lifted my basket and frowned when I saw my brand new fabric was torn and smeared with mud. I must have cursed under my breath, because Vincent laughed and lifted a sleek black eyebrow at me.

"Sorry," I apologized, "I don't usually curse like that."

Vincent shook his head, "Do not ever apologize, there is no need." He took the basket from me and pulled the fabric out to look at it. "I will buy you better fabric than this and better clothing than this. You won't have to want for anything anymore."

I stopped walking when he said that and looked at him, "You are going to buy me clothing? Why?"

Vincent grinned again. I knew, in that moment, I was never going to get my way if he forever flashed that grin at me, "I plan to keep you very well, Vivienne. You will want for nothing as long as I am around."

"How long do you plan on staying around?" My voice wavered when I asked him that simple question.

I closed my eyes so I didn't have to see his grin. I felt his fingers upon my chin and suddenly his lips were against mine. My eyes flew open and saw his midnight blue gaze upon me as his lips lingered. I swallowed hard and suddenly felt nervous. I had just experienced my first kiss and it was with the most beautiful man I could ever dream up.

"What was that for?"

He continued to linger at my lips, placing nips along my jaw, "That was for closing your eyes as you spoke to me. How could I resist when you were there for the taking. If I have offended you I do apologize, though I do not regret my choice to kiss you."

Again I blushed and he shook his head, "Do not blush chérie, for if you do, I might be forced to kiss you again."

I couldn't help it; he was saying such beautiful things and turning my world upside down. So when I blushed again, I felt his lips upon mine. This time, I opened my mouth and let him kiss me fully. I don't remember how long we stood there, just beyond the gate to the marketplace, but it felt as if we were the only ones in the world.

He pulled away from me slowly, placing a kiss on my nose and smiling, "I told you not to blush, chérie."

I let out a small laugh and nodded, "You did and I did not listen. Now I know better."

He nodded, "Oui, you do. Now let us get you back to your teacher. I am sure he is missing you by now."

"André is most likely upset that I did not meet him at the gate." I looked around carefully as I spoke, trying to spot him. After several moments, I was worried and wondering why André was not waiting for me. With a sigh, I turned back to Vincent, "Would you walk me back to the cottage?"

Vincent took my hand in his again and smiled, "I would love to, chérie. As long as I am with you, I am the happiest man on earth."

I smiled again and nodded. We began walking down the dirt path that led to the cottage. After a few quiet moments, I turned to Vincent, "I asked you a question before and never received an answer."

"What question was that, Vivienne?"

When I didn't respond right away, he squeezed my hand in encouragement, "I asked you how long you plan on staying around."

"Oh," he replied softly and turned his head so I couldn't see the grin that would forever turn my knees to putty. When I prompted him to respond with a tug of his hand, he turned back to me, "Forever."

We walked slowly around the bend in the road that would take us to the cottage I shared with André, "Forever is a very long time, Vincent. I don't know if you'd want to keep me around forever."

"What makes you say that?" he asked me.

I squared my shoulders, "I have a purpose with André. He teaches me more than just the ways of the gods; he is teaching me to become one of them."

"No one can become a god, Vivienne," he replied a bit smugly, "You are a mortal, a human, there is no way you can become a god."

I sighed; knowing that he wouldn't understand what André had offered me. Even having met Vincent, my mind still went to André and would always belong to him. I wanted a taste of the worlds both men were offering me; the immortal world of André's and the loving world from Vincent. I wanted to become a goddess, to rule with André as the flame and fire itself, but a part of me longed for the embrace of Vincent. And that part of me terrified me beyond all recognition.

I felt Vincent tugging on my hand again and I turned my gaze upon him, "You're daydreaming again."

"I know," I replied, "I tend to daydream a lot. André says that one day my daydreaming is going to get me in trouble, but I think it helps me escape and analyze the world around me."

"What were you thinking about? Or is it private?" he asked me softly.

I lowered my head slightly, answering him in a whisper, "Private. In my head, no one else is there but me. I like to keep it that way."

Vincent nodded, "I understand, I get that way on occasion as well. In your head, things aren't always clear, but at least no one else is telling you how to do something."

"Exactly," I replied, lifting my head up to meet his gaze again.

I suddenly stopped on the path and sniffed the air, smelling smoke. In a panic, I looked up to the treetops to see smoke billowing out from the cluster of pines where our cottage rested. I let go of Vincent's hand, gathered my skirts and ran as fast as I could around the bend, stopping dead in my tracks when I saw the sight before me.

Where the cottage once stood was only a pile of smoldering ashes and black smoke. I ran toward the ashes, my sights set on finding something that would tell me if André made it out alive. I could feel my foot starting to burn as I approached the pile of charred wood, but I was intent on making sure André was safe. My gaze shifted from right to left over and over again before it fell upon a piece of wood that wasn't burned. I pushed at the board with my foot and beneath it I found André's brown robe and upon it his emerald broach. It didn't occur to me right then that he hadn't been wearing the broach that day, only that it was something of his to give me hope. I picked it up, held it to my chest and staggered away, only to fall to my knees at Vincent's feet.

"Vivienne?" he said softly and knelt beside me, pulling me into his embrace as silent tears streamed down my face.

"He's gone," I kept whispering, as if doing so would make him appear from the woods. But he didn't. The only piece of André I had left was in my hands and I was now forced to face the world I had rebelled against with every fiber of my being.

"Shhh," Vincent cooed, "it's all right. Just cry."

I shook my head, "You don't understand. André is my everything, how am I supposed to get through this world without him? How am I supposed to learn without him at my side?"

Vincent shook his head as he held mine. His thumbs wiped away my tears, "I don't know the answers Vivienne."

I pulled my head away from his hands and lowered my gaze to the emerald in my lap. My fingers played over the stone, watching as the color seemed to change beneath my touch. I watched as Vincent's elegant fingers gently touched the top of mine and moved to hold my hand in comfort.

"Here," he pulled the robe away from my lap and wrapped it up. He placed it in his shoulder bag and helped me stand, "Come to my home, stay with me until we can send word to your family."

I nodded, "It's just my mother. I don't have anyone else. But that sounds nice, Vincent. Thank you."

He smiled at me; a soft comforting smile that told me everything would be all right in time, "No need to thank me. I am at your service for anything you may need or want."

I don't remember much after we left the charred remains of the cottage. Nor do I remember ever seeing the robe or emerald again, until the day Vincent gave me my pendant nearly six hundred years later. All I do remember is having the distinct feeling that André was not dead, merely gone from the realm, perhaps to the Otherworld to be with the other gods.

I guess only time would give me the answers I sought for that day, or still seek to this day. What I do know is that fate still owes me for what she has taken from me and if our paths ever meet on this plane or the next, I will ask for my reward.

Chapter Six
Moonlight

Aeron hated the moon in the mortal realm.

It looked so dull compared to the bright silvery glow it cast in the Otherworld. He felt a pull in his realm, felt the moon's magic; but here, it was merely a rock in the sky. With a sigh, Aeron pulled himself away from the balcony of the hotel room that he and his sister were sharing. He still hated the idea of remaining in the mortal realm, hated the feel and the hurried pace.

"Will you stop sulking," Renée stated from one of the double beds. She was lounging with her arms behind her head, multicolored hair in a fan on the pillow. She still wore her mortal guise, but she changed her appearance to look more like herself and not the punk teenager she wanted the mortal realm to see her as.

Aeron turned around to face her and shook his head, "Comfortable?"

"As a matter of fact, I am," she responded with a smile and closed her eyes, "You need to relax. There's nothing we can do tonight about Vivienne and Vincent, so we must wait until morning."

He growled under his breath and sat down beside her on the bed, forcing her to open her eyes, "I told you that I didn't want to be here and you said it would only be a couple of days. So let's plan this out so we don't have to spend more time in this shit hole of a realm than we have to."

"Language, brother, language," Renée made a tsk noise under her breath and sat up. Her hair fell around her shoulders in a wave of color as she moved to stand, "You trusted me two hours ago. What has changed?"

Aeron glared at his sister and growled low in his throat, "What's changed? Are you kidding me?! Renée, you have done nothing but drag your damn feet since we even entered this realm."

"Why are you so impatient to get Vivienne and Vincent back together?" she asked him calmly. Renée made her way into the tiny bathroom and shouted back to him, "I'm the one that should be upset that we're not moving more quickly." She poked her head around the doorway and winked at her brother, "I have a plan, so trust me."

Aeron rolled his eyes; she always had to have a plan. Damn fate. He knew exactly what would happen if this plan of hers was to come to pass. But what was he doing? He was standing there, watching her and aiding in her madness. He had the knowledge and the power to stop his sister, but part of him was curious to see if she would go through with this plan of hers.

"Well?" she asked, coming out of the bathroom. She had changed her appearance again. She now looked like his sister, not the punk teenager she was only five minutes before. She wore a black silk robe with belled sleeves. On her feet were soft slippers of the same color, and her raven black hair hung loose about her shoulders in waves of midnight.

Aeron rolled his eyes again, "Well what?" He moved to sit on the small chair by the faux wooden desk, "You know bloody well I will follow you with whatever path you choose, sister. But what I won't do is watch you drag your feet when we both want the same thing. So you have until sun up tomorrow, or I am leaving without you and reuniting Vivienne and Vincent alone."

Renée let out a soft smirk, "Alone? I doubt it. You need me brother, so stop being so dramatic."

Aeron laughed loudly at her remark, "Now that's rich. You're telling me not to be dramatic?"

"But you don't deny that you need me," she replied with a laugh. Renée sat on the edge of the bed, leaned back and rested on her elbows and forearms. After a few silent moments, she sighed and glanced over at Aeron, "I agree to your terms brother, we'll leave first thing in the morning. Until then, we rest then we will start with Vincent and then bring him to Vivienne."

* * *

"Are you really going to stay looking like that?"

Renée rolled her eyes, piercing green and defiant beneath long black lashes and a ton of black eyeliner. She continued to apply the cherry red lipstick upon her lips and nodded, "Yes. Until he is convinced of who we are, then I will make myself known to him. You might want to disguise yourself as well, brother."

Aeron shook his head and pulled on the worn leather jacket, "No, Renée. I go out there looking like myself."

"You are too clean, too otherworldly," Renée replied, waving her hand up and down, gesturing at his appearance, "You still have your godly glow. So please, don't draw attention to us and change your appearance."

With a wave of his hand in front of his face, Aeron shifted his appearance slightly. His blue eyes, vibrant and intense, shifted to a honey brown and his hair, black and thick, shortened to just above his ears in a shade of coffee brown.

With an annoyed look in his eyes, he raised a sleek dark eyebrow, "Happy now?"

Renée smiled, showing her brilliant white teeth encompassed by crimson lips and nodded, "Yes, I am." She tore her gaze from Aeron to look out the window, watching as the sun began to shine upon the world, "Its dawn. Vivienne will be opening the bookstore at seven, but she always gets there around six. Before going to Vincent, I would like to check on her, make sure we don't have to change our plans yet."

Aeron nodded, a few long pieces of coffee brown hair falling into his dark eyes, "All right. It will take us a little while to get over there if we are to do it the mortal way."

"I think it's a good idea that we act as mortal as possible while we are here," Renée replied. She sat down on the edge of the double bed she slept in and pulled on the black, thick-soled combat boots.

Aeron stood at the open window, listening to the sounds coming from the city known for its late nights. He heard the soft noises of alarm clocks and water running for morning showers, noises never heard in The Otherworld. He longed for the silence of his realm, where the only sounds in the morning were birds chirping in the trees outside his home. As his thoughts moved to his home, his eyes searched the sun. Like the moon, it was not as beautiful in this realm as it was in his. This sun was harsh and bright; where in his realm it was warm and welcoming. For the life of him, he couldn't understand his sister's need to stay in this realm and part of him knew that he never would.

"Are you alive over there brother?"

Aeron pulled himself away from the window and locked onto his sister's gaze. With a curt nod of his head, he motioned toward the door, "Shall we head on our way? It's almost seven."

Renée followed him closely and silently as they made their way towards Magique Books. It took them about fifteen minutes to get there, remaining silent and knowing that what they were about to do, would change the fate of the world for the better. Renée knew, deep in her heart, that without the love of André in the world, it was less bright; in both realms. So now, it was up to Vivienne to bring him back.

"You know that it's going to take a lot of convincing on our parts," Aeron said softly as they walked down the block toward the bookstore.

Renée stopped and glared at her brother, "Yes I know. You don't always have to be so condescending when you talk to me Aeron." She rolled her eyes again and rested her back against the red brick wall of the bookstore, "I know what I am doing. So will you please trust me?"

Aeron sighed and nodded, "Fine. I just see a terrible thing if this doesn't work out the way you want them to."

"As do I brother," she replied softly, "as do I."

As Renée began to walk away, Aeron grabbed her shoulder and pulled her back, "Then why, if you foresee the same outcome I do, are you going after this foolish mission?"

"Because brother," she replied with a stern look in her eyes, "I have a duty to fulfill to our father. I promised him before he vanished, that if anything were to happen to him or Vivienne that I would come look for him. He also gave me the ability to release the emerald's power if he weren't around."

Aeron turned his gaze toward the street to watch a woman pass them. Once she was past, he turned his gaze back to this sister, "Then why are you only acting now? You have had nearly eight hundred years to fulfill that promise to father."

"Every vision I have had said that Vincent would come back to Vivienne of his own volition," she began in a harsh whisper so that no one passing would hear her, "So now, because he has dragged his immortal feet for one hundred seventy five years, I have to pick up his god forsaken mess."

Aeron groaned, "You have had eight hundred years Renée! You could have released the emerald's power anytime within in the last millennia and we wouldn't be in this mess. Every day we stay in this realm, we are one day closer to losing our power and immortality."

"I know!" Renée yelled. "I will get you back to our realm as soon as we are through here, Aeron."

Her face was red with anger and frustration. She was seething with the words her brother was saying to her. She knew all of what he was saying to be true, but she had to fulfill her vow, no matter the cost.

"No matter the cost?" Aeron asked as frustration and annoyance seeped from every word. When Renée nodded, he continued, "You better be willing to stand by that statement in the end Renée."

She nodded and started to calm herself, "I am, brother. No matter the cost, we are going to get André back."

Aeron's gaze, frustrated and annoyed, shifted from his sister to the bookstore to see that Vivienne was there and had opened for the day. He groaned and started to walk in the opposite direction, Renée close on his heels, "She's there and wondering why Vincent hasn't come yet. She knows she's seen him."

Renée nodded, "This I know, brother. She wonders this every day and night. We need to make sure everyone is convinced today. I want to bring Vincent here by afternoon."

"It isn't going to take very much to get Vincent down here," Aeron stated, "What's going to take some work on our part, is having him work with our plan. Because once he knows where Vivienne is, he isn't going to want to listen to us."

Renée nodded, "I agree. So how do we approach him?"

Aeron stopped walking and stared at his sister. With a growl in his voice, he roared at her, "You told me you had a plan."

"I do," she replied sheepishly, "when it comes to Vivienne. Vincent is yours."

He growled low in his throat and fisted his hands, "Bloody hell Renée! Fine, I'll take care of Vincent. You better be ready with this plan for Vivienne, because I'm ready to go knock down a door."

***

"Vinny! Someone is buzzing in."

Vincent turned off the shower and poked his head out of the frosted glass shower door. His long, shaggy black hair hung in wet tendrils that streamed down his muscled chest. Grabbing a towel, he wrapped it around his waist, slipped on a pair of black, slide flip flops and walked out to see Steve near the apartment buzzer.

"Well, who is it?" Vincent asked, towel drying his hair.

Steve shrugged, "They said they needed to talk to you. I'll ask." He turned around and pressed the white talk button, "Who is this?"

"An old friend," said the deep resonant voice on the other end of the buzzer box.

Steve turned to Vincent and raised a sleek brown eyebrow and smirked, "Old friend? How old, Vinny?"

Vincent rolled his eyes at Steve's inquiry, groaned and shook his head. Stalking towards the buzzer, he placed his hand on the button and yelled into the box, "Who the hell is this?"

Silence.

"Tell me who this is now or I'm coming down there and I won't be happy," Vincent was grinding his teeth by this point, especially when he once again received silence. Again, he yelled into the box, "Who's down there?!"

Just then, there was a knock on the door. Vincent and Steve held gazes for a brief moment. With a sigh and a roll of his dark eyes, Vincent placed his hand on the curved French handle and pulled the door open. His eyes grew large when he saw who was standing on the other side of his door.

"Well, I had a feeling that you weren't lost," Vincent said with a sneer.

Aeron stepped into the apartment, Renée close on his heavy booted heels. He smirked, a slow tug of his lips into a sly smile, "Well, I didn't exactly have a convincing excuse."

"So my only question to you is who are you?" Vincent turned his gaze to Renée and winked at her, watching her gaze as he stood there in nothing but a towel.

Aeron nudged Renée with his elbow, breaking her gaze from Vincent's half naked form. He cleared his throat and rolled his eyes, "My name is not needed at the present time, neither is my sister's. What we can tell you is the information we have concerning a certain red headed woman that has stolen your heart. Or rather, you've stolen hers."

Vincent's eyes, usually dark, turned black and blazed with anger, "You know where Vivienne is?!"

"Yes," Aeron replied with a smug nod.

"And you knew this the other day when you just happened to bump into me?" Vincent asked, his voice full of longing.

Aeron nodded and closed the door behind him, "Yes, I did."

Vincent glared at him, anger seeping from his dark eyes, "Tell me now and I won't have to hurt you."

Renée laughed, a soft yet mischievous sound that escaped her crimson lips, "Hurt us? No, no, no my immortal friend."

"How do you know I am immortal?" Vincent asked, now growing suspicious of the two unwelcome guests. His gaze shifted back and forth between Aeron and Renée, trying to figure out how they knew who and what he was.

Renée smiled slyly and a sparkle twinkled in her clear blue eyes, "Let's just say Fate has a way of coming back around and rewarding those she finds in her favor."

For a moment, Vincent was silent, looking back and forth between the two again. Suddenly, as if hit by lightning between the eyes, he lifted his head to glare at Renée; with a soft laugh, he shook his head, "Fate, you're Fate."

"Oui," she replied with a grin. She pointed at his towel, "We'll wait for you to make yourself more presentable. Then we'll talk."

Vincent rolled his eyes and then nodded, moving quickly to his bedroom to change. Moments later, still towel drying his hair, Vincent came back five minutes later fully clothed. He wore black Dockers, neatly ironed and belted with well-worn black leather at his hips. The shirt he wore, a crisp white button down, was loose about his neck and had the sleeves rolled up to his elbows, exposing well muscled forearms.

Renée looked him over with a curious eye and nodded, "Not as good as the towel, but it will do."

Aeron pushed at his sister's shoulder and shook his head, "Renée."

"Renée? So you do have names." Vincent grinned and brushed back his long raven black tresses with his fingertips.

Aeron rolled his eyes and cursed himself under his breath. With a nod of his head, he answered Vincent, "Yes, we have names. Since it is important now, I am Aeron and this is Renée."

Vincent eyed them again, "Well you know me already, but this is my friend Steve."

Aeron glanced over at Steve and nodded. With a tilt of his head, he raised his eyebrow toward Steve, "You look very familiar."

Steve laughed, "Well I don't know buddy. I've never seen you a day in my life."

Vincent snapped his fingers at Aeron to get his attention back, "Can you please tell me more about Vivienne. Where is she?"

"In due time," Aeron replied, his voice calm and even, "I need you to be patient and listen to us before you do anything brash."

As soon as he said that, Vincent had Aeron by the throat and was holding him up against the wall. Through clenched teeth, Vincent sneered, "Like this?"

Aeron laughed as his throat was being crushed by Vincent's strong hand, which only enraged Vincent further. When Vincent squeezed tighter, Aeron rolled his eyes and looked down at him, "I can't be killed moron."

Just then, from behind Vincent, Renée pulled him away from her brother. Holding her hand out before her, as if gripping his neck just as he held Aeron's, Renée lifted Vincent off his feet. With a flick of her wrist, she sent him flying across the room, crashing into the glass coffee table in front of the modern black leather couch.

As soon as he crashed, Steve ran toward his friend, "Vinny!" He turned to glare at Renée, "You bitch!"

Renée walked over to Vincent, pushing Steve aside while ignoring his derogatory statement, and knelt beside Vincent, "Are you ready to listen to us?"

Vincent looked up at her, touching his head to see that it was bleeding, "How did you do that? What are you?"

"Gods," Renée replied as if that was a statement Vincent heard every day. With a smile she offered Vincent her hand and reluctantly he took it, helping him to his feet, "So are you ready to listen or do I have to send you through the window as well?"

Vincent's eyes widened and he glared at Renée, this young girl dressed in 80s punk clothing with a wild ferocious look in her crystal clear blue eyes. He shook his head and laughed, "Gods? Are you serious? What would gods want with Vivienne or me?"

Aeron groaned and stalked the room, pacing it as if to leave a mark on the floor. His hands behind his back as he paced, he glanced over to Vincent, "Are you really this dense? Because I really saw this conversation going a whole lot better. Nor did I see having to take you to Vivienne with dried blood in your hair." He rolled his eyes and sighed, "The emerald, Vincent. That's what this is all about."

"The emerald, Vivienne's stone?" Vincent asked, moving his hand to his pocket where he always kept it.

Renée held out her hand palm side up, forcing Vincent's hand from his pocket. From his clenched fist, the emerald flew to hers and she smiled. With her eyes locked on the stone, she answered him, "Yes Vincent, the emerald. You've never believed the stories about this stone."

He nodded, "You're right, I don't believe them."

"Yet you took it from her anyway," she replied, her eyes never leaving the perfect green stone, "you felt the change in her, and knew that something was wrong with the woman you married. So you stole away from her, taking her fire."

Vincent shook his head and closed his dark eyes, "I never meant to steal her fire. I just wanted my wife, my love, to be the same woman that she was when she was young. But instead I was gifted with a beauty beyond anything I could have comprehended, with a power that I never wanted to see her have!"

Renée lifted her head and held Vincent's gaze and she transformed instantly into her goddess form. Her blue eyes pierced into Vincent's with a rage she had been holding back, "Did you even know the kind of power Vivienne possessed? That she was more important to this realm that you realized?"

Vincent stood in awe of what was going on before him. The punk girl, beautiful in her own way, had transformed into the most ravishing and intimidating of beauties. With a hard swallow, he cleared his throat, "What are you talking about? Yes I know that Vivienne has magic, but she's not important to anyone but me."

Aeron laughed, "So you think. It was another that had her love before you."

"André." Vincent said his name in a low voice and growled his name.

A sly grin tugged at the corners of Renée's full lips. Slowly, she started to walk around Vincent, as if she were an animal stalking her prey, "Yes, André. It is with your help that we are going to bring him back."

"Over my dead body!" Vincent growled and sat on the edge of the leather couch. Anger was pouring out of him as he watched Renée with his arms folded across his wide chest, "André left Vivienne and I took care of her. She was a mess when André left. It was I that held her at night as she wept for a man that never loved her as much as I have. It was I she built a life with, not André. Why in hell would I help you bring him back?"

"Because we are demanding it," Renée stated, her jaw firmly set as she spoke. "You do not question us. We are the ones in control here, if you do not cooperate willingly, then we will make you."

Aeron moved to stand beside his sister, causing Vincent to shift his fearful gaze, "Either help us or we just take the emerald from you and go to Vivienne without you. We were trying to be nice and reunite you two." Aeron wrapped his hand around the collar of Vincent's button down shirt and lifted him off the chair, "But if you are going to jerk us around, I am more than willing to bring you to the brink of death and let you sit on the edge, begging me to finish you off."

Vincent's eyes grew wide when Aeron lifted him off the chair. Once the words were out of Aeron's mouth, Vincent nodded, "Fine. I'll do what you want me to do." Above anything else, even the loss of Vivienne, Vincent feared death. The only other reason for his immortality was Vivienne.

Renée rolled her eyes, "Aeron, stop showing off and let him go."

Aeron let go of him hesitantly. Wanting to ignore his sister, Aeron annoyingly smoothed out Vincent's shirt, making him growl in response. Aeron let a smug grin tug at the corners of his mouth, "Good. I'm glad that we have an understanding."

"Don't think that for one minute this has anything to do with whatever you two have planned. And don't think that any of this is for André. The bastard can rot wherever the hell it is you believe in." Vincent stated, standing up and grabbing his jacket.

Vincent turned to Steve to see a look of perplexed anxiety on his young face. With a shake of his head, Steve leaned close to Vincent's ear, "I don't like this Vincent. What if something goes wrong?"

"Nothing will," Vincent replied with an assurance he didn't even believe himself. He silently laughed to himself, noticing that Steve didn't call him Vinny, "Just stay here. Don't worry."

Steve sighed and pursed his lips together to keep himself from saying something stupid, "Just don't get yourself killed all right? I really don't want to have to explain that to anyone."

Vincent laughed at his friend and patted him on the shoulder, "Who would you have to explain it to, Steve? I don't have anyone."

"Just go, okay?" Steve said with a roll of his eyes. He turned his gaze to Aeron and Renée, and clenched his teeth. Setting his jaw, he spoke with a purpose in his voice that not many had heard before, "Just remember that this man is my best friend. I may not have the ability to kill gods, but I can always try."

"Don't provoke, Steve. Just stay here, I'll come back," Vincent smiled at his friend and then turned his gaze back to Fate and Knowledge, "Let's go, but just know that I am doing this for Vivienne. I don't like either of you."

"That's all right, Vincent," Aeron replied with a smirk, "We don't like you either. You are simply a means to an end —or a beginning rather."

"I have one question before we leave," Vincent said softly. When Aeron and Renée looked at him with questioning eyes, he continued, "How did you find me?"

Renée grinned and placed her hand up to her head, using her fingers as if it were a phone. Softly, in a soft French accent, she spoke as if she were frightened, "*Vincent? Vincent LaTorche? Please come quickly, father.*"

Vincent's eyes grew wide with a mixture of horror and anger. Without thinking twice, he maneuvered himself and slapped Renée across the face, "You vapid bitch! How dare you use the love for my children against me!"

Renée yelped at the shock of being struck and quickly brought her hand to her cheek. Glaring at Vincent, she shook her head, "Stupid fool!"

"Knock it off Renée, you're fine," Aeron shrugged his shoulders and laughed, "You can call us all the names you wish, Vincent. What we did still got you to us. Everything happens for a reason. Your reason for being just happens to be our way to get André back."

Vincent let his shoulders fall in defeat. He was truly beginning to believe that his only purpose in life was to be a means to an end. So, if that was to be his lot in life, then so be it. He would help these two bring back the one man he truly despised if it meant that he would get to see Vivienne at least one more time.

When the three of them reached the door, Renée placed her hand on Vincent's shoulder, pulling him to face her, "We are losing time. No more walking."

"What?"

Vincent's question was lost on a breathless whisper as Renée whipped her dark robes around them and in a flash of light they were transported from his loft apartment to the sidewalk in front of the bookstore.

Vincent glared at Renée, who was once again in her human guise. Once again her perfect goddess form was clad in black, purple and combat boots and her hair was a mass of colors and curls pulled back into a ponytail at the back of her head. Her blue eyes, clear in her goddess form, were now masked by a façade of black mascara and eyeliner.

Tearing his eyes from Renée, he shifted his gaze to the sign above them. "Books de Magique" stared back at him and he growled with anger, "You've got to be kidding me!"

Renée grinned again and patted him on the shoulder, "I am Fate after all. I had to step in before the time was right."

"Before the time was right?!" Vincent was roaring with anger now and he pushed Renée's hand from his shoulder, "You twist and mold things to your desires and you expect us all to follow what *you* want for us! All I have to say is that this plan of yours better work. I refuse to be any part of your wicked games after this."

Renée rolled her eyes and watched him turn his back to her. She let that sly grin tug at her lips again and turned her gaze to Aeron. She held it as she spoke into his mind, *"If he continues like this, we'll kill him when we have no more need of him."*

Aeron nodded and placed his hand on the doorknob. Turning his gaze to Vincent, he winked, "You're choice, Vinny, Fate or Knowledge first?"

Vincent rolled his eyes when Aeron used the name only Steve called him and tried to ignore the sudden nervousness that he was feeling. With a shake of his head, he shifted his dark eyes between Aeron and Renée. With an encouraging breath, he placed his hand on the doorknob and turned the handle.

Chapter Seven
Love and Hate

The Gods, when they came to be, not only created The Otherworld and the human realm, but also a prophecy that could destroy their perfection.

The prophecy surrounded a simple jewel —an emerald —born out of the brightest star in the heavens that was said to unleash a powerful flame upon the realm. When in the hands of the witch born to wield it, she would be able to control the elements and keep balance in the world. It was said that only she would be able to keep peace in a world of chaos and war. For centuries the emerald was kept safe, away from the human realm, and its location was known only to the Gods.

André was not only the keeper of the emerald, but he was also the creator of the human realm. He loved the humans, coming and going from the realms as he pleased and he vowed that one day he would remain there with them. Intent on watching over the humans he loved so much, he took the emerald from its hiding place in The Otherworld and left.

It was within the human realm that André built his home, leaving behind his children in The Otherworld. For centuries André moved from place to place, waiting for the chosen witch to be born. As the years continued to roll by, he changed his appearance, keeping himself apart from, yet amongst the humans.

His visions brought him to Gaul, now France. It was there that his visions told him that the woman would be born, so it was there he would wait for her. André waited nearly three hundred years for Vivienne, learning of her name the New Year's night she was born.

That night the wind blew wildly and the only sounds that could be heard above the howling wind were the lusty wails of a newborn child. André stood on the hill above the small hovel, bundled tight in a brown fur cloak and watched through the window as the High Priestess of the small French village gave birth to her first child. The moon shimmered down its silvery glow upon the fresh white New Year's snow, causing it to glisten like the rarest diamond.

He remained standing upon the hill until morning dawned in the eastern sky, setting the morning sky ablaze with color. When he knew that the child slept and Celeste was alone, he made his way up the path to the small hovel. André's hand hovered above the weather worn wood and closed his honey brown eyes.

In his mind, he saw into the small fire warm room and watched as Celeste sat in the rocking chair holding her daughter. He heard her softly singing an old lullaby. It was a song that he had sung for years, humming the tune and teaching her the words while they lay naked and sated after a night of loving. Suddenly, he longed for those nights again, remembering the feeling of perfect joy as he held Celeste in his arms. As he heard her start the song over again, he could not help himself and softly sang along with her.

Sleep my love and peace attend you,
Guardian Spirits the Gods will send you,
Softly the drowsy hours are creeping
Hill and vale in slumber sleeping,
Your loving gaze I am keeping
From dusk till morning light.
While the moon her watch is keeping
as the dreary world is sleeping.
The spirits gently stealing
Visions of delight
Breathes a pure and wondrous feeling
From dusk till morning light.

André finished the song softly, his voice almost a whisper as he closed his honey brown eyes. A single tear slid down his cold cheek as he finished the song that had brought him much happiness over the years. A gust of wind blew violently as he stood on the doorstep, listening to Celeste as she sang to her child. In that moment, when the wind blew and the sky opened up to pour soft fresh snow upon the earth, André had a vision, a vision he hadn't expected to have, not yet; a vision of flames and a rising power.

"André, come in from the cold."

André smiled softly when he heard Celeste's musical voice call to him. Placing his hand on the door, he pushed it open. The fire warmed the small space he entered, but he knew that most of the heat was not from the roaring flames that filled the hearth at the north side of the room. His eyes, full of eons of wisdom, noted the tiny details that made it truly Celeste's home. Half melted candles sat idly the mantle above the hearth and trinkets hung from the windows to keep out evil spirits.

André's gaze shifted to Celeste, sitting quietly in the rocking chair by the roaring fire. A soft smile tugged at the corner of her lips as she cooed at the baby in her arms. André made his way over to her — them —the only sound in the silent room being his boots on the wood floor. It seemed as if it took forever to stand next to Celeste, André felt as if every footfall made the room grow larger.

She looked up at him through strands of wild red hair, her fierce dark blue eyes piercing into his very soul, "Hello André."

André closed his eyes as she spoke. Her voice was like music to his ears, as if the heavens sent a choir in the soft harshness of her timbre. With a smile, he opened his honey brown eyes and gazed at the child in her arms, "Hello."

Celeste shifted in the rocking chair, her arms gripping the baby tighter, "I have not seen you since the fire festival. Why do you come this night?"

"A vision." Andre stated matter-of-factly, his gaze not shifting from the infant in Celeste's arms. "What's her name?"

Celeste's full lips curved up into a loving smile as she kept her gaze glued on her daughter, "Vivienne Déesse."

André smiled at the middle name Celeste had chosen for her daughter; Goddess. He pulled his hand from inside the large belled sleeve of his fur cloak and gently touched the child's cheek. Suddenly, he brought his hand back as if she had burned him and his gaze flew to Celeste.

"Do you know whom you have in your arms?" he asked, his voice more scolding than he had intended.

Celeste glared at André, a sudden flare of fire in her dark blue eyes, "She is my daughter, André and nothing else. I know of the thought in your mind and I wish you would just let it be. She is not going to be like you."

"But she is my child!" André roared, his booming voice shaking the newborn baby awake. When Celeste stood and began rocking Vivienne, she just glared at him and shook her head. André sighed and sat on the edge of the rocking chair, "Celeste, she is not only half god; she is the emerald's keeper. Feel her fire, Celeste. You know it's true."

"Shhh, it's all right Vivienne. Don't cry," she cooed towards her daughter. Celeste turned her back to André, something she had never done, and placed Vivienne in the basinet. When Vivienne had stopped crying, Celeste stood up straight and stared out the window into the wild, cold night.

"Celeste? Are you even going to look at me?" André asked, his voice shaky and uneven with a lack of confidence.

Her hands gripped the edge of the white basinet and she hung her head. In a soft whisper that was barely audible to André's ears, she replied, "No. What you have to say I do not want to hear."

André stood and slowly made his way over to Celeste. Gently, he laid his hands on her slim shoulders, hung in both grief and defeat and pleaded with her, "Celeste, darling. Please, listen to my offer and if you don't like it then you can banish me from your life and Vivienne's life forever."

"You cannot have her André. You weren't even supposed to come back. Our night together was supposed to be just that, one night."

Straightening her shoulders, she turned to face him and brushed his healing hands away from her, "I knew what she was when she came from me not seven hours ago. And right then and there I made the choice to bind her knowledge of the emerald's power and her inevitable obsession with its power."

"There will be no obsession with the emerald as long as I have her near me," André replied, his voice unwavering with assurance. He smiled at her and pulled Celeste into his warm embrace, holding her head against his shoulder, "I can help her with her powers and mold her to become the woman and goddess she is destined to be."

With a growl, Celeste pulled from André's embrace and pushed him away. Her blue eyes usually calm and collected with an unspoken power that stated her position as High Priestess, blazed with blinding fury. With a stern and stable voice, she spoke to André in a harsh whisper, "No! You will have no power over her. She will grow up not knowing the blood that runs in her veins. She is to have a normal childhood, grow up, marry a strong man and die an old woman—nothing else—no fire, no magic, none of it André!"

"You can't just make choices without me Celeste!" André shouted, taking hold of her shoulders and shaking her sternly. "She is my child as well and I will not let you just bind the magic that is in her blood. No one bound yours when you were born."

"I am not half god André!" she replied in a harsh whisper and pushed away from him again. She pointed to Vivienne, now asleep in the basinet and started pacing the room, "You expect me to just keep her as she is, no change and just accept the fate that you are thrusting toward me because there is nothing else I can do about it?! I don't think so André, I will do with *my* daughter as I please."

André watched her pace about, keeping his warm gaze upon her frame as she moved. Even in the robes of a priestess, her form was still perfect and well proportioned. Her waist, even after carrying a child, was small and curved to full hips. Her breasts, full of the milk that would sustain the life of his child, were high and firm in her priestess robes. In that single moment of watching her by the firelight, his thoughts drifted off to the night they shared together at the fire festival. He could vividly recall her naked and sated lying in his arms as the flames danced in the fire pit beside them. Above them, the stars twinkled and smiled down upon them, keeping their love a secret.

When André grew silent, Celeste turned to face him, "André?"

He shook his head, breaking free of the trance of a time long lost. His face instantly grew hard with annoyance as the memory broke free from his mind and he pulled his cloak about his shoulders again. Making his way to the door, he pulled it open, letting in the wild wind and shouted back to Celeste, "I will be back in twelve years when it is time to collect *our* daughter. You will not keep her from the fate she is destined to have. Do what you must in the time I am giving you with her, but never tell her of whom her father is."

* * *

To a god, forever doesn't mean much. A day can come and go in a blink, but as André waited twelve years for his daughter to grow into adolescence, each day was agony. Before the knowledge of his youngest child, André would sit on the porch of his mortal realm home and watch the sun rise and set, hearing the pixie songs in the blazing glory of the morning sun. At night, as the moon shined its silvery glow upon him, he would think about the mortals he loved so much. He would think about Celeste. But after he learned of Vivienne, the moon seemed to almost lose its glow and the sunrise refused to sing.

Every year on the morning of Vivienne's birth, André would stand on the hill above the small hovel to watch his daughter. As the years slowly inched onward, he remained hidden from her gaze, yet ever watchful as she grew up. He watched as his flame haired child grew each year, coming soon to stand at the shoulder of her tall mother. Even at the age of twelve, Vivienne was stunningly beautiful and he had this awful feeling that she was going to be a handful.

A thought struck him each time he stood on the hill above the hovel; he watched Vivienne intensely, but he hadn't with any of his other children. His other children were born in The Otherworld, with him close by. The mothers were of that realm, so André didn't have to watch over them as he did Vivienne. But he was drawn to Vivienne. Perhaps it was because of who she was destined to be, or perhaps it was because André truly did love this child.

Celeste knew that André watched them, always keeping his ever-watchful eye upon them as Vivienne grew to adolescence. Each year on Vivienne's birthday, Celeste would sit at the window and look up at the hill André stood upon. She wondered if he could see her, watching him as intently as he watched them. It was in those precious few moments in the morning before Vivienne awoke that Celeste would think of a time when she loved André; loved him enough to let him give her a child. But as always, when Vivienne awoke and stepped from the warmth of her bedchamber, Celeste's thoughts came back to the real world and to the responsibility she had to her child.

It was that responsibility that kept her from wanting André to take Vivienne. Celeste knew she had no control over what André was going to do inevitably, but she could try. She wanted Vivienne to have as normal a life as possible and that wouldn't, couldn't happen if André got his way. Each day, Celeste could feel Vivienne's magic growing stronger, even without training. Her basic magical instinct was almost perfect and that fact scared Celeste. What scared her even more is what her daughter could do if she did have André's training.

If twelve years to André took forever, then they flew by for Celeste. New Year's eve, she sat in her small hovel in the rocking chair beside the roaring fire. Vivienne slept on a dark green blanket at her feet, her cheeks pink from the warmth of the fire, or perhaps from the fire within her. Her flame red hair fanned out behind her as if it had been placed like that intentionally instead of Vivienne haphazardly flinging her hair over her shoulder as she found a comfortable place on the floor. Celeste knew that André would be along any moment, but for now, she kept her gaze on her daughter's tall, slim adolescent form, draped in plain white nightgown.

She thought of the gowns Vivienne could wear if she married a man of wealth and title, could envision a day when Vivienne was not clad in the simple and plain frocks, with patches and simple stitching on the hems, that were all Celeste could afford. Celeste's visions were almost too real, too attainable and for some reason that scared her. She wanted that kind of life for her daughter, and after the four years she would spend with André, she would have that vision come to life.

"You believe that?"

Celeste lifted her head to see André standing in the doorway to her small hovel. She pulled her lips tight, keeping herself from yelling at him and waking Vivienne. Instead, she turned her head to the fire, stealing her gaze away from the one man she wished to gaze upon forever.

André almost couldn't hear her whisper of assurance as he closed the door, but he knew she had answered him with a yes. He remained with his back to her for a silent moment, causing the tension in the room to thicken. He finally turned to face her, his eyes soft, "She won't have the life you see for her. She's meant for so much more than lovely gowns bought by a rich husband."

Celeste watched as Vivienne shifted in her sleep. When her eyes didn't open, Celeste turned her gaze to André, "She can have anything she wants. Neither you or I have a say in what she is meant to have."

"Then why are you so dead set on contradicting everything that I have said?" he asked in a harsh whisper, "You and I both have a different vision of our daughter, mine just happens to be more real."

"Real?!" she harshly replied and stood, the blanket on her lap falling to the wood floor. She stalked toward André and jabbed her finger at his chest, "You want to offer her the power of a goddess, something she believes is not tangible in this realm. I have taught her to be aware of what is around her, not of what could be around her."

André laughed softly, holding back the normal boom of his voice, "Could be around her, are you kidding? You see a world of glitter and wealth for her, a world that could only be attainable if she meets and marries a nobleman. I want to give her a world where she won't need a man like that. She can have anything with the wave of her hand."

"Instant gratification," Celeste stated with a roll of her eyes, "and that has worked so well for you."

André growled low in his throat, his jaw set as he stared at Celeste. With his teeth clenched and his voice in a harsh whisper, he answered her, "Is that how you think I live my life? Yes, I do sometimes wish items into existence with a wave of my hand, but those moments are few and far between." He softened his features and his honey brown eyes glowed with a mischievousness she had not seen since the night of their mating, "You weren't an instant gratification."

"I wasn't someone you conjured from thin air either," she replied, stepping away from him as his eyes softened toward her.

As she turned away from him, he reached for her, placing his hand on her hip, "No, you weren't. You were given to me by Fate herself. You are a goddess in this realm that holds power over me and my immortal heart."

Celeste knew she shouldn't let his words weaken her, even if she wanted to believe them to be true. She glanced down to his hand on her hip and sighed, "André, we can't do this. There has been too much time and too much said between the two of us." She turned to fully face him, "We can't go back now."

"I can snap my fingers and everything that has happened between us can disappear," he replied holding up his hand, ready to do what he offered.

Celeste placed her hand atop his and shook her head, "And take Vivienne from both of us?"

André held Celeste's gaze until she said Vivienne's name, then it moved to his daughter's slumbering form. In a whisper that was barely audible to her mortal ears, he shook his head, "No. We both need her."

"No, you need her," Celeste replied, taking her hands from his, "I just want her to have the best life she can have. If I had to, I could live without having her near. But you, you need her to complete the prophecy."

"Celeste," André said her name softly, hoping to bring her gaze back to his.

She shook her head, keeping her back to him, "Just go. When Vivienne wakes at dawn then you can come back and claim her. I want nothing to do with your plans for *our* daughter."

"You won't even come to see her?" André asked seriously. He stood at the door, his hand on the doorknob and waited for her answer.

Celeste shook her head, "Not until I come to get her from you the year of her seventeenth winter. You can have your four years with her, but I grant you no more than that."

"And if she chooses to stay with me after my four years?" André asked, "What then?"

Finally, Celeste turned to face him, her dark blue gaze piercing into his ethereal soul, "She won't have a choice. You don't have the nerve to tell her who you are or what you are, so when the time comes, she'll come back with me. And even if you do muster up the courage to tell her you are a god, you won't be able to tell her you are her father because you're afraid she'll hate you."

"She won't hate me," he replied sheepishly, holding her gaze.

Celeste lifted the right corner of her lips in a smug smirk, "You just keep telling yourself that as you teach her your magic and your myths. In the end she won't choose you. That I know for a fact."

* * *

Leaving Vivienne with André for four years was harder than Celeste thought it would be. She truly believed that she could go about her life, letting her daughter think she didn't want her, and be all right until the day she went to claim her back. But the knowledge that her daughter truly despised her caught her off guard.

The week before Vivienne's seventeenth birthday, Celeste set out on the five-day journey to André's cottage. Tucked in the middle of a cluster of tall pine trees, the cottage was warm and inviting with classic stone walls and a thatched roof. Celeste let out a mournful sigh of sorrow as her two horse drawn sleigh pulled up the worn dirt path. There had been so many times over the four years Vivienne was with André that Celeste had wanted to run up to the door, burst in and take Vivienne from him. Even a short trip under the pretense of Vivienne's fictional father passing didn't ease her mind. It wasn't only Vivienne she wanted back; it was André as well.

Dawn was just breaking over the darkened valley as her sleigh pulled up outside of the small cottage. She lifted her head, clad in soft white fur and pulled down the wool scarf that covered her face to gaze up at the chimney producing gray smoke. She listened intently to the woods around her, hearing nothing but the rustling André was making from inside his small warm home. A smile tugged at the corners of her aged crimson lips as she thought of André, a god, doing morning household chores.

After a few moments of private thoughts, Celeste dropped the reigns and stood, letting the heavy fur blankets fall off her lap. The valley was cold and Celeste was thankful that she thought to wear her white wool dress and fur cloak to shield her from the elements. Pulling the hood about her graying red hair, she made her way to the wooden porch, just in time to have the door whipped open in front of her.

A gust of wind took her hood away, causing her red hair to escape its clutches. André stood in the doorway, clad in his usual brown robes, speechless at the sight of her. He held her startled gaze for what seemed like an eternity before he awkwardly stepped toward her to guide her out of the cold.

"Here," André started, moving out of the way so she could enter, "let me take your cloak. Warm yourself by the fire."

Celeste nodded her head in silent agreement, not trusting her voice just yet in front of André. She watched him closely as he took her cloak from her wool-clad shoulders and hung it on the hook by the fireplace. He was different somehow, not the scatterbrained man that had taken her daughter four years before. He was calmer here in his home than he was when he visited hers; perhaps he magically protected this cottage differently than she protected hers.

"Are you going to say anything?" André asked when he could no longer stand the silence.

She smiled at him softly and smirked, "What is it you wish me to say André? Hello? How have you been? Has my daughter learned enough to come home?"

André let out a sigh of defeat and shook his head, "I wish you weren't so cold towards me Celeste. I did love you once."

"Once," she answered boldly and cast her eyes down, "but no longer."

He growled at that statement and moved to place his hands on her shoulders firmly, causing her to look up at him, "Now Celeste that's not fair. You knew who and what I was the night you made love to me. I had no idea that we would create such a beautiful child. Why can't you just accept the fact that our daughter is something this world needs? She's someone that I need."

Celeste cast her gaze to the floor. André had never exposed himself so openly to her before, laying his heart on the line in hopes that she would accept his offer to bring Vivienne into the other realm to be a goddess. After several silent moments and encouraging looks from André, Celeste finally lifted her head to meet his pleading gaze, "I still want to tell her of what I want her to have. I will compromise one thing."

"What's that?" André asked, folding his arms across his chest in a gesture that was meant to be intimidating.

A deep breath of encouragement was all Celeste needed, "Instead of making her come with me today, I will give her until spring. She will then make her choice of staying with you or coming home with me."

"You'd really let her choose? You'd let it be her decision?" André asked as if the offer Celeste had made wasn't expected.

She nodded and smirked, "I'm not as cold hearted as you may think André. I love Vivienne. I may be hard on her, but it's for her own good. She will be more than just a priestess, either way she chooses."

André nodded and smiled, "You're right. Do you still stand by your statement that she won't choose me?"

Celeste didn't know how to answer right away. Part of her wanted to scream yes at the top of her lungs, but the other part, the more mature part, said no. She tilted her head and stood, pacing in front of the fire, "I want her to have the best possible life she can have. With whatever she chooses I will support her. Though, yes, I do think she will come home with me in the spring."

He was silent for a moment, considering what Celeste was telling him and trying not to let his anger take over. When the teakettle began to whistle, André nodded and stood, "The water for tea is ready. I'll go wake Vivienne if you wish to set up the tray."

Celeste nodded, sensing the awkwardness of André. Even though he was a god, human emotions got the better of him. She never understood why either. André seemed to favor the human realm above his Otherworld, but he never said why. With a smirk, she thought that perhaps it had to do with his precious Emerald prophecy.

After pouring the tea from a plain black kettle, she sat at the table and waited for her daughter. In Celeste's mind, she saw Vivienne vividly, knowing each and every inch of her form. But the image in her head was from four years prior and was the image of a young, naïve, adolescent girl. She tried to picture Vivienne as an adult, her hair vibrant and her eyes piercing, but she couldn't somehow. Her mind blocked whatever Vivienne had become.

From outside, a noise jolted Celeste out of her trance. Standing, she looked out the frosted window to see a woman, dark hair cascading down a body draped in blue silk. With a roll of her eyes, she moved toward the door and opened it. A growl escaped her lips as she glared at Fate, "What are you doing here?"

Renée laughed softly and placed her finger over her lips, shushing Celeste's voice, "Quiet, priestess. You mustn't let your daughter know I am here."

Again, Celeste rolled her eyes, "Answer me. Why are you here?"

Renée smiled and stepped upon the freshly fallen snow, hearing it crunch under her slippered feet, "I am here to make sure that the correct choice is made. You know I can't let you have your way."

"I truly wish you would leave us be," Celeste replied in a harsh whisper, ignoring Renée's statement that she would not get her way, "Let Vivienne make her choice without your influence."

Renée tilted her head to one side and laughed, the firelight playing with her eyes with wicked amusement, "You know I can't do that, priestess." She lifted her arm, placing her hand palm side up. There, in the small of her flawless palm appeared a clear orb and within that orb an image began to form, "Watch closely, for I know you see what is happening. The woman you see is Vivienne, in all her magical and goddess glory. You cannot take what is rightfully hers, given to her from not only André but Fate as well."

Celeste watched the orb for several moments, noticing an orange lick of flame near Vivienne's feet. Quickly, she lifted her gaze to her daughter's face to see it distorted in pain. Celeste growled and waved her hand at the orb, causing the image to distort and disappear, "No! You have now made up my mind and I don't care how much André hates me for this, but neither you nor he will have Vivienne!"

"Heed my words Celeste," Renée replied in a harsh whisper, "You cannot take fate into your own hands when she is appearing before you. I came to you as a courtesy, now you will know my wrath."

In a swirl of silk and snow, Renée vanished into the dawning morning. Celeste was now fuming, her anger seeping from every ounce of her being. She closed the door, a bit too loudly and turned to see André coming through the door with a concerned look upon his perfect face.

"What was that?" he asked her in a sharp whisper.

Celeste growled again and sat at the table, "Your first born daughter."

"Renée was here?" André moved toward her slowly, but shied away when Celeste growled at him, "What did she say to you?"

"Doesn't matter," she snapped, "I take back my offer. She will still be with you until spring, but at that time, she will come back with me. And that is final."

André cursed Renée silently, but his gaze still held Celeste's, "You can't do that and you know it."

Celeste smirked, but never replied to André's statement. That was when Vivienne, her wild red hair loose about her shoulders and her eyes full of anger and wonder, came into the room. Celeste's eyes smiled at her daughter, but no tug of her lips was seen. The conversation went as she had thought it would, Vivienne roared her anger at Celeste, but it was André that calmed her.

When Vivienne's temper soared, causing the fire in the hearth to ignite with her anger, Celeste was truly frightened. She hadn't thought Vivienne's power was that great and a sudden pain of guilt struck her gut as she told her she would see her in the spring. When Celeste left the house, she heard Vivienne slam her bedchamber door and she laughed. André followed Celeste out onto the porch. Silently, they stood in the cold, listening to each other's angered breathing.

"Did you have to upset her like that?" André's voice was soft as he spoke, his head hung in defeat.

Celeste turned to face him, her eyes blazing with anger, "Yes. She needs to know that this world is harsh, she can't keep thinking that she can have whatever she wishes by simply snapping her fingers."

"But she can," André snapped quickly, "She deserves whatever it is she does wish."

With a growl, Celeste wrapped her fur-lined cloak about her shoulders and stalked toward her sleigh. When she was halfway there, she turned and stalked back to André, "You can't keep lying to her. You want her to chose you, then tell her the truth —all of it. Then we'll see who she comes to."

André was mad, his breathing coming out in short gasps. Perhaps it was the cold that had suddenly made him go crazy, but he took Celeste's shoulders and pulled her towards him. "You drive me mad, but I can't help but want to love you." With that said, he pulled her against him for a kiss that was more anger than it was passion.

Celeste was taken aback by the sudden show of affection, but still melted beneath his lips. After a brief moment of weakness, she pulled away from him and slapped him across the face with her bare hand. She pushed him away, placed her gloves on her hands and walked away from him.

"Where are you going?" André roared after her. When Celeste didn't answer him, he growled and asked again, "Where are you going?"

Celeste stopped at the sleigh, her back to him. She shook her head and pulled the hood back up to cover her red hair. When she was settled in the sleigh, she finally turned to face him, her eyes filling with tears, "That kiss changes nothing André. What did you hope to happen, that I would change my mind?" She shook her head and wiped away the tears, "You aren't the same man that I loved all those years ago André. That man no longer exists, only the shell of a once powerful god."

With that said, she snapped the reigns, sending her horses into a full gallop out of the cluster of trees. André stood there for several moments after she left, thinking maybe she would turn around and come back. But when that didn't happen, he placed his hand against the cheek she slapped and let a single mortal tear fall down his immortal cheek.

Chapter Eight
Reunion

"Hello Vivienne."

The man's voice I hear makes my body freeze in place. It is a familiar voice, but I don't recognize it right away. In my hand is a book, the title and content escaping me as I try to place the voice. I don't want to lift my head for fear that it is Vincent and I don't recognize him. Again, I hear the voice.

"Hello Vivienne."

I can no longer stand the torment my own mind is creating. I place my finger in the book to save my page and lift my head. Who I see is not Vincent, but a tall man with midnight black hair, and clear blue eyes, wearing tattered jeans and a weathered brown leather jacket. I tilt my head at the sight of this man and wonder who he is and how he knows me.

"May I help you?" I ask, praying my voice does not fail me.

The man smiles revealing perfect white teeth. The look of this man is almost ethereal and for a moment I fear that the gods have come for me. His gaze locks with mine and I don't like the feeling that he is staring into my soul.

"May I help you?" I ask again.

He shakes his head and slowly saunters back to the counter where I sit, "No, but I believe I may be able to help you." He nonchalantly looks at a few books as he walks towards me, "My name is Aeron."

I know the name instantly and quickly get to my feet, taking a guarded stance, "You are Knowledge. I knew that you were a god!"

Aeron rolls his eyes at me, "You are far too clever for your own damn good Vivienne." With a sigh, he nods his head toward the door and the punk girl from the day before walks in.

"Hello Vi," she says with a smirk and laughs sarcastically.

I am frustrated already and don't like where this morning has gone. It started so peacefully with a warm bath in my claw foot tub. I soaked for a good hour, keeping the water hot with my own fire.

"Stop daydreaming," Aeron states, moving to stand next to the girl, "André always said that would get you into trouble one day."

"You know of André?" My voice wavers as I say his name, I can't help it.

Aeron rolls his eyes and nods, "Of course we do." He smirks when the punk girl moves to stand beside him, "We are his children after all."

"You are his children?"

I can't believe what I am hearing. I knew that André was a god and somewhere in the depths of my mind I knew he had to have had children, but I never thought I'd ever meet them. I feel as if I want to hide from the day and will this morning to start over again. Why couldn't it have been Vincent at the door?

"Will you two cut it out, you are upsetting her."

This time I know its Vincent I hear. My body, still frozen, feels as if the only thing containing me is my tight skin. My eyes growing wide and flashing black, shift from Aeron to Vincent and I swallow hard.

"Hello Vivienne." His voice is exactly as I remember, soft, melodic and deep. As I look at him, the only thing I don't recognize are the lines around his eyes that make him look older when I know that isn't possible.

I don't dare speak, I don't trust my voice, but the silence in the bookshop is deafening and I can't stand it. With a tear swelling in my eye, I clear my throat and give Vincent the fakest smile I can muster.

"Vincent."

He starts to walk toward me, his gaze never leaving mine. The grin tugging at his lips is a look I hadn't seen in almost two hundred years and I've missed it. He gets within three feet of me, my hand itches to reach out and touch him, but Aeron pulls him away.

"Not yet, Vinny," he says to him and I cringe at the name he calls Vincent. With a wink, he pushes him even further from my grasp.

Vincent places his hand on Aeron's shoulder and growls at him, "You can't keep me from her!"

Aeron laughs, "You think so? You've voluntarily kept yourself from her for one hundred seventy five years. What are a few more minutes? You'll get your chance to touch her soon enough. But not until we get what we've come for."

My eyes move quickly from Vincent and to Aeron, "What do you mean? What have you come for?"

"In due time, my dear," Aeron says with a sneer, "I can't tell you everything all at once. That wouldn't be any fun."

I smirk at his statement. None of this is fun, no matter what he thinks. I shake my head and shift my gaze once again to Vincent who is staring right at me intensely. I shiver from the energy he is exuding towards me and wonder why he and I ever failed. He lifts his left hand to drag his fingers through his hair and I see that he still wears the Fleur di Lis ring I gave him on our wedding day all those years ago. I smile at this and wish I had put mine on this morning.

"So are you ever going to tell me why you're here?" I ask Aeron, breaking my own trance. My eyes move to the punk girl and eye her cautiously, "And who are you?"

Aeron laughs, "Come on Vivienne, how is it you don't recognize her?"

He nods towards Renée who in a flash of blue and silver light, transforms into her goddess form. Her blue silk robe cascades down her perfect body like the ocean lapping against the shore. Her midnight dark hair falls in perfect wavy tresses over her shoulders and down her back, coming to the top of her rear. My eyes move to hers, clear and blue against her porcelain skin and I feel as if I know her.

"You do know me, Vivienne," she says softly. Her voice is almost as melodic and calming as André's.

I shake my head at her in attempt to both clear my mind of cobwebs and also to place this goddess beauty that is standing in my shop, "I'm sorry. I feel as if I should know you."

Renée laughs and moves close to me, placing her hand on my forehead. Instantly, she takes me to a buried memory of the day in the market when I lost André. He was standing at a wagon speaking very intently to a woman with long dark hair. His face was pulled tight and his honey brown eyes were angry. Suddenly I opened my eyes to see her within inches of my face and I gasp.

She mockingly gasps back at me and grins, pulling her hand away from my head, "You know me now?"

I nod and clear my throat, "You're the woman from the market. You made André mad that day."

"From what I remember, it was you that he was angry towards," she says with a smirk that makes me want to smack her, "You were the one he made run away."

I shake my head, my anger seeping from my pores and if I don't control it I could burst the bookstore into flames, "No! You said something that made him act like that toward me! I did nothing but love him."

"Love him?" she replies with annoyance and shakes her head, "You don't know do you?"

Aeron places his hand on Renée's shoulder and shakes his head, "It is not for us to tell her."

"Tell me what?!" I roar so loudly and forcefully that the book shelves and picture frames in my store rattle against the walls. I can see in everyone's face that I have frightened them and calm myself. With an encouraging breath I close my eyes and speak softly, "Please, tell me why you are here and why you are testing me like this. Is Vincent really here? Is this all a test? What do you want from me?"

When I collapse to the floor on my knees in tears, Vincent pushes past the two intruders to kneel beside me. Taking my soft delicate hand in his strong artistic one I smile through the rush of tears. He pushes a piece of flame red hair behind the shell of my ear and whispers, "Do I feel real to you? Do I feel as if I am a dream that keeps you from wanting to close your eyes?"

I shake my head and turn so my gaze fixates on him, "You feel more real to me than the countless nights I have spent awake hoping you would be next to me. But I feel with Fate in my presence she will take you from me again if I don't do as they ask."

He closes his eyes as if in pain and places his forehead against mine, "Trust me Vivienne. Renée won't take me, no, can't take me from you ever again. You and I are forever."

"How touching," Renée says and pulls Vincent to his feet. She locks her gaze on him and smirks, "Don't tell her that I can't take you away from her. You don't know what I can or can't do."

I pull myself to my feet and push her away from my husband, "Stop this! You are torturing us both and you aren't even telling us what you want."

Aeron laughs at this, bringing my gaze to his, "You think Vincent doesn't know what's going on? Go ahead Vivienne. Ask Vincent why we are here."

Slowly I turn to Vincent and look at him. His gaze, fierce and piercing, locks on mine and I shiver, "What are they talking about Vincent? Do you know why they are here?"

He nods to me and lowers his head. His hand is toying with something in his pocket and with a hesitation I have never seen from him before he pulls his hand out, revealing to me the stone he stole all those years ago, "This is why they are here."

"You still have my emerald!" I don't recognize the childlike voice I produce and reach my hand out toward the stone, instantly feeling the heat I have missed for one hundred seventy five years.

It is Aeron that stops me, taking the stone from Vincent. With a smirk playing upon his perfect face, he tosses the stone in the air, watching as my gaze never leaves it "Not yet my dear. You must first learn why."

Tearing my gaze away from the emerald, I look at Aeron, "What are you talking about? What's so special about my emerald?"

"You really don't know?" Renée gasps mockingly, "Shocking. Did André teach you anything?"

With that statement I can't help but roll my eyes, "You know better than anyone the answer to that stupid question. André taught me what he needed me to learn. If he had wanted me to know about this stone then he would have said something."

"He never had the chance," Renée blurts out, her voice filled with annoyance, "You just had to go and fall in love. André wanted so much more for you. It makes me sick that you are his favorite."

"I was his favorite? Favorite out of whom?" I roll my eyes at her, "I never meant for life to end up this way." Quickly my eyes shift to Vincent and plead with him, "Don't get me wrong, I love you Vincent, but I wanted more than to just become a wife and mother."

"I know," he replies softly. I can tell in his dark eyes that what I have said has upset him, but it is the truth and I won't lie.

Renée steps in between Vincent and me and stares at me intently, "Don't even speak to him right now. What needs to be said is between you, Aeron and I. Vincent is only here as an incentive for you to do what we want."

"An incentive? What kind of incentive do I need?" I am starting to get upset with how the morning has unraveled. "Will you please just tell me what you are doing here and why you want my emerald so damn bad?!"

"Well," she begins with a soft yet sure voice, "every story about the emerald, every myth you have ever heard is true. The power lays in wait for the chosen witch to take it and rule. It is this woman, this witch, who can create a better and more peaceful world. She has the power to sit at André's right hand and stop the darkness that has covered the mortal realm for so long. Only she can overcome her own darkness and sadness to become the phoenix. Then she can rise from the ashes and be given the greatest of all gifts; the gift of fire and life."

Renée lifts the emerald up so it is eye level with me, "This, Vivienne, is your fire. Your fire isn't André and it is not Vincent. This emerald and this alone is your fire, the wind you have always wanted to catch and ride away."

My eyes widen as she tells me this and I can't help but let out a little gasp of surprise. I felt strong when I wore the pendent years ago and loved that feeling. And after Vincent took the emerald from me I longed for that fire again. But now, knowing that's the reason why I felt that way, it made me long for it again.

"So this is what my mother and André kept from me?" My eyes shift from the stone to settle on Renée.

She nods matter-of-factly, "Yes. And if you hadn't run away from him in the market that day and run into Mr. Broody over here, then you would have been rewarded a long time ago with this knowledge."

"And power," Aeron adds quickly.

Renée grins, "Yes, and power."

The mere mention of the word power and I am suddenly yearning for it. Every nerve ending in my body is humming for even the smallest about of energy and power that I once received from that stone. And I want it again. Without thinking twice, I reach my hand out to touch the emerald, only to have Renée pull it away and tuck it into her hand.

"Not yet, Vivienne," she begins again. She smiles at me; a smile that is more loving than I'm sure was intended. "First, before getting the stone back, you have to do something for us."

I roll my eyes at her power trip. With a sigh, I nod and hold her cold gaze, "What would that be?"

I watch as a grin tugs at the corners of her crimson lips, a grin that looks much more sinister than I hope it is, "What is it that you have longed for most? What is it that you have wanted and waited for that you have yet to receive?"

I smile and my eyes shift to Vincent. I chew on my bottom lip, suddenly feeling as if I am a young girl again seeing him for the first time. I open my mouth to give Renée my answer but she shakes her head, shifting her gaze between Vincent and I. With a sigh and a roll of my eyes, I speak softly, "What? Vincent is whom I want! Why must you insist on standing between us? It's as if doing so would keep us apart any longer!"

Aeron growled low in his throat and moved to stand in front of me, shielding my gaze from Renée, "Stop it! I don't want to hear anymore of this trivial nonsense! You will help us, blindly if you have to. But you will help us nonetheless. Got it?"

With a frustrated sigh, I pull the dark brown wig from my head and let the long mass of red tumble over my shoulder and down my back. I run my hand through the hair that has fallen into my eyes, letting my green gaze fall on Aeron. I lift my chin in an attempt to look intimidating, but I know I fail miserably, "Fine. Just tell me what any of this has to do with the emerald? I am so sick of all this cryptic bull shit!"

Aeron rolls his eyes again and snatches the emerald from Renée's grasp and shows it to me again, "Yes, what Renée tells you about the emerald is true. It has immense power and can only be wielded by the chosen one. The only problem with that is we need something from the stone and the only one that can release the power is you. So you need to figure out how to crack this thing open and give us what we want. Then you can run along and have your happy life with Vincent. We'll never bother you again."

"Crack it open?" I growl low in my throat and glare at Aeron, not yet brave enough to touch the emerald, "I haven't exactly dedicated my life to this, you know. How am I supposed to know how the magic works?"

Aeron sighs and lowers his hand, shielding the emerald from my gaze, "André had to have taught you something about the stone, something that would one day help you when you needed it most."

I shake my head at him, firm in my knowledge that André didn't teach me anything about the emerald, "No. André taught me many things, but this stone was not one of them. The only emerald I remember from my childhood is the one he wore as a broach on his robes."

Aeron shakes his head when I tell him what I remember, "He wore the stone in front of you on a daily basis and never told you what it was?" He turns to Renée and growls, "What was going through his mind? What could he possibly gain by not telling her who she was to become?"

Before Renée has a chance to answer Aeron, I extend my hand out to turn Aeron's face back toward me. I not only surprise myself by doing that, but Aeron as well, for he gasps at my touch. Shaking off my sudden embarrassment, I hold his gaze, "André told me that he could make me a goddess if I had chosen to stay with him instead of going to my mother. But something tells me you both know about that. Thinking back on it I know I would have chosen André, but I can't say that now. Not when I have a family that I love more than any power you could give me."

Renée smirks at my admission and shakes her head in what I can only perceive as disgust, "Are you sure about that? Power is something that everyone strives for, mortal and immortal both. What makes you say with such certainty that the power of this stone wouldn't change your mind?"

"Because," I begin with a sudden feeling of confidence, "I have a family and love in my life. No power is greater than that."

Aeron laughs at my statement, "No power greater than love? How cliché."

When Aeron rolls his eyes, I nod my head and smirk, "Regardless of how cliché that is, it's the truth. I love my children and I love Vincent. No matter what the two of you tell me, you can't make me choose power over them."

This time it's Renée that laughs. Her blue eyes, piercing and fierce, hold mine as she lets out a sarcastic smirk, "We'll see about that."

With a wink, she tears her gaze away and holds her hand out to Aeron, silently asking him for the emerald. Aeron hesitates for a moment before handing over the stone, but gives in anyway. I can see that there is doubt in his eyes for what Renée has planned. I still wish I knew what they truly wanted, but I know deep down that they aren't going to give up the whole deal, no matter how much I beg.

"Vivienne," Renée begins, holding up the stone to my eye level, "I ask you again. What is one thing you have wanted for the past eight hundred years?"

I move my gaze between Renée and Vincent. Hesitantly and with a whisper, I answer her, "André."

Renée grins and nods, "Exactly. How badly do you want to see him again? What would you do to see him again just once?"

In a voice I barely recognize as my own, I whisper, "Anything."

My eyes dart quickly to Vincent who hangs his head at my barely audible voice. I mouth, "I'm sorry" to him and he just shakes his head and turns toward Aeron and Renée who are watching me intently.

"Are you sure you'd do anything Vivienne?" Aeron asks, his voice and posture sure that I will answer positively. When I nod my head he lets out a laugh that fills my bookstore with its robust sound and seems to almost shake the books loose of their sturdy homes. "Very well then, since you have agreed to give us back our father..."

"Wait," I interrupt Aeron quickly and shake my head, "how am I supposed to bring André back? I have no power to bring back the dead."

"Who says he's dead?" Renée smirks, her hand still stretched out with the emerald in clear view.

My eyes move from Renée's piercing gaze to the emerald in her hand, "Then where did he go?" Renée doesn't answer me; all she does is lift her hand higher so the stone is in my direct view. Again, my gaze moves from the stone to her and my eyes widen as I realize what she is silently telling me, "He's in the stone?"

"Makes sense," Vincent replies from behind Renée and Aeron.

"Makes sense?!" All of a sudden I am angry with Vincent for him even thinking that it was a possibility André was with me the entire time, "What do you mean, makes sense?!"

Vincent sighs and pushes past Aeron and Renée, "Think about it Vivienne. When we got to the pile of rubble where the cottage was, the only place that wasn't burnt was where the emerald hid. Then when I gave it to you all those years later, it was a magical connection that you hadn't felt since André was alive."

My anger doesn't go away as Vincent starts to explain himself, "You took the stone from the rubble when you asked me to go with you? Why did you wait six hundred years to give it back to me?!"

"Vivienne, that's not the point I'm trying to make," Vincent replies. When Renée smirks from behind him, he turns toward her and glares; "You have no say in this right now. So knock it off!"

After Vincent snaps at Renée, I reach my hand out and place it against his cheek, forcing him to look at me again. When he does, his eyes are sad and full of a longing that I had only hoped to one day see again, "Vincent stop, please. You have tried for centuries to keep André away from me, from both my physical being and spiritual. I miss him more than I miss the wind I chase. Don't keep him from me again. If there is a chance for me to have him in my life again then I want that chance."

"What if that chance comes with the price of not having me next to you?" Vincent asked, pulling away from my touch.

I drop my hand to my side and sigh, "We have been apart for too long. You won't leave me again just because I want my mentor back. Would you truly leave me because I need to see André again?"

Vincent looks to Aeron and Renée before turning his gaze back to me, "No, you're right. I don't like it, but I'm here with you till the end."

I ignore his comment about the end and turn to Renée, "Okay, what do I do? How do I release him?"

She shrugs at me, "I don't know. I was hoping you'd be able to tell us."

I roll my eyes and for some strange reason I have the feeling that she's lying to me, "And you're supposed to be all-knowing gods?"

"Just take the stone," Renée snaps and places it in my hand, "Use that fire you have stored up inside yourself. Maybe that will work."

The stone is cold to the touch, which surprises me. I remember it always being warm when it hung around my neck. I wrap my fingers around the cool green emerald and close my eyes, wishing and hoping that whatever magic is in me will open the stone and release what's inside.

With that hope, I start to feel a heat coming from inside my fisted hand. I stagger backwards, hitting the small of my back on the glass countertop. There is a powerful magic coming from inside the stone that I have not felt in centuries and I know that it's André wanting to come out again. Finally, I pry my hand open to see the stone float above our heads, an array of lights casting their glow within the confines of my bookstore.

From the stone, a wild wind begins to blow papers and books into the air and circle where the four of us stand frozen in place by the power of the emerald. Suddenly a beam of light shoots from the emerald directly towards me and hits me in the chest. I want to fall down, but the light is keeping me cemented to the floor, unable to move or deter the overwhelming power I am feeling.

I close my eyes and I can hear Vincent shouting at me, telling me to step away from the emerald's light, that's it hurting me. But I am feeling a warmth and safety I didn't know existed until now. It's building inside of me and I love how it feels. It's consuming me and I know it will knock me out if I don't stop it. But I don't want to give this up.

This power is amazing and it's mine. All mine.

"Mine!"

Chapter Nine
Memories

"What happened?"

Vincent stumbled backwards onto his back and placed his hand on his head. Trying to regain balance, he got up to his knee before standing fully. Standing beside him were Knowledge and Fate, seemingly unaffected by the sudden shift in the plane of existence. Both only smirked at Vincent's obvious question and stood there as they gazed around at their home realm.

The world around Vincent was one he'd never seen before. It was one of stunningly beautiful skies and crystal clear waters, but that's not what he focused on; instead his gaze shifted to Vivienne who was lying motionless on the dirt path at their feet. Quickly, he ran towards her and knelt beside her, cradling her head on his lap.

Vincent placed his head against hers and rocked back and forth, trying desperately to wake her up, "Vivienne? Please, Vivienne open your eyes."

"That's not what's going to wake her up," said a man with a low, sure voice.

Vincent lifted his head, the sun blindingly harsh. A dark shadowy figure blocked out the bright light and Vincent squinted until his eyes focused on who stood before him. With a smirk, he looked back down at Vivienne and shook his head at the unwelcome man in front of him, "Go away André."

"How do you know who I am?" André asked, folding his robed arms across his wide chest.

Still cradling Vivienne's head in his lap, Vincent shifted his position on the ground so he could look up at André, "How wouldn't I know who you are? Vivienne released you from the stone. There would be no one else I would have expected."

With a smirk, André knelt down beside the motionless Vivienne and placed his hand on her forehead, "She's had the power of the emerald pierce through her heart. She must be placed in the waters of the Healing Caves and then she'll wake after a day or two of rest."

Vincent let his gaze fall from André, his honey brown eyes full of worry for the woman he had left bereft and broken nearly eight hundred years before, to Vivienne. A tear fell down his cheek and he nodded, but his voice failed him and let André see his vulnerability, "All right. Where is that?" Vincent lifted his head and finally looked at the world around him, "Where are we?"

André stood, his brown robes falling around his aged form and he squared his shoulder as he proudly told Vincent where the stone had taken them, "We are in The Otherworld; the place that was created by my own hand before yours was created. Here, the gods live and flourish and are able to come and go as they please as long as they use the boat on the River of Time."

Vincent shifted on the ground so he could see all that André was describing. All around them, the four seasons seemed to bloom in unison, changing only when they touched the wooden bridges that connected them. Where they sat on the dirt path must have been summer, for the above them apple trees blossomed with ripe red fruit and the sweet smell of cherries was carried on the calm, warm wind. To the left a cooler wind blew carrying the promise of shorter, cooler days and changing leaves. The bridge that led to autumn was covered in vibrant green vines that wrapped around every inch of its oak. Vincent watched as crows descended from the top of tall oak trees to swoop down and hop on the ground toward pumpkins ripening in the garden just beyond the bridge.

Beyond the changing trees and the robust gardens was the bridge that led to winter. On the autumn side squash vines with large green leaves threatened to take over the wood, but as the vines approached winter, ice and snow layered over them with a thick covering. Long threads of ice hung from the bridge and every withered, dying tree as the dark of the year took over. Where the other seasons held life, whether it is a bird, squirrel or deer, there was a presence. But in the winter, there was no life. Nothing stirred within the confines of ice and snow, just the promise that soon spring would come and the flowers and trees would bloom.

"Vincent?" André stood in front of him, his arms across his wide chest, "What are you staring at?"

Vincent shook his head and stared up at André, "What? Oh, I just have never seen a place like this before."

"And never will again," Renée replied and helped Aeron lift Vivienne off the ground and place her on a plush pillowed cart pulled by a sterling white pony. "This place is not for your eyes, as you are not made of our blood. Regardless of the fact you have made yourself live this long, you are still mortal."

Vincent growled and shook his head, "Wait a minute. What do you mean not of your blood? I know I'm still "mortal" as you put it, but so is Vivienne."

At that comment, André stopped moving and paused the processional to the Healing Caves. With a smirk, he quickly moved towards Vincent, holding his gaze the entire time, "You are arrogant in your assumption that Vivienne is not of godly blood. If you hadn't interfered in her fate, she would have still had the chance to live forever."

Vincent watched as André made his way toward him and he took a guarded stance. With a similar smirk that André had given him, Vincent replied, "How? Vivienne is as mortal as I am. She was born in a simple town and lived a simple life."

Renée rolled her eyes at this. She petted the pony as she eyed Vincent, "You really are this thick aren't you? I can't believe you haven't figured it out yet."

"Figured what out?!" Vincent was now getting angry. Renée was talking in riddles again and André was staring at him as if he should know this great secret that he was never privy to. "You speak more riddles than I care to hear. So please, just tell me what it is before you drive me insane!"

Again, Renée rolled her eyes, knowing that Fate would have to step in and help guide Vincent along and pulled André toward where Vivienne lay motionless on the pillowed cart. Looking at Vincent, she pointed to André's and then Vivienne's faces, "Do you see anything similar—perhaps a feature that is the same?"

Vincent moved closer, trying to figure out what Renée was speaking of. He shifted his gaze between André and Vivienne, comparing eyes, scars, mouth shapes, and ears and then he saw it. It wasn't a feature that could be seen if they weren't looking for it. This was a feature that he had adored on Vivienne since the day they met, yet hadn't realized it was there until he saw her magic. Suddenly, with Vivienne and André so close together, their combined auras shinned bright in the summer sun. It was then that Vincent saw it, saw that Vivienne and André had the same aura.

"It can't be," Vincent whispered breathlessly, "you are her father?"

André smirked, giving Vincent a sly smile and nodded, "Aye, I am. And she does not know."

Vincent shook his head again, as if doing so would clear it completely of what he had just heard. After a moment, Vincent held André's piercing gaze, "How could she not know? How could you have her live with you and train with you and have her not know you are her father?"

"It's complicated," André replied sorrowfully, "Her mother and I met and slept together the night of the fire festival in her small village. Celeste was the most beautiful mortal woman I had ever seen and I knew, the moment I saw her, that I had to have her. We danced and spoke of her life; I was intrigued by every single detail she had to tell me. But it was when she told me she was a priestess and would never be allowed to marry that I knew I had to give her at least the gift of a child.

"We loved each other the whole night," André continued, holding Vincent's curious gaze, "But as the morning dawned, I kissed her goodbye and never looked back. But Fate," he pointed to Renée and rolled his eyes, "brought me back to Celeste nine months later. I walked into the hovel she lived in and found her there with the most precious of babes. Pink and perfect, Vivienne lay against her mother's chest and I fell in love all over again, before I learned that Vivienne was more special than just the daughter of a god."

"You learned that she was the keeper of the emerald," Vincent stated bluntly, his eyes fixated on Vivienne's slumbering form.

André nodded and lightly touched Vivienne's cheek, "She is more than I could have asked for and perfect in every way. But, you know that already." He smirked and pulled his hand from Vivienne's face and turned to Vincent, "But in the end, Celeste didn't want my influence in my daughter's life. I told her that she could have twelve years with her until I took her to train her and hone her skills as a witch and goddess in training. I could never bring myself to tell Vivienne that I was her father. I found it was easier to tell her I was a god."

"You know she loved you," Vincent stated harshly, beginning to pace along the dirt path, jabbing his finger toward André, "She mourned you for years after we were married. I was never good enough to live up to the memory of her precious André. I don't care how hard it was to live with your daughter and not be able to tell her who you truly were. I am the one she chose and I am the one she loves now."

André dropped his head in defeat, his warm honey brown eyes full of sorrow, "I never gave her any inclination that I was anything more than her teacher. She was the one that built me up in her mind to be more than I appeared to be."

Vincent rolled his eyes at André's remark and shook his head, "Oh poor you, André. I have hated you for more years than I care to count and have longed for Vivienne even longer. I know that what I did was my fault, but now I am here, helping her achieve her goal. So just wake her up and let's get this over with. I don't want to be here any longer than I have to be."

"Again you don't get it," Renée stated from beside the pillowed cart, "Once Vivienne achieves her goal you won't be able to be a part of it. She's here to stay with us in her rightful place as the Phoenix Goddess."

Vincent's eyes widened at Renée's admission. He shook his head and reached down to grab Vivienne's hand, "No. I have been without her for too long. I won't let you take her again."

"And it was your fault you didn't have her," Aeron replied softly, his voice almost as soft as the wind, "If you hadn't left her then, and she was able to capture the power of the emerald all those years ago, you would have still lost her."

It took all of Vincent's willpower to not haul off and hit Aeron across the jaw. Instead, he growled low in his throat, "Watch your tongue Aeron! You don't know what she would have done. In my heart I know she would have given it up for me and the children."

"You keep telling yourself that," Renée said with a smirk and motioned for Aeron to start the pony again up the path.

Vincent stood watching them for what felt like lifetimes, but knew it was only moments. Shaking his head to clear it, he jogged up the slight incline to catch up to the cart, "So once you heal Vivienne, are you going to tell her the truth?"

André kept walking up the path, trying to ignore the truth in Vincent's question. When Vincent caught up to him, he stopped André and pulled him so they were face-to-face, "Answer me old man. Are you going to tell Vivienne the truth or do I have to do it for you?"

It was that statement that finally made André's temper spark. André twirled around quickly, his robes spinning upwards as he moved and with his hand cupped in the air he lifted Vincent off the ground. Vincent struggled against André's phantom grasp and kicked his feet dangling three feet from the dirt path. André's eyes flashed black and then red as a powerful wind blew his robes about his aged form. Vincent was slowly loosing consciousness and when his struggling stopped, André lowered his arm and dropped Vincent to the ground.

"I will take care of Vivienne when I am good and ready!" André growled harshly through clenched teeth and short, labored breathes,

"Vivienne is not your concern now. When she awakens, you will be allowed to say goodbye. You must leave after that."

Vincent brought his hand up to his throat, massaging the bruises left from the invisible hold, "Not my concern? She's my wife!"

"A fact that neither concerns nor affects me," André replied bluntly. He turned around on his heel and continued on with the processional.

***

"Don't you think you were a bit harsh on Vincent, father?" Aeron asked, helping him lift Vivienne off the pillowed cart.

André shook his head, "I only spoke the truth Aeron. You know that."

As they walked into the Healing Caves, the torches hanging on the stone walls burst into flame. Foot by foot the torches lit the long path that lead to the pools of water that would heal Vivienne and bring her back to consciousness. Renée led the procession down into the damp cave, holding out her hand to let an orb of blue light help guide their steps. The pools were lit from beneath with the same blue light that Renée held and were heated by boiling hot rocks. Once they arrived at the water, Renée took Vivienne from her father and brother, stripped her from all her earthly clothing and slipped on a black silk robe.

"I'm ready," Renée said softly, watching as her brother and father appeared from around the corner, "I'll guide her head and shoulders if you'll take her feet Aeron."

Aeron nodded and helped Renée place Vivienne in the warm, healing waters. As soon as Vivienne was submerged in the warm water, her porcelain skin slowly began to turn pink from the heat. André sat on the edge of the pool, the cool stones a comforting contrast to the heat of the water and watched his youngest daughter twitch.

"Is she supposed to be doing that?" Aeron asked, standing behind his father with arms folded across his wide chest now clad in a blue silk robe.

André didn't lift his head to look at Aeron, only nodded, "Yes. The heat of the water is calming her very frantic and scattered mind. I'm trying very hard not to enter her dreams, but the way she is smiling is making me want to help guide her back to us."

"I'll do it," Renée volunteered almost immediately with an energetic sneer, "I have no problem whatsoever going into Vivienne's mind. I quite enjoy it there."

Aeron rolled his eyes and eyed his sister cautiously, "You say that almost too eagerly, Renée. Why don't you let father have some fun for once."

"Why? He doesn't want to do it," Renée snapped defiantly, reaching down towards the pool to place her hands on Vivienne's head.

André stood at that comment and pushed both Aeron and Renée away from him, his hands firmly on their chests, "Knock it off, both of you. Is this how the two of you have acted towards each other since I imprisoned myself?" When Renée nodded, André shook his head and pointed to the cave opening, "Out, both of you. Leave Vivienne and I so we may have a few moments of peace."

Aeron and Renée left the cave in a huff, growling at their father as they did so. After they were no longer visible, André turned to gaze once again upon his daughter in the healing waters of the warm pool. With an encouraging breath, André dipped his hand into the water and placed it on Vivienne's head. Closing his eyes, he let his mind wander into her dreams to see what she was seeing, to help guide her back to him.

***

André opened his eyes and rubbed them as if he had been sleeping for centuries. He felt a sudden pain of cold before he took the time to inspect his surroundings. Before long, he knew exactly where he was; outside the small hovel that Celeste and Vivienne shared when she was a young girl. For a moment, he wondered why she brought him to stand outside, but soon a noise brought his attention to the window and he glanced into the fire warmed room to see a version of himself he barely recognized. The man standing in the room looked defeated and longed for the touch of the woman standing three feet away from him, yet he made no attempt to touch her. He watched as Celeste scolded and yelled at him, but it was Vivienne's adolescent form sleeping on the floor near the hearth that held his attention.

Suddenly, as if pulled from another place, he left where he stood in the cold. He was transported to the next morning and he was standing outside the worn wooden door of the small hovel. Remembering what he had done that day, he knocked softly, Celeste opened the door and again, her beauty took him back.

"Why are you just standing there staring at me?" she snapped, "Come in, it's cold."

"Good morning, Celeste." André walked inside, unsure of what was going on and why he was reliving this painful memory. He looked around the room, unchanged in years and moved to stand by the fire.

She just rolled her eyes at him and moved to the door at the far end of the hovel and opened it. André heard her say to Vivienne that she wanted her to meet someone. He could hear Vivienne's voice, soft and innocent, ask her who it was. Celeste told her it was an old friend and she should just come out because her mother wanted her to.

When Vivienne stood in the doorway, her eyes widened at the sight of André as if he were a giant. She wore a simple white dress with dark blue lacing up the sides and a blue shift on beneath. Her hair was braided back away from her porcelain face dotted with brown freckles that framed intense, piercing green eyes. He watched as she swallowed hard and nervously walked into the warm room rubbing her upper arms, "Hello, sir. It is nice to meet you."

Celeste moved to kneel in front of Vivienne and held her hands, "This is André, and he is an old friend of mine and a very powerful man. I have asked him if he would like to teach and train you in the magical arts."

Vivienne nodded and shifted her gaze from Celeste to André and then back again, "Why are you making me leave? Did I do something wrong?"

"Oh no, no, no my dear," Celeste shook her head and pulled Vivienne in for an embrace, "I just know that you have wanted to do some studies for a while now and I can't let you stay here and have me

teach you. That's not how things work. It won't be for very long, just a couple of years."

Vivienne's eyes widened nervously, "Years? I will be away from you for years?"

Celeste nodded and turned slightly so she could glance and point at André, "André is a very nice man and will take wonderful care of you. Don't worry my love."

Kneeling down beside Celeste, he took one of Vivienne's hands, "Would you like to see a demonstration first?"

Celeste smirked, and rolled her eyes in annoyance. She shook her head and voiced her sarcasm, "Sure, go ahead. Dazzle her with your talent."

André could tell that Celeste didn't want to prolong this any more than she had to and now she had to just sit back and let André win over his daughter with tricks. André turned his attention to Vivienne and held out his hand, "You see anything in the palm of my hand? Do you see any sparks or flint?"

Vivienne examined his hand and shook her head, "No, I don't."

"Good. Now watch," André grinned and held her gaze as he silently said an incantation and fire erupted on his palm, "I can teach you this."

Vivienne fell back onto the floor, her eyes wide with amazement, "How did you do that? Are you some kind of sorcerer?"

"You could say that," he replied with a smirk and closed his hand, the fire vanishing as he did so, "So does that convince you? Will you please stay with me and learn from me?"

Vivienne jumped to her feet and grinned, "Yes! As long as you will teach me that trick and any others, I would love to learn from you!" She turned to her mother and hugged her about the waist, "Oh thank you mother! Thank you for allowing me to meet André."

Celeste smoothed out Vivienne's hair and held André's gaze. With a sigh, she said softly that she loved Vivienne and then glared at André, silently telling him that she would never be able to forgive him for what he was about to impart on her.

Once Vivienne was packed and settled in the horse drawn sleigh, she said good-bye to her mother. Waving until she was out of sight, Vivienne settled against André and thanked him over and over again. As she continued to voice her appreciation, André's eyes began to droop and he felt as if he were being pulled from this memory. Before long he was fast asleep in the sleigh, waiting for whatever Vivienne was going to show him next.

The room was still dark when André opened his eyes. Yawning, he sat up from the soft plush mattress beneath him, rubbed his face and beard and looked about the familiar yet strange room. It was a place he had not seen in centuries, yet it still held a feeling of home to him. Taking in a deep breath, he stood and donned a brown robe and opened the simple white curtain that guarded the small window on the north side of the room.

"I'm back in the cottage," he whispered to himself in awe.

In the clearing behind his house, he gazed upon a doe grazing near the brook and he smiled. He hadn't seen that kind of peaceful image in a very long time. Letting the curtain fall back into place, he turned his head toward the door, wondering if Vivienne was in the cottage.

Going to the door, he pulled it open to the fire warmed room. The only light in the room was coming from the dying fire in the hearth beneath the black cauldron. He stood in the doorway for several moments, looking around at the room. Everything was exactly as he remembered it to be, with nothing out of place except for the lack of Vivienne's presence.

Venturing forth, he strode toward the door that led outside. That's where he found Vivienne. She was young, maybe fifteen or sixteen, and she was sitting in the grass, her hands out before her, making a buttercup bloom and die as she opened and closed her hand. André smiled at the sight before him, but remained in the doorway as to not disrupt her concentration.

André watched Vivienne, her green eyes glazed over with quiet power, as she not only controlled one buttercup, but also had a circle of them around her. A smile tugged at the corners of her soft pink lips as the flowers bloomed around her. André knew this was the first *time she had controlled her powers so precisely and loved watching it again. Just like the first time he watched her, she exuded power, but this time, something was different and he couldn't figure it out.*

"André, what are you doing?" She asked him quietly, her voice barely hitting his sensitive ears.

André laughed and pulled himself away from the doorframe and walked down the two wooden steps to the grass where she sat. The moment his feet touched the grass all the buttercups vanished and she looked up at him, her eyes no longer glazed with power, "I was simply watching you explore your power. How did you know I was there?"

"I always know when you're watching," Vivienne replied softly and stood. She wore a simple blue dress with white laces holding the sides together. Her long flame red hair was tied back with a loose braid that she had done herself and stray strands were licking the sides of her long black eyelashes.

André let out a soft laugh and smiled, "I'll always watch over you Vivienne, whether I am there or not."

"Well it's a good thing I'm not letting that happen," she replied with a smile and gazed into his warm honey brown eyes. With a tilt of her head, she eyed him curiously, "There's something different about you André. You seem older to me today."

It was at that moment André realized that he had entered her memory as he was in the Healing Caves. He reached out to touch her shoulder and willed himself to look a bit younger, "Oh? Perhaps it's just the light."

When André seemed to change as the sun shifted above them, Vivienne blinked her vivid green eyes. Shaking her head, she turned, but kept her gaze upon him, "Perhaps you are right. The light seems to be playing tricks on me."

André smiled and silently breathed a sigh of relief. He didn't need her figuring out that he was appearing to her as a different version of himself. With a lift of his head, he gazed upon the porch where she was heading and couldn't help but picture her as she was in the Healing Caves. Here, she was young, naïve and vulnerable, but there, where she lay unconscious, she seemed older. Just from seeing her, she seemed a changed woman and part of him couldn't wait to meet the newest version of her.

"André?" Vivienne asked from the porch, her hand outstretched toward him, "Are you coming? It's time to make tea."

He nodded, but didn't move, "Why don't you start and I'll catch up soon. I'd like to enjoy the sunny morning if you don't mind."

"Of course," she replied, eyeing him curiously again, "Just don't take too long. You told me you were going to tell me something important today."

André tilted his head and thought for a moment. Then it dawned on him, he told himself every morning that he would tell her who he truly was. But, as always, he couldn't bring himself to do it. He wondered, why on this morning of all days, he had told her he had something important for her.

"André?"

He shook his head to clear it and smiled at her, "Of course. I almost forgot. Go inside and I'll be along shortly."

When she was inside, André turned on his heel and almost ran to the edge of the pond near the cottage. What was he doing in this memory and why was she thinking of this day? He tried to recall this day, but it seemed to start like any other—trivial talk in the morning, tea after lessons and then a walk to the market in the afternoon. For the life of him, he couldn't figure out what was so special about this memory.

While he slowly walked around the pond, he could hear Vivienne singing in the house. That was a sound he hadn't heard in a very long time and he missed it greatly. After a few moments of just listening to Vivienne, he turned and made his way back towards the cottage, but didn't go in. Instead, he stood outside the window on the porch and watched her move about the room. Even though the Vivienne in front of him was one he remembered more vividly than his own life, there was something different about her. She seemed taller than a few moments before when she was sitting in the grass with the buttercups blooming around her. It was as if, all of a sudden, she had aged before him and she was now seventeen. That meant this was his last spring with her.

He turned away from the window then, realizing that the memory he was in, was a mash-up of all her memories while she was growing up. He turned to look at her again and noticed that her hair was no longer braided back away from her face, but now hung loose about her shoulders the way her mother wore hers. A smile tugged on his lips and he couldn't help himself when he tapped on the window to get her attention.

Vivienne quickly turned toward the window to see André. Her eyes were wide with surprise and she placed her hand on her chest as if to keep her heart contained there, "André? What are you doing?"

"Come outside," he replied, ignoring her question.

With a sigh, she tossed the rag in her hand on the table and bounded outside, "What's wrong? Why are you outside so early?"

André let out a soft chuckle and took her hand, "Do you remember the day I caught you here with the buttercups?"

"Yes," she replied wearily and lifted a sleek red eyebrow at him curiously, "It was only a year ago. Are you all right André? You look a little worn down."

André smiled again and tugged her hand so she would follow him, "I feel better than I have in a rather long time my Vivienne." When they reached the clearing by the pond he pointed to the ground and told her to sit, "Do the buttercups again. I want to see them one more time."

"One more time?" She asked sitting on the grass. Looking up to him, her green eyes glazed with tears, "André, you are frightening me. You're acting as if this will be the last time you get to see me. What's going on?"

André smiled at her and pointed to the ground once again. He ignored her statement and held her gaze, "Buttercups, please."

Vivienne eyed him curiously, keeping her gaze on him as she slowly descended to the grass, "Why is this so important to you André? It's just a simple power control that I learned my first summer here."

"I know," André replied with a nod, *"But you are so much more controlled now, I would like to see how you have progressed."*

With a sigh, Vivienne nodded in agreement, *"All right."*

As Vivienne closed her eyes, André watched as the small, delicate yellow buds broke free from the spring grass and shot up towards the heavens. André closed his eyes as well and listened to the energy hum around Vivienne, feeling her energy as he stood three feet away from her. Suddenly, André opened his eyes when he felt more than energy exuding from her presence.

"Vivienne?"

She opened her eyes, but André only saw black orbs staring back at him. All around her the delicate buttercups bloomed past blossoming and started to wilt. Just then, within Vivienne's eyes, flames burned against the black depths and caused André to take a step back.

"Vivienne, perhaps I was a bit hasty when I wanted you to do this power control," André said wearily.

She didn't reply, didn't even acknowledge the fact that André had spoken to her. A powerful wind lifted her flame colored hair and blew it about her shoulders. With her arms extended out, palms down toward the wilting buttercups, she began muttering a chant that was inaudible to André's ears.

"What am I doing?" André asked himself out loud, *"I can stop her. I can stop this at any moment. All I have to do is let go of these memories."*

As André said that, he tried to will himself back to The Otherworld and let go of Vivienne there, but to no avail. Vivienne was keeping him with her in this dream and the longer she had control on her powers, the longer he would be here with there. André continued to shout at Vivienne, but she remained immune to his verbal tenacity. When it seemed she could take no more of his shouting, the perfect circle of wilting buttercups burst into flame and encircled Vivienne in orange and red.

***

André opened his eyes and stumbled back from the Healing Pool. The cool rocks beneath him broke his fall as he seemed to be thrust backward from where Vivienne lay calmly in the warm water. It took André a few moments to compose himself before getting back to his feet and when he did, he held onto the small of his back where he had been impaled by a large rock.

"Vivienne," he sighed, her name coming out in a whisper that was meant only for him. He reached into the now scalding water, hot from the fire burning in her blood, and lifted her from it; her skin was pink and warm from the water. Knowing that Aeron still stood beyond the opening of the caves, he shouted back to him, "Aeron, please come help me."

Aeron bounded in like an excited child receiving a present. When he saw that André was injured, he took Vivienne from his grasp and placed her on the pillowed cart, "Father, what happened? You've been in here for hours. Vincent is getting quite stir-crazy back at Renée's cottage."

André shook his head and sat on the edge of the cart, pushing Vivienne's feet out of the way, "I don't give two shits what Vincent is doing. Who I care about is laying beside me in the throes of a very powerful dream. I could not shake the power from her and she thrust me out when I believe I grew too annoying for her."

"Annoying?" Aeron replied with a snicker, "What were you doing, shouting at her to stop?"

André stood up slowly, heard his back crack and eyed his son carefully, "Shut your mouth and get her back to your sister's cottage. We'll make her warm and let Vincent see his wife before we make him leave."

"Wow," Aeron replied astonished. He guided the pony slowly back down the hill, careful not to jolt Vivienne, "You're becoming soft in your old age, father. The man I knew would have sent him packing before he hitched a ride to our world."

André replied with a laugh and patted his son on the shoulder, "You're right, I would have, but when it comes to Vivienne, there's no way to tell her no, even when it comes to Vincent."

"I still don't like him father," Aeron said bluntly, crossing the bridge into winter, "I don't know what it is about him, but something just doesn't settle with me."

André placed a blanket over Vivienne as they crossed into winter and pulled his own brown robes about his aged form, "I only just met the man, but from the few moments I have spent with him, I know he is not good enough for my Vivienne. He stole the stone from her first of all and then left her for more than a century. That's not the kind of man I want for my daughter."

"Well father, I hate to break it to you, but you left her too," Aeron stated as they approached the cottage, "And why did you leave her like that? You had to have known she would stay with him the day you saw them together in the market."

André nodded and looked to Vivienne sleeping peacefully on the cart, "You're right. I did know that she would choose him and it hurts me to know Celeste was right as well. But she was looking at me differently, almost as if she needed something more from me than I could give her. She loved me differently that I had intended and it was my fault for not letting her know the truth, but I did what had to be done. I just didn't think it would take this bloody long to have all the pieces fall into place."

Aeron stopped the pony when they reached the cottage and tied it to the post near the porch. Knowing that André's back was still hurt, he lifted Vivienne, blanket and all, from the cart and carried her inside. There, they found Vincent sitting by a roaring fire and Renée sitting beside him, both silent until the door opened.

"You're back," he exclaimed, jumping to his feet, "Is she all right? Is she healed?"

André ignored the questions and headed toward a room at the far right corner of the cottage, Aeron close on his heels. He placed Vivienne on the plush mattress and covered her with several warm blankets before moving to light a candle.

"Are you going to answer me?" Vincent asked from the doorway.

André shook his head and knelt down to start a fire in the fireplace near the bed, "No. The only thing I am going to say to you is this. Enjoy the time you have with Vivienne now, for when she awakens, you will have to say your good-byes and leave The Otherworld."

"Leave? You are really serious about that?" Vincent asked astonished, "You can't keep me from her. I promised her that I would be with her till the end."

"Well then I suppose you should not make promises you can't possibly keep," André replied sternly, his gaze never settling on Vincent. "Look, you have to realize that Vivienne doesn't belong in your world. She is a goddess and will be treated as such. You may have your night with her so I suggest that you make it count. This is my gift to you. Either take it or leave now, it's your choice."

Vincent let out a sigh and hesitantly agreed to André's gift, "Fine."

Once André was out of the room and the fire roared in the hearth, Vincent took off his crisp button down shirt and settled into the bed next to Vivienne. He kept thinking about what André had said that Vivienne was a goddess and should be treated as such. He had always treated her as if she were a goddess and queen, for that's what she was to him. He had been without her for too long and now that he was with her again, he wasn't going to let Aeron, Renée and André take her from him. But a thought plagued him as he settled against Vivienne, a thought that perhaps André was right. Maybe Vivienne did need to be here with her family and learn more about her powers and her heritage. Maybe she needed to be here, without him, even though that hurt him more than anything. She, in his mind, needed more than just him and his need for her was a selfish one. Everything he had done was selfish, so why stop now? So, in the morning, he would take her to André and after he told her the truth, Vivienne would make her choice.

As he snuggled against Vivienne, a smile crossed his face as he moved to embrace her warm body tighter and he placed a kiss on her cheek. He settled his head beside hers on the pillow and with a smile, whispered in her ear, "I love you Vivienne. Don't worry, no matter what happens I will always be at your side and in your heart, even if that means letting you go."

With that said, Vincent let himself relax beside his wife and fall asleep with her for the first time in almost two centuries. He would deal with what happened today tomorrow, but for now, he just needed Vivienne's embrace.

***

From the other side of the closed door, André, Renée and Aeron stood silently, each holding the other's gaze. It was Renée that broke the silence and in a whisper spoke to her brother and father, "This isn't good. He cannot be here if your plan is to work."

André nodded and growled low in this throat, "One way or another, we'll get Vivienne to accept her powers in this realm and not just in her dreams."

"I hope you are right father," Aeron said softly.

André tilted his head to one side and let a sly grin form, "You already know the answer to that Aeron, and stop doubting yourself. And stop doubting me. Tonight, we'll let them have each other, but tomorrow is a new day and a new beginning."

Chapter Ten
Awakening

"Vivienne, are you awake?"

I glanced up from the book I was reading to see Vincent walk though the large oak door of our bedroom. He was dressed in a long-sleeved men's dressing gown he wore to sleep. I smiled when I saw his face. I was always so happy to see him, "Yes, darling. I am awake."

Vincent closed the door behind him gently, the clicking of the lock echoing in the quiet room. I was lying on the bed when he came in, a book on my lap as he sauntered over to me, hiked up his dressing gown and climbed onto the bed beside me.

I leaned over to him, kissed his cheek and returned my eyes to the book on my lap, "Are you all right, my love?"

Vincent nodded, "Yes."

I put down my book and looked over at him, "You're lying to me Vincent. I distinctly remember you telling me that you would never lie to me."

"I'm not lying to you Vivienne," he replied and rolled over to look at me. Bending his elbow, he rested his head on his hand. With a twinkle in his eye, he settled his other hand on my leg, "I will never lie to you. I love you."

I drop the book on the bed and slid down so I was nose to nose with Vincent, our lips just a breath apart, "I love you too. But you were really quiet tonight at dinner. Even the kids said something to me when you went to have brandy with Monsieur LaRoux."

He shook his head, rubbing his nose against mine, "I just have a few things on my mind, that's all. I want to run something by you."

I laughed when he rubbed my nose and pulled my head back. Running my hand through his long black hair, I smiled, "What's that?"

"What do you think about locking this place up for a few years and see America?" His eyes lit up at the very thought of travel, something we hadn't done in at least a hundred years. "Think about it Vivienne. We can pack up only the items we need and just travel. We can go see New York City or any other city you wish to see." His hand settled on the pendant around my neck and his thumb played on the stone, "It can be just you and me. The only magic we take with us is the tincture and the magic we create."

I pulled back at that moment, my hand on the emerald that made me feel powerful and strong. Climbing out of the bed, I paced closer to the fire roaring in the hearth, "I don't know Vincent. Going to see America sounds wonderful, but why do I have to leave my stone here? You gave this to me. I wear it with pride."

Vincent sat up on the bed, "You should wear it with pride, and it's beautiful. But I want this trip to be just you and me."

"I don't know, Vincent." I repeated it again, only because I didn't know what else to say to him. He wants me to give up the one thing that has given me back my fire. "Do you know how much this stone means to me, Vincent? I feel powerful with it around my neck. Nothing can harm me if I have it with me."

"I know how much it means to you," he says to me, climbing over the bed and walking over to me. Raising my left hand, he points to my wedding ring, "Shouldn't this mean more?"

I looked down to my hand, the silver Fleur di Lis ring sparkling in the fire light, "Of course it means more."

Vincent suddenly pulled me into his strong embrace and pressed a searing kiss to my lips, silently letting me know he intended on making love to me. That had been his way of telling me for over six hundred years. But I never denied him.

Vincent led me to the large four poster bed we had shared for six centuries and laid me down upon it. His gaze was piercing as he rose above me and I suddenly felt the same way I did on the night of our wedding. He was dominating above me, rising over me and molding my body against his. His hand circled my throat and easily unclasped the pendant from my neck. Part of my brain was still working, telling the other half that he was only doing this to distract me. But then he swept his tongue against mine and my mind went blank.

It was sometime during the night or maybe just before dawn, that I felt Vincent leave the bed. Naked, I rolled over to watch him walk across the room wearing only a blanket wrapped around his shoulders. He knelt before the dying fire and stoked it back to life. Soon it was roaring.

"Come back to bed." I opened the blanket up to him invitingly and smiled. With a grin, he nodded, but didn't come over right away. I sat up slightly, the satin sheet falling to drape over my hip, leaving my top bare. With a slightly raised eyebrow I stared at him, "Vincent, what's wrong?"

He stood and it almost looked for a moment as if he were going to run back into my arms. But he didn't, instead he shook his head and stared at me with a sparkle in his eye, "I'll be over soon. I have something I need to take care of. Just go back to sleep."

I lay back down and groggily nodded in agreement, pulling the thin satin sheet back over my naked body, "All right my darling. But don't be long."

Vincent never came back to the bed that morning. When I woke, it was past ten o'clock and he was not even in the château. I dressed quickly in a hunter green gown with white French lace. I placed my long red braid into a bun at the nape of my neck and put on small pearl earrings. I looked at myself in the small mirror in from of me and examined my face, neatly made up with soft colors around my eyes and a cool mauve stain upon my lips. Tearing my gaze away from myself, I opened my necklace drawer to pull out my pendant, but I noticed it was gone. Instead, in its place was an envelope with my name on it written in Vincent's perfect script.

I pulled out the envelope with shaking hands and opened the ivory flap to see the matching paper inside. What I read on that paper made my eyes swell with unwanted tears.

My Darling Vivienne,

I will one day return to you not only my presence, but the emerald as well. Just know that leaving you was the hardest decision I have ever made, but I can't sit idly by your side and watch the magic of your pendant steal away your passion and your warmth. You tell me that the pendant has brought your fire to you, but I believe you are wrong. The fire you sought was found the day you and I were married and fueled further when we had our three wonderful children. I have not told them where I have gone, but I know deep down you know where I am venturing to next. I am sorry that you are not with me. But perhaps someday, when you realize that you have all the magic you have ever sought already, I will return to you. And when the dark night seems endless, just think of me.

Yours forever and ever,

Vincent

"You told me forever, Vincent."

Anger poured from every pore. The unwanted tears spill down my cheeks and smear the black ink on the paper, the words so perfectly scripted spreading and running off the page.

"Mother, do I hear you crying?" Adrienne walked in slowly and saw that I was hunched over my vanity, clutching the letter in my hands. She knelt down beside me and gazed up into my eyes, "Mother? What's wrong? Where's father?"

I cried harder when she mentioned her father and wiped my eyes with the back of my hand, the freshly applied makeup smearing on my hand, "He's gone with my necklace. They are both gone from my sight and my presence."

I handed her the letter. When she was finished she looked up at me and shook her head in disbelief, "I don't understand."

"Neither do I," I answered her honestly. I lifted my tear filled eyes and held her worried and curious gaze and as I tried to speak, my lip quivered in fear, "But what I am supposed to do without him?"

***

I can feel my head pounding before I even open my eyes.

I don't want to open them yet for fear of a bright light making the pain worse. My only response to that fear is to cuddle deeper in the heavy blankets that surround me, cocooning me and shielding me against the cool harshness of the room. I smile against the warmth and then I feel a hard, warm body next to mine and my senses go on alert.

I don't know what to expect when I open my eyes and deep down I hope that it's Vincent. I turn my head towards where the warmth is coming from and when my eyes open, I don't see harsh sunlight. Instead I see soft silvery moonbeams streaming through a small window at the foot of the bed. Finally my eyes focus on the form next to me and I see long black lashes against high cheekbones. I smile softly, the kind of smile you give when you wake up next to a lover, a lover that I haven't seen in far too long. Laying next to him all I can think of is that last time we lay like this, naked and wrapped up in each other. We loved each other so fiercely that night; I should have known something was wrong that morning. Trying to wipe that memory from my mine, I sit up slightly, letting the blanket and silver robe fall from my bare shoulders and I touch Vincent's cheek.

He smiles against my touch and snuggles against my hand. He must have realized who was next to him for when he opens his almost black eyes they seem to light up at the sight of me, "Vivienne, you're awake."

"Yes," I reply, my voice softer than I have ever heard, "it seems that I am. Where are we Vincent?"

Vincent doesn't move away from me or move to sit up. Instead he just pushes my hair back away from my eyes, leans in to kiss my lips gently and whispers, "Shhh, it doesn't matter right now. I just want to be here with you for a few moments. To hold you and touch you and kiss you."

"You're scaring me," I say to him, pulling away slightly from his touch, "why are you whispering?"

He shakes his head at me. He moves in to kiss my forehead, then my nose, "I don't want anyone to hear us. I just want you to myself for a little while."

I shake my head at him, "No. Not yet." I slide away from him in the large plush bed, away from his warm embrace and pull the silver robe around my shoulders.

"What do you mean, not yet?" His voice is angry and his eyes are just the same, "Vivienne, I haven't been able to hold you in forever."

"And whose fault is that?" My anger is just as strong as his and I can feel his pretty strongly, "I'm sorry Vincent, but just because you want to hold me now doesn't make up for the fact that you left me almost two hundred years ago!"

He hangs his head in what I can only assume is defeat, "I know, Vivienne and I am sorry. You have no idea how sorry I am."

I push away from him again, this time getting off the bed and letting my bare feet touch the cold stone floor beneath me, "But why did you do it? Why did you leave me like that and take the emerald from me? Why did you have to steal away from me in the night and leave me cold and alone?"

Again, he hangs his head and I growl low in my throat because that look is starting to annoy me, "I didn't like what the emerald was doing to you. You weren't the same woman I fell in love with; you were different and I couldn't handle it."

"So the only thing you could come up with was leaving me?" I am shouting now, completely ignoring his earlier statement of telling me to be quiet, "You are a selfish, inconsiderate fool and you make me wonder why I ever longed for you in the first place. You, Vincent LaTorc are just another person to let me down. First my mother, then..."

"Don't say André," Vincent roars. He crawls across the bed toward me and sits with his feet dangling off the edge, "Don't say his name. You have done nothing but compare me to him our entire marriage."

"Compare?!" I am beyond angry at this point and I slap him across the face, "Compare you to him? How dare you. I love you and have never, *ever* compared you to André."

Vincent brings his hand up to this cheek where it has started to redden from my slap. In the corner of his eye, a tear wells up and falls, "Never? How is it that our children are named after him?"

I roll my eyes at his question, "Our children are not named after André. Okay, well André is named after André, but that's it. The girls aren't named after him."

Vincent rolls his eyes in response to mine, "See, he has to live up to this image of André you've built up in your head, we all have. I saw what the emerald was doing to you when you wore it; it was as if you found André again even for a brief moment."

"Again," I exclaim, throwing my hands up, "a selfish remark from my dear husband. Well answer me this then; why, if I long for André so badly, did I want you back? Why did I lie awake at night wishing it were you keeping me warm? Why was it you I cried for every night for nearly two hundred years? Answer me that!"

Vincent growls low in this throat and almost leaps off the bed at me. Taking me about the waist, he twists and tosses me on the bed, coming down on top of me. With a twinkle in his eye, he grins, "I answer that the only way I know how."

"How," my voice is a raspy whisper because he has knocked the wind out of me.

Again, he just grins at me and brings his lips to meet mine. His kiss, a feeling I miss, is not like the thousands of kisses we have exchanged in years previous. This kiss is ignited by rage and fueled by his passion. His tongue sweeps inside my mouth and I cannot help but sweep mine in his. As he kisses me, his hands roam up and down my silken clad sides and I arch to meet his touch. The kiss that is bruising my lips slows and becomes tender and sweet and we pull away from each other and I stare at him.

"Did you really cry for me?" He asks me this as he nuzzles his lips against my neck.

I nod and pull his head up so our eyes lock, "Yes. I love you, Vincent. I have loved you since the moment I met you almost eight hundred years ago. I never left you; you were the one that left me. I waited for you, stayed in the castle for a hundred years before moving down to Paris with the children. I thought I saw you once."

He grins at me and nods as if recalling the memory, "You did. It was 1955 and your hair was short. I didn't like it at all. The dress you wore was unflattering and you looked as if you were a stranger in your own skin. But as you turned and your eyes landed on me, I saw your fire. I knew that you were still in there somewhere."

"It was a wig. I still wear a wig when I'm at my shop. My real hair is too bright, too vibrant. Someone is bound to figure out that I'm not normal." My voice is soft as I bring my right hand up to run my fingers through his thick black hair, sweeping it away from his onyx colored eyes, "I wish you had run to me. I would have welcomed you back without a single thought or question. I just needed you."

Vincent drops his forehead against mine and closes his dark eyes. With a sigh, he opens them again and stares at me, "I just couldn't. I knew what I had done was wrong and it was not up to me whether or not you had this great power. But that selfish part of me, that part of me that stayed away from you, just couldn't let you have it. Not because I wanted your power, heavens no, but because I didn't like the woman you were when you had the stone."

My hands are still on his head, my fingers playing with a curl of black at his neck, "Again, Vincent, that isn't your call. Granted, I have no idea what kind of power Fate and Knowledge were talking about, but if that power is made for me, shouldn't I see what it's like? What if it's something good for this world?"

"And what if it's not?" His gaze pierces into mine and I can't help but stare at the black depths hovering above me, "I can't stand to think what this will do to you. What if I lose you again?"

I sigh and move slightly beneath him, letting him fall to my right. I turn to face him, resting my head on my hand and my elbow on the pillow, "I don't know how to answer you Vincent. None of this makes any sense to me. All I want is to go home with you and see the children. Can we just go?"

Vincent shakes his head at me and I scowl. He snickers at me and kisses my pouting lips, "Don't look at me like that. We just can't right now."

"Why not?"

He smirks again, "Well, I don't know how to get back to New York from here."

"From here?" I sit up slightly but he stops me from leaving the bed, "Where are we Vincent?"

His gaze holds mine as I watch his lips move, but I don't hear him right away. I ask him again what he said and this time I hear him correctly, "We are in the Otherworld."

"What? We are in the Otherworld, really?" I sit up and lean against the plush pillows. Then, as if lightening hit me between the eyes, I turn quickly to look at Vincent, "Did Aeron and Renée bring us here?"

Vincent nods and through tight lips, lets out a barely audible, "Oui."

I get up off the bed and move to look out the window, but Vincent stops me and pulls me back to the bed, "Don't look outside yet. Don't open up this little cocoon we have. I want to hold you here a bit longer before having to face what's out there."

He holds the blanket open, inviting me back into his warm embrace. Again the memory of our last night together comes flooding back into my brain as he lifts the blankets. I go to him without hesitance and lay against his shoulder. Snuggling up to him, I lift my head and place a soft kiss against his chin, "Vincent, what have you been doing the last one hundred seventy five years?"

He smirks and plays with the hair that has fallen into my eyes. Brushing it back, he answers me, "Mostly just going from place to place. I have seen many places over the years. I first came to America and saw the south, but I left as the civil war was about to break out. In 1918 I moved down to New Orleans and lived in the French Quarter. I stayed there for thirteen years before going up to Chicago. It was amazing down in New Orleans. Each night was like a party and it was almost like being home again; I just wish you had been there with me to see it. I don't think I truly lived without you in my life. I met a friend a few years ago, his name is Steve, and he's a good guy. It's strange to befriend a mortal though. I always thought that mortal friendships were messy because I never stayed in one place for very long."

I smile at him talking about his friend and touch his cheek, "I'm glad that you were able to talk to someone. Does he know that you are immortal?"

"He does now," he says softly, his voice barely audible, "Steve would tell you that all I do is mope about and brood about the woman I let go. He would tell you that the only reason I go out at all is to hopefully get a chance to happen upon you. But I never knew where you were until Aeron and Renée tricked me into going to New York."

"Tricked you?" I laugh and lay back against the pillow, bringing him to hover above me, "How did they trick you?"

He sighs and kisses my forehead, "I received a voicemail message that told me that you were in trouble and that I could find you in the city. The message ended with 'come quickly father'. I thought it was one of the girls, so I got down to New York as soon as I could."

"Where were you?" My fingers play with the midnight black hair at the nape of his neck, curling around my forefinger.

Vincent smiles and continues to play with my hair splayed out on the crisp white pillow, "Boston..."

"Boston?" My voice hitches when I say that and my eyes cast down, "I wonder if that's why Adrienne was moving there."

Vincent shakes his head and cocks an eyebrow, "I haven't seen the girls in about a hundred years..."

I pull back from his touch for a moment, "Wait, you've seen the girls? Where? When?" I hear a hint of pain in my voice when I ask him this.

He closes his eyes and rests his forehead against mine, "Yes. It was in France, 1901. I was walking through a market outside of Paris when Audrey saw me and then called Adrienne over. We exchanged hugs and I begged them both not to tell you they saw me."

I swallow hard and let a tear fall down my cheek, "Oh. I think I remember that day. It was the end of summer and I usually went with them to the market but I had fallen a week before and broke my leg. Regardless of the fact we are immortal and we heal quicker that mortals, broken bones still heal slowly."

Vincent smiles softly at my comment and wipes the tear off my cheek, "They told me you were at home hurt. I fought the urge to run to you. I very badly wanted to rush in and heal you myself, even though I didn't have the power to do so."

"I know you would have tried," I give Vincent a fake smile and try to hide the hurt in my voice and in my eyes. I need to change the subject because if I don't, I'll end up saying something I'll regret, "How long have you been in Boston?"

"I've been there for about fifty years," he responds hesitantly, "I'd actually heard of your bookshop and wanted to go there for quite a while. Some of Steve's friends at the bar, who think they are of the occult persuasion, told me your shop had the best selection of occult books. They told me that a pretty French woman owned the shop."

I laugh at him softly and shake my head, trying to hide a blush that had suddenly flushed my cheeks, "You have to be joking with me. I barely make enough money to keep the shop open. It's a good thing that you left me with enough money to stay comfortable."

His eyes close when I say that and his forehead rests against mine, "I am so sorry Vivienne for every ounce of pain I have caused you. I never meant to hurt you, I was selfish and inconsiderate."

I shake my head and clasp my hands on either side of his head, pulling him back to look at me, "But you are here now. I love you Vincent and will never let you leave me again. I just want this moment, this single moment, to last as long as it can."

Vincent lets a playful grin form, pulling back to show me his perfect white teeth, "I think we could do that."

I giggle as his lips descend to mine and I move so he rests on top of me, "Good."

***

"Vivienne, it's time to wake up."

I shake my head and pull the covers over my head, "No. I want to sleep more."

Vincent pulls the blankets back and I open one eye. I really want to see the soft silvery moon light again, not the harshness of the sun streaming through the small window now. I can't help but sigh at my own frustration and then eye my husband curiously as I notice what he is wearing. He is clad in a black, shiny robe and his hair looks wet. I press the heels of my hands into my eyes and force myself to wake up and sit up, only to find out that I am bare beneath the warm blankets.

"Vincent," I hold the blanket up to my chest and swing my legs over the edge of the bed, "why are you dressed like that?"

He holds out a similar robe to me, this one threaded in silver, "This one is for you. Put it on quickly, our presence is being requested in the spring."

I take the robe and slip it on while eyeing him curiously, "The spring? What are you talking about?"

He sighs and holds out his hand to mine, "We don't have time for an explanation. You just need to come with me."

Without hesitation I take his hand and let him lead me outside. Upon my feet is a pair of soft silver slippers that to my surprise guard me against the chill of winter. What also surprises me is the scene in front of me as we exit the small cottage tucked into a pile of white fluffy snow. Off to the left of the small wooden porch is a pony tied to a post and hitched to a pillow-covered cart. For some strange reason I have a feeling of lying on those pillows. Vincent tugs on my hand when I don't follow him right away and for a moment I can't move and am paralyzed from continuing on and following him without question.

"Where are we going?" I ask, turning my head slowly and holding his questioning gaze.

Vincent smiles and moves onto the porch next to me, his hand still holding mine, "Like I said before. Our presence is required in the spring."

It's then that I notice that The Otherworld has all the seasons existing at once, the only connection are bridges over crystal clear water. I look to the island that was spring, the green leaves lush with morning dew and flowers in every color bursting to life with encouraged vigor. A smile tugs at the corners of my lips and I turn once again to face Vincent, a look of child-like wonder on my face, "This place is beautiful. No, beautiful is not a strong enough word. It's magnificent, ethereal, stunning; I can't choose."

Vincent grins at me and tugs at my hand again, "Come, we'll be late if you don't hurry."

"Vincent you are frightening me. Late for what?" My child-like wonder doesn't cease as I gaze around at the winter wonderland around me. Vincent is eagerly trying to get me to move quickly, but I want to stand and enjoy the beauty. I've never liked snow before, but I never really had a chance to experience it in this sense. In France the snow always came quickly and left just as fast, especially when I lived in Paris; and in New York, unless there's a big storm, the snow doesn't stick.

"Just come on will you?" Vincent says, again a bit too eagerly.

I pull on his hand to make him stop as we reach the bridge leading away from winter, "Vincent, why are you moving so fast? And who are we going to see, Aeron and Renée? If so, then let them wait. I have no need to see them again so soon."

By now Vincent is standing on the winter bridge and begging me silently to come with him. When I don't give in to his piercing stare, he groans, "Vivienne, please. I can't tell you why, but you must come with me."

With a sigh, I place my hand in his and step onto the ice covered bridge. My slipper-covered feet move slowly across the smooth ice and I'm careful not to fall. As Vincent and I walk, hand in hand, across the bridge into spring, I am silent. I have the strange feeling that Vincent is keeping something from me, but I can't put my finger on it. Why, after the night that we had just shared, is he acting this way? I feel as if he is trying to push me away all of a sudden.

While my mind wanders, I follow Vincent without question and block out what is going on around us. As we enter into spring, I feel the difference in temperature and want to shed the silk robe from my shoulders, but I can't for I am bare beneath it. This is why I like the layers of my modern clothing; if I am warm, all I have to do is shed my sweater. With a sigh, I look around me and listen to the birds sing their mating songs. These sounds make me smile and long for the French countryside. I stop when I see a doe drinking from a small spring and watch silently as she nourishes herself.

"Always daydreaming."

For a moment I can't move. The low, smooth voice I hear is one that I would never be able to forget, but I fear that my mind is playing tricks on me. I swallow hard as my head slowly turns to my right and my breath catches in my throat when I see André. He is staring at me with a piercing gaze from his honey brown eyes and he smiles at me. His face is covered in a light dusting of brown and silver whiskers, I almost don't recognize him.

"André," my voice sounds breathless to my ears and I feel a smile cross my lips.

His gaze moves quickly to Vincent who is still beside me holding my hand tightly and then moves back to me. He doesn't move close to me and this bothers me. "Hello my Vivienne. I hardly recognize you; your power is just pouring off of you."

My gaze sobers and I tilt my head to one side, "My power? That's all you have to say to me? I haven't seen you in almost eight hundred years and all you have to tell me is that my power is pouring off of me?"

André stares at me again, his gaze moving between Vincent and me as if he were waiting for Vincent to do something. With a sigh, he lowers his shoulders and relaxes his stance, "I am sorry Vivienne."

Vincent squeezes my hand and lets it go, a silent message for me to go over to André. I look at him quickly and he nods, giving me reassurance and I slowly make my way over to the man I have longed to see for most of my life. My walk to him was the longest walk I have ever made; even the walk down the aisle to Vincent wasn't as long as the ten feet to André. I don't know what I am going to say when I get to him. Part of me wants to yell at him for leaving me the way he did and part of me wants to know why he never gave me more instruction when it came to the emerald.

"You're confused." André states as I move closer.

I tilt my head to one side, eyeing him cautiously and I nod, "Yes, I am. Where have you been?"

"I've been with you always, Vivienne," André says softly and begins to pace in front of me on the dirt path. I watch as his gaze shifts from me to Vincent and back again and points to his chest, "I was about your neck and close to your heart. I felt the power and fire inside you as the pendent hung from your neck until one day, the light and fire was gone and it was dark."

I could feel Vincent behind me, seething with a quiet anger. With a turn of my head, I grab his hand and encourage him to stay calm, "It's all right, love." When he nods at me, I turn once again to André and move close to him, "So you were in the emerald the whole time? I longed for you, begged for you; why did you not make yourself known to me?"

"I couldn't," André replied and continued to pace as I moved towards him, "I was stuck in the stone, placed there to only be released by you when it was time."

I roll my eyes and I am suddenly annoyed, "When it was time? How was I to know when it was time if I didn't even know you were in the stone?"

André uses his head to nod behind him where Aeron and Renée sit in their silk robes upon twin tree stumps, "Aeron and Renée were to come to you, tell you when it was time and give you the knowledge to release me." He then shifts his gaze to Vincent and glares at him, "But you interfered. You weren't supposed to interfere."

I hear Vincent growl low in his voice from behind me, "You were the one that left her André! Did you expect her to just carry on without anyone after you vanished?!"

"Well I wouldn't have had to leave if it weren't for you!" He roars back at Vincent and I suddenly feel as if I am just in the way. André, usually calm and collected, at least in my memory, was now seething with anger towards Vincent.

Vincent rolls his eyes and folds his arms across his chest, "If it weren't for me? I happened upon Vivienne in the market and fell in love with her. It was you who couldn't stand to see her with anyone else, you selfish coward. You wanted to keep her under your tutelage so you could mold her into some kind super goddess? Well she didn't want your power then and she doesn't want it now! All she wants..."

"All I want is what Vincent?" I interrupt him before he has a chance to say anything that he or I will regret. "Don't tell André what I do or don't want." I turn to face André and stalk toward him and jab my finger in his chest, "And as for you, you don't have a say in anything when it comes to me with Vincent. I chose him, not just because you left me, but also because I fell in love with him. You offered me power once and if given different circumstances, I would have gone with you blindly. Now," I sigh and close my eyes, "now all I want is peace. I don't want a world with unspeakable power. I just want to be."

I watch as André glares at me, his eyes still full of rage, "You just want to be? Well, my darling Vivienne, if it weren't for me, you wouldn't exist at all!"

"What are you talking about?" I stagger back from him until my back is flush against Vincent. His strong hands encircle me and I feel that he is trying to keep me calm while André roars in anger.

André laughs, a laugh that I have never heard before. It's almost maniacal and devious, "I can't believe you have never been able to figure it out Vivienne. Most of all I can't believe your mother didn't tell you after I vanished."

Again, I shake my head and try to remain calm within the circle of Vincent's embrace, "What are you talking about André? You're scaring me."

"Do I have to do the same thing to you that I did for Vincent?" Renée asks softly from behind André. I watch as she slides off the tree stump and saunters over to where we stand on the dirt path. I take my gaze from Renée and pull from Vincent to look at him questioningly. I hear Renée is just behind me and she places her long delicate hands on my shoulders, "Yes, he knows."

"What does he know?!" I whirl around quickly and face Renée, a tear threatening in my eye, "What does everyone but me know?"

She moves to stand beside me and lovingly wipes the tear from my cheek. Tasting the tear, she grins and then points to André, "Look at him very carefully, do you see the godly glow around him?"

I smirk, "Yes, I've always been able to see that. You're not telling me anything new, Renée. I know already that André is a god."

"Yes," she replies softly. She is almost acting sisterly and I laugh to myself. I don't like the evil grin that has formed on her face as she conjures a mirror and holds it before my face, "Look at yourself very closely, Vivienne. Do you see that same ethereal glow?"

I look at myself closely, examining every corner of what is exposed to me on the mirror hanging in thin air before me. My hair looks disheveled, that's the first thing I notice. I need a brush. Suddenly, as if someone heard my thoughts, my hair straightened and smoothed out before my very eyes, coming to rest over my left shoulder. The exposed part of my right neck seemed to glisten in the sun as if it were sprinkled with glitter. It's never done that before. I bring my hand up to my neck and try to wipe it away, but to no avail; that's when I see the glow has spread to my hands, face, and hair and as I look down, the rest of my silk clad body. I look up, the mirror gone and hold André's eyes, now filling with tears.

"I…I'm a god?" My voice is barely recognizable to my own ears. It sounds like the wind on a cool spring day and seems to just rush out of my lungs.

André shakes his head at me and smiles lovingly, "Only half, the other half is from your mother."

I feel as if I can't breathe, my throat feels thick and I try to swallow, "So that would mean you are…my…"

"Father," Renée blurts out impatiently and rolls her eyes in disgust.

***

André is my father.

I keep going over it in my head; trying to figure out how I didn't know. But I have no idea how, just from looking at him, I can tell. I look back on my life and I have to laugh at myself. I always thought that I looked like my mother —we had the same features, at least in my mind we did. I wish that there was a picture of her; I miss seeing her face.

"Vivienne?" It's Aeron's voice that breaks my trance and brings me back to consciousness.

My eyes open slowly; above me I see Renée, Aeron and Vincent. I have no idea where André is. I press the heels of my hands into my eyes and try to sit up, "What happened?"

"Careful," Vincent says his hand on the small of my back, "I think you hit your head when you fell."

I fainted? I need to stop fainting when something happens, everyone is going to start thinking I can't handle big things. I try to hide my insecurities and smile at Vincent and then franticly look around for André, "Where is he?" My eyes dart to Aeron and Renée, "Where did he go?"

Aeron points to where he and Renée had been sitting before on the twin tree stumps. I smile at him and got to my feet slowly, the silk robe falling to cover my exposed knees, "André?"

He looks up at me as I walk towards him. He looks as if he has been crying. A small laugh escapes me as I think of a god crying, but then I think about the fact that he is my...father. André, the man that I have longed for with every fiber of my being is actually my father.

"Vivienne," he says my name in such a soft whisper that I can barely hear it.

I just stand there and look at him. So many thoughts fly through my head that I don't know where to begin. Silent and scared, I place my hand on top of his and laugh at the similarities, "How could you not tell me?"

"Your mother told me not to," he answers quickly.

I pull my hand away from his and fold my arms across my chest. With a laugh, I shake my head, "Because my mother told you not to? Are you joking?"

André just stares at me, blinking his honey brown eyes as if doing so will make me forget what I've gone through. I've wanted nothing more than to have André in my life again, to have the first man that ever loved me the way I was, not the way I could be. Instead, I have the shell of a god cowering before me like a broken and beaten animal and I don't like what I see. What happened to the powerful sorcerer that taught me how to wield fire with a wave of my wrist? Where is the man that taught me how to bloom buttercups from the fresh spring earth and have them wilt the next minute?

With a sigh, André shakes his head at me, "You hate me. You are looking at me the same way your mother did all those years ago and it pains me to know she was right."

"She was right about what?" I ask and I can hear a hint of teenage defiance in my tone. I have to hold back a smirk when I think that and try to keep a sober face while talking to André.

André laughs, obviously noticing my daydreaming, "She was right that in the end you'd choose her and what she wanted for you. She wanted you…"

"I know what she wanted for me, André," I interrupt, my voice snapping a bit too harshly, "You don't have to tell me what she wanted for me. I lived it remember? And I didn't choose her or what *she* wanted. I chose what *I* wanted and I wanted to live with you and learn more magic and become what you offered. But now," I sigh, "Now I just want Vincent."

I hear Vincent smirk behind me. I don't even want to turn around to see the childish face he is making towards André. I am so torn over what I want. I have longed for both men for so long, I have forgotten what I need. After André and before Vincent left, what I wanted was to be a good wife and mother. After Vincent, all I wanted was to hide away and live a peaceful and quiet life. People would come and go as they pleased and I would go through the motions for my family, but I know that they saw through my façade.

"What are you thinking about?" André asks me. His voice is low and his face sympathetic. I hate that look.

I shake my head, "I'm thinking that all of this is just too much. Why now? Why did you have to tell me this now?"

"I told you," he replies quickly.

"I know," I roll my eyes and hold up my hands to stop his excuse, "I know. My mother told you not to. Well then answer me this André. Who was my mother to you? How did she hold that much power over you?"

André smiles softly and I can only wonder as to why. It's almost as if he's recalling a memory. He leans against the tree stump and folds his arms across his chest, the sleeves of his robe draping down across his abdomen, "Celeste, your mother, was the most beautiful woman that I ever met. One look from your mother sent me over the edge and I knew that even though she was mortal, she was the woman I would love for all my days."

I shake my head as if doing so would clear out the cobwebs in my memory, "So you loved my mother? But I remember her hating you."

"Towards the end she did," André says his voice soft, "When it came to how we would raise you, she wanted her way and nothing else. I wanted a certain life for you as well, but we couldn't compromise —I wouldn't compromise."

I fold my arms across my chest and shake my head, "Compromise? What would you two have to compromise about?"

"Celeste wanted to raise you without magic and without my influence," André says to me bluntly, "I wanted none of that. I knew, the moment you were born, that you were the vessel that would hold the emerald's power. You were the most important child in the world —in the realms —and I couldn't let your mother control how you would grow up. You needed my influence, even if it were to just help develop your instinctive power of fire…"

"Wait." I hold up my hands again to stop him and shake my head, "You both moved me around like puppets. My mother wanted me to have this grand life, but I got it. You wanted me to have a powerful life and you gave me the freedom and knowledge to gain that power.

I got bits and pieces of both of you —why are you so intent on making me your way? Why do you have this need to make me more than I want to be?"

"Because I am your father!"

His shouting makes me take a step back. His voice is harsh and demanding in those few words and I am not at all sad that I have never heard them before in my lifetimes.

"I'm sorry Vivienne," André whispers, his voice soft and less demanding, "But you have to realize what you mean to me," he points to Aeron and Renée behind me, "what you mean to us. You have to realize what you mean to the world."

I shake my head and let out a nervous laugh, "But I don't know what I mean to the world. All I've ever known was that I have magic in me —that I have fire in me and when the emerald was resting on my chest I felt as if that fire was coursing through my veins. But I didn't understand why. You never told me why, André."

"I never got the chance before, but now I plan on telling you the reason why you are so important, not only to me, but to the world." André watches me intently and pulls himself away from the tree stump. He starts to pace slowly, his robe dragging on the dirt path beneath his feet. With a smile, he turns his head towards me, "You, my Vivienne, are the fire that heats the world. You were always meant to be immortal, just not in the way that it happened. Your heart, your fire, is passion and strength that helps everyone in the world overcome every obstacle they come across. Even hiding away in your bookshop, your heat and passion did its job."

I shake my head at him and shrug my shoulders, "But why? Why am I so special? Why is the emerald so special to me?"

"Because you were made for it," André continues, "You are the vessel for the emerald's power —a power that enhances your own. In anyone else's hands the power is chaotic and uncontrollable. But within you," he sighs and smiles brightly, "within you the power is exceptional. You would glow even more brightly than you did the day with the buttercups."

I can't help but let myself smile at him recalling one of my favorite memories. With a blush on my cheeks I move towards him, "So all this power, where has it been hiding, only within the emerald?"

André shakes his head, "No, the power has been within you all the while. The emerald is only the enhancement, only the way the power is projected into the world."

"I don't understand any of this André." I start to pace as I think about the years I spent with André. I try to recall all of the knowledge he bestowed upon me, but for the life of me I can't recall a single thing that he would have said about the emerald, "When were you going to tell me about all of this? When were you going to tell me I was so special?"

"I told you how special you are everyday, Vivienne," he states impatiently, "How dare you even think that I never told you how much you meant to me."

I ignore his impatient reply, "So, all the while you were teaching me and molding me into some kind of super witch, you couldn't bring yourself to tell me you were my father? Did you think you were protecting me or something?"

"All I ever wanted was to protect you Vivienne," he says to me, his voice soft and reassuring, "even my disappearance was for your protection."

I stop walking towards him and laugh at his remark, "Really? How? Because I just remember feeling rather alone, empty and unloved. If it weren't for Vincent, I don't know what I would have done."

"Vincent is the reason I disappeared," he admits quickly and bluntly.

I stare at him blankly, "What? You were the one that yelled at me in the market place and when I went to look for you, you had vanished. So how is Vincent the reason you left?"

"I saw you with him," André began, his head hung and his voice low, "After you ran from me and Renée, I ran after you and watched as you bumped into him. At first I thought it was cute, how you looked at him with wide doe eyes. You had never looked that anxious before, you were always so sure of yourself with me. So I stood around the corner from where you two were and I heard everything that Vincent said to you. I heard him tell you that he was enamored with you and your eyes twinkled and your smile grew. You were in love with him from the very start and I knew that. So, as to not confuse the issue and the answer I knew I was going to get that day, I disappeared. And Fate and I let you have your moment."

"Ha!" I hear Renée from behind me and I turn around. "I didn't let her have anything."

With a roll of my eyes at Renée I turn back to face André, "You're right, I did fall in love with Vincent right away and I'm still in love with him. But, as Vincent has most recently made clear, I was obsessed with you André. I had this need to connect with you, to have you show me more than what I was born with. I needed to know where my limits were when it came to my magic. I never got to know those answers because you left me. And as it turns out, you were just afraid that I wouldn't want what you offered because I fell in love. So, answer me this, father," my voice is a little snider that I intend it to be, "why can't I have both?"

"Because we can't always get what we want, Vivienne," André grabs my shoulders and holds firmly, his fingers most likely leaving bruises, "I'm sorry, but if you want the life of a goddess, you can't have the life you presently have."

I pull away from him, pushing his arms from me violently, "What if I don't want to be a goddess?"

André lets a sly grin tug at his lips, a much more maniacal smile than I'm sure he intended. With a smirk, he leans once again against the tree stump and folds his arms across his chest, "Then you have a choice to make."

"What kind of choice?" My voice is barely audible to my own ears and I'm sure that Vincent, who is now holding my hand, can feel my fear.

André doesn't move a muscle when Vincent grabs for my hand, though I see his eyes dart to where we are joined. Lifting his gaze back up to me, his face is sober and his are eyes focused, "Chose me, become a goddess, no more than that. Become the Phoenix and live forever with unlimited power."

"Or?" My voice wavers.

"Or," André begins, "chose Vincent and give up your immortality and your power. Your children and Vincent will continue to have the ability to be affected by the potion, but you won't. You will live a mortal life and die an old woman."

My eyes grow wide at his statement, "You would truly do that? You would strip me of everything I have worked for if I don't choose you? What kind of father is that?!"

"A father that demands his daughter does as he asks!" He is shouting now, his voice demanding. He pulls himself away from the stump and starts to stalk towards me, his arms animated as he explains himself, "I sat back and let your mother have her way, well no more Vivienne. You either chose me or chose Vincent; but make sure that your choice is well thought over, because you will not be given a second chance."

My eyes shift away from André and I look at Vincent, tears streaming down my cheeks, "Vincent."

He shakes his head at me and kisses me softly, "Shhh, Vivienne. It's all right. Don't choose something just because André or I want something from you. Either way, I just want you to be happy." He pulls me into his embrace and whispers in my ear as I sob on his shoulder, "I love you. I can stop taking the potion; we can grow old together like we're supposed to. I just want you to know that whether you are beside me or in another plane of existence, you are and always will be my one true love."

"I love you too," I pull back slightly and stare into Vincent's dark onyx eyes, "I don't want to lose you. Could you even love me as an old cone of a woman?"

Vincent laughs and wipes away the tears that are hanging on my jaw, "I would love you as a withered old woman, with one leg and a patch over your eye. Just as long as you love me back, I'm the luckiest man in the world. Like I said, if you do choose me, I'll stop taking the tincture and I'll grow old with you. For better or for worse and till death do we part —that was my promise."

With a tortured laugh, I smile at him and kiss him softly, "Thank you Vincent." When he nods at me, I turn to face André and pull away from my husband. I take in a deep breath and square off my shoulders, "I'm sorry André. Though I have longed for you for so long and would have wanted nothing more than to sit next to you till the end of time. I…"

"You what, Vivienne?" He interjects when I hesitate to finish what I am saying. His teeth are clenched and I can tell that he is angry.

I sigh again, "But I love Vincent. I have always loved Vincent. He is the one I choose."

With a growl he throws his hands up in the air and stares at me straight in the eye, "Then so be it Vivienne. I had so much planned for you and you're going to throw it away for love? Mortal love?!"

"It's not mortal love André!" I shout at him, tears still streaming down my face, "What Vincent and I have is beyond mortal or immortal. It's beyond time!"

André stalks towards me again and once again grabs at my shoulders, "If you have longed for me for so long, why are you turning me away now?" He doesn't wait for my answer, "If you want to push me away, then so be it."

André lets go of my shoulders, shoving me away from him. With an outstretched hand, he sends Vincent flying into a tree behind him, knocking him out cold. I let out a stifled scream and turn to run towards Vincent. I need to make sure he is all right. But André grabs my shoulder and spins me towards him violently. I am frightened at what I see in his piercing gaze. The fire in his eyes is full of anger and frustration —both directed towards me and I can do nothing about it.

Tearing his gaze from me, he closes his eyes as if what he's about to do will hurt him more that it will hurt me and he places his hand on my chest. It's almost as if doing so will stop my heart. I feel as if a heat is rising inside me and balling up beneath his palm. I start to gasp —my breath feels caught in my burning lungs and becomes short and shallow. I try to tell him to stop, that he is hurting me, but I can't seem to form words and I can feel myself starting to get drowsy. I force myself to open my eyes just as André pulls back his hand from my chest and a ball of pulsing green energy is suspended above his palm.

"I'm so sorry my Vivienne." I hear him say softly as I begin to black out, "I'm so sorry, but you have left me no choice."

*****

"Vivienne?"

I hear a voice that I don't recognize. Even the voice in my own head I don't recognize —I don't sound like the way I should. I want to move and to open my eyes, but something is keeping me from doing so.

"Vivienne, darling wake up."

It's a man's voice I hear and even that is unfamiliar.

I moan and try to move my hand, but my whole body feels like it's been encased in stone. Finally I feel my muscles loosen and I move my arm and bring my right hand up to rub the heels of my palms into my eyes. I open them and focus on a blurry image of a man with dark hair and eyes staring down at me. The man, wearing a black t-shirt and worn dark wash jeans moves towards me, but stops when I pull away. He softens his features, a gesture that is meant to make me feel reassured. That's not a feeling I have. I pull away as he reaches for me, pushing my body into the plush mattress beneath me.

"Who are you?" I ask, my voice a scared whisper.

The man smirks and moves to touch my cheek. I pull back once again and he stares at me questioningly, "Vivienne, what's wrong? You know who I am."

I shake my head and slide off the bed. I look around to see a well-manicured apartment with black and chrome details and large windows looking out over New York City, "No I don't know who you are, or where we are for that matter."

"Vivienne, I'm your husband —Vincent."

I shake my head and feel a tear fall down my cheek. I am frightened and don't know who this man is or where I am. My breathing is heavy and I swallow hard, "Husband? I have no husband."

"What? Vivienne, stop it. You're scaring me."

"I'm scaring you?!" My voice cracks as I shout at him.

His eyes, already soft when looking at me, start to well up with tears. He hands grip my shoulders, his fingertips biting into my skin, "Vivienne, please tell me you are just playing a game with me. Tell me this is revenge for not having me around for so long. Tell me anything; just don't tell me that you don't remember me."

I am so confused by his ramble that I can't help but to start to cry myself. Tears slide down my cheeks and splash against his hands as my head bows in defeat. Shaking my head, I start to cry harder, "I'm sorry. This isn't a game or a trick. I can't tell you what you need to hear. I don't know you."

Chapter Eleven
Fate's Revenge

"Who does she think she is?!"

Aeron shook his head at his sister and followed her as they crossed the old wooden bridge into winter, "She's our sister, Renée. And Father's favorite."

Renée whipped around, her silver silk robe and raven black hair slicing the cold air as if it were a knife. Her breath comes out in short gasps, visible in the cooler air at the end of the winter bridge, "I hate that she is Father's favorite! We both took a backseat when Vivienne was born and I hate, *hate*, that she turned down André's offer. She had no right!"

"Had no right?" Aeron laughed and continued to follow his sister as she stalked off in a huff, "It was her decision to take or deny the power. Who are we to say that she had to choose André? The choice was hers to make."

Renée stomped into her cottage, slamming the door in a failed attempt to ignore Aeron. When Aeron opened the door he growled at her and Renée folded her arms across her chest, glaring at her younger brother, "When did you choose her side Aeron? I thought you were with me in this? You know, with me till the end, no matter what it takes."

"That was to find André, which we did I might point out," Aeron snapped quickly, using his foot to close the door behind him and shutting out the cold of winter, "Our goal was to find our father and we did that. So answer me this, why are you so mad that Vivienne didn't take the emerald's power? She told us in her bookshop she wouldn't take power over love. I don't know why you are so surprised."

Renée glared at her brother with annoyance and let her arms and shoulders drop. Aeron had to keep himself from laughing out loud at how ridiculous she looked. When she heard the barely audible smirk she growled in response, "Must you always be so ignorant Aeron? Do you really think that André was my only reason for getting our sister to come here?"

Aeron sighed and flicked his tongue against the bottom of his top teeth, "Of course not. I know you better than that Renée. I just can't believe you couldn't see any of this coming. Where in your all-knowing plan did you think any of this madness wouldn't ensue? If you continue down this course, Renée, I'll have no choice but to choose Vivienne's side."

"Don't you dare," Renée growled, her jaw set and her teeth clenched, "I warned you once Aeron, cross me and feel my wrath."

Aeron laughed at his sisters audacity, "Warned me? Sure, Renée. But remember that I did warn you as well if you did decide that this was your plan. Our sister is more powerful than both of us combined and you know it. Even without her powers, she could still take us on. So you just keep telling yourself that I fear your wrath."

Aeron shook his head and covered it with the hood from his silken robe. With his hand on the door, he pulled it open, letting in the wild winter wind. As he was about to walk through, Renée slammed the door closed, keeping him inside and the wind out, "Don't you dare walk out on me brother!"

Aeron turned to face her; his eyes wide as she yelled and threatened him, "Don't start Renée. I have no patience for you right now, so my advice to you is let me leave now before I really get angry."

Renée let out a low laugh, a low rumble in her chest that came out as if thunder brewed there, "Before you get angry? Aeron I haven't seen you angry in generations! Knowledge doesn't get angry. Now, so you don't have to see me get angry, I'm going to let you go. But just be on your guard brother. I plan on so much more when it comes to Vivienne and the emerald. And you'll just have to tune in to see the powerful ending."

***

"I know she's up to something."

André stared at his son, clad in a dark blue robe as he sat on the shore of the summer island. A soft breeze blew through the apple trees above them and picked up the ends of Aeron's hair as he dipped his feet in the cool water.

"Renée is always up to something," André replied sitting next to his son.

Aeron shook his head, "I know, but it's different this time. There's something about Vivienne that Renée just can't get out of her head. What I want to know is, if Vivienne had taken the offer and taken her power in full, what would Renée have done? What would we have done? I realize that the world needs her that you need her father, but I don't understand this obsession Renée has for our sister."

André lowered his head, watching as the water lapped against Aeron's bare feet. He was caught up in the rhythm of the water, drowning out all other noises around him, only hearing the sounds of summer. When Aeron pressed him to answer or acknowledge his comment, André snapped his head up as if brought out of a distant memory and spoke. "I know what she's waiting for. I know what she wanted from the beginning."

Aeron sat up straight and bore his gaze into his father's eyes, "You what?" He pulled his feet from the water warmed by the hot summer sun and stood up. Defiantly, he glared at André, "And if we hadn't brought you back you would have allowed all of this to happen?! This isn't good André! I curse the Spirits for all that has transpired recently and I want nothing to do with any of it anymore!"

André rolled his eyes at his son, "Calm down Aeron! I swear, you are more dramatic than your sister at times." With a sigh, André motioned for Aeron to follow him up the path towards the Knowledge House. "I've taken the green orb of energy I pulled from Vivienne and placed it under glass to confine it. If the energy escapes in any way, it will find the first powerful being and fill them with unspeakable power."

"Wouldn't it find Vivienne? It is hers by right," Aeron asked, trying to keep up with his father.

André nodded as he turned the bend toward Aeron's cottage, "Yes it would if there were no other god-like beings in the way."

"So what if Vivienne didn't get the power?" Aeron asked, "What if one of us got it? What if Renée was the one?"

André kept his gaze forward, his jaw set as he hesitated to answer Aeron's question. Finally, after a few moments of silence, he spoke, "That's exactly what Renée does want, Aeron. I hate to think that I didn't protect this prophecy better."

Aeron stopped on the hill and gasped at his father's audacity, "I'm really starting to regret bringing you back André. I really don't like any of this." With a shake of his head and a roll of his eyes, Aeron let out an annoyed huff, "You're damn right you should have protected the prophecy better! So now, Vivienne is out there in the other realm without her memory and you have a very pissed off goddess of a daughter; so please pray tell what you plan on doing about this!"

André twirled on his heel to glare at his son. His honey brown eyes, usually warm and wise, flashed black, "You have no idea how much it pained me to do that to Vivienne! But she deserves what I have done to her. In the end I know she *will* choose us, no matter what happens; I know she will take her power."

Aeron watched as his father stalked away from him and up the steepest part of the hill. André's anger was not something Aeron missed within the past eight hundred years. Letting his father have his childish tantrum, Aeron followed up the hill slowly. Aeron let his mind wander to a time when he was younger, to a time when André still would come and go between the realms and when life in The Otherworld was just a little bit simpler. While all along The Otherworld had always been beautiful, when André went away both Aeron and Renée felt the difference in the air. It seemed as if a light was gone, brightness in the sun and stillness in the moon had faded when André trapped himself in the Emerald. And now that he was back, that light still hadn't fully returned. The moon and sun still seemed to lay hazily in the sky, hovering above them empty and cold until Vivienne would take her rightful place beside them.

"Aeron! Come quick!"

Sprinting up the hill, Aeron moved as quickly as he could toward his father's frantic voice. The Knowledge House seemed too far away from where he was and with every step it seemed to be moving further away. André was in trouble. Suddenly a realization hit him; it wasn't André who was in trouble. Vivienne's power was gone. He just had this feeling and it was justified when he saw the summer sun seem to dim above him. With a growl of frustration, he ran faster, the silk of his robes bunched around his knees as his long strides brought him up the steep hill.

Aeron burst through the glass doors of The Knowledge House, the golden columns stretching towards the glass ceiling. Beneath Aeron's feet, black marble floors stretched out before him, cut only by stark white walls with gold filigree. In the middle of the expanse of black, gold and white, was a pedestal with a broken glass cylinder and beside it, André on his knees, his face contorted in pain.

"What happened?" Aeron rushed to kneel next to his father as he frantically looked around, "Where's Vivienne's power?"

"Where do you think it went?!" André lifted his head, anger and pain mixing in his eyes. André stood, his brown robe sweeping the floor as he began to pace, "I can't believe she did this!"

"Really father, you can't believe I did this?" Renée stood in the doorway to The Knowledge House, her silky silver robes replaced by a dark purple gown with a deep V-neck that accented her chest. Her raven black hair blew about her form from an unseen place. Surrounding her was a green aura that pulsated from the power she had stolen.

"Renée!" André said his daughter's name through clenched teeth and let a low rumble come from his chest.

She let out a maniacal laugh that started deep in her chest. A grin tugged at the corners of her crimson lips as she started pacing the black marble floor, keeping her gaze upon her father, "Oh please father. You chose Vivienne above me and Aeron a long time ago. She was a weak woman and would have made an even weaker goddess. She doesn't deserve this amazing power."

"You don't deserve it either Renée," Aeron shouted, his face red with anger and frustration towards his older sister, "It isn't meant for you. This can only end badly and you know it!"

Again she let out a menacing laugh and a sly smile, "No, Aeron, you know how it can end. I have the power to change anything I want to the way I want it. I am omnipotent."

André growled low in the throat at her arrogant admission, "You egotistical bitch!"

"Tsk, tsk, tsk father," she replied, shaking her head as she continued to pace around them, "is that anyway to talk to your first born?"

"What do you hope to prove by this Renée?" André asked with a smirk, "This power is too great even for you. It will consume you and you won't come back from it. Fate will have destroyed fate!"

Renée rolled her eyes at her father and moved towards the door, "Stop being so dramatic father."

"Don't do this Renée," André followed after his daughter, "I beg you, please just give back the power. There are other ways to get Vivienne back. Don't do this because you are mad!"

Renée whipped around to face André, anger making her face red, "You think I'm doing this out of anger?! You are a fool father, an utter fool. If you think I've done any of this because I was angry then you are sadly mistaken."

"Then why have you done this? Why are you on this power trip?" André stalked towards Renée, jabbing his forefinger in her chest in an attempt to appear more intimidating. Instead he came across as scared as he felt.

"Why?" She laughed her hand against her heart as she stared at André with a mixture of contempt and annoyance. Then her face sobered and her dark blue eyes pierced into André's, "Because I can."

***

"Is she sleeping again?"

Vincent nodded at Steve and turned his gaze back out the window overlooking the landscape of New York City now covered in a soft blanket of fresh snow. With a sigh, he pinched the bridge of his nose and squinted, "I don't know what to do. I finally got her sedated, but she's just so frantic. She doesn't know who I am."

Steve stood, adjusting his worn jeans, and walked over to Vincent. Placing his hand on Vincent's shoulder, Steve dropped his head, "Where were you Vinny? You were gone for almost two months! I've been back and forth between Boston and New York hoping that you'd show up again."

"We were in The Otherworld," Vincent replied, pulling himself away from the window, "I remember Vivienne telling me that time moved differently in The Otherworld than it does here, but I never thought it was that drastic. We were only there for two days."

Steve let out a frightened laugh and ran his hands over his hair, brushing his hand against the short buzz, "Two days? I've been pretty scared shitless over here, waiting to see if you were dead or not. I had no clue that you'd come back with an amnesiac wife." Starting to pace, Steve sighed and tried not to think of how badly the situation could have turned out. He turned his gaze back at Vincent and gave him an encouraging smile, "So tell me about this Otherworld. What is it like?"

"You really want to know?" Vincent asked with a smirk. When Steve nodded, Vincent smiled and began softly, his voice low, "It's magnificent. Think of the most beautiful place in the world and this place would change your mind. There are four islands, each a different season all blooming and dying at once. The smell of cherries and apples in the summer drifts with you as you cross the bridge into autumn. Then you get a whiff of pumpkins and the air starts to chill slightly and you smell snow on the air as you get closer to the bridge leading to winter. Though winter is cold and dead, crows dot the white ground, leaving behind them tiny prints in the snow as they hop.

"The spring was my favorite," Vincent continued with a smile, "Watching Vivienne in the spring was breathtaking. She seemed more alive in The Otherworld that I had ever seen her before. Though she had no magic surging through her at that particular moment, there was an ethereal glow about her that made me love her even more, yet at the same time, frightened me beyond anything I had ever been scared of before. The thought that she might not choose me, made me realize that she deserved to have all the power that André was offering her."

Steve shook his head and held up his hands as Vincent started to trail off, "Wait a second. Who is André and what kind of power was he offering your wife? What the heck happened over there?"

"Everything I've always feared," Vincent answered, keeping his gaze on Steve, "Come to find out, Vivienne does have a father and he was her mentor. It is the man that I have hated with every fiber of my being for leaving her the way he did and having her compare me to him every step of the way. Sure," he continues with a shrug, "she told me that wasn't true, but she loved him. He was first."

Steve gave Vincent a blank stare, "What? The dude is Vivienne's father? I'm so confused."

"You and me both," he replied and sat on the piano bench. He took a deep breath, and turned his gaze back to Steve; "André was Vivienne's mentor when she was still mortal. He taught her magic and how to hone her skills as a fire witch. Well, come to find out, he lied to her and never told her who he truly was. And because she didn't choose him when he offered for her to become a goddess, he took her memory away. And because the bastard has always hated me, this was to punish the both of us."

"Wow," Steve sat on the large plush chair beside the piano and let out a huff, "wow. How is it that you could have kept all of this to yourself all these years?"

Vincent smiled softly and looked to his feet clad in stark white socks, "I preferred to be by myself after I left Vivienne. I was guilty for taking the stone from her and even though I knew it was wrong of me to do so I wanted to keep her safe." He lifted his head, "And this is exactly the reason why. She doesn't deserve this; doesn't deserve to be lying in our bed sedated because I can't stand to have her not know who I am."

"So it's all about you again?" Steve shook his head and stood, "I can't believe how selfish you are being. Your wife, who you haven't seen in what, two hundred years, is in on your bed without a clue as to who you are. And all you are doing is thinking about yourself?" Steve set his jaw and started moving towards the door, "I thought you were a better man than that Vincent."

When Steve called him by his given name, Vincent pulled him back, grabbing his shoulder a bit too violently, "What would you have me do? Huh? You want me to fight gods for my wife's memory back?"

"No!" Steve shouted back, lowering it when he heard Vivienne murmur in the next room, "What I want you to do is fight for your wife, not for yourself. Do it for her, do it for your children."

"My children," Vincent sighed breathlessly and then grinned at his friend, "Steve you are a genius! Maybe she remembers them."

Steve laughed and playfully punched Vincent in the arm, "Now that's a thought."

Vincent stopped and shook his head, "Wait, I have no way to find them."

"Why don't you try Vivienne?" Steve suggested, "I stopped by the bookshop a week after you guys were gone and saw that someone had locked up and cleaned inside. There was a sign on the door that said closed for vacation." Vincent laughed and rolled his eyes. Following along, Steve snickered, "Well, long story short, I was not the best of teenagers and broke into a few places. I still know how to pick a lock and got inside the bookstore."

Vincent laughed harder, "All right? What did you take?"

Steve smiled coyly and pointed to his book bag near the door, "Her purse, ledger and date book are in my bag. I think I saw a cell phone."

"You should be in trouble," Vincent smirked and pointed at him, but hugged his friend, "But I'll let this one slide."

Steve pushed away from Vincent and rolled his eyes. Tossing the red and black patent leather purse at Vincent, he smirked, "Just look for the cell phone will ya? And don't hug me."

Vincent smirked and dug through Vivienne's purse. Inside, he found a matching wallet, two half packs of mint gum, a dozen or so pens without caps and zipped inside a pocket, her flame red cell phone. Vincent laughed to himself at the thought of Vivienne carrying a flame red phone and thought, *"Always the fire witch."*

Flipping the phone open, he opened up the contacts and scrolled through the one hundred fifty contacts. A slight pang of jealousy hit him as he saw a lot of men's names, but he kept telling himself they were clients of the bookshop. After flipping through all the names, he settled on Adrienne's number. It appeared to be local.

Looking at Steve, he took in a deep breath and clicked on Adrienne's name in the address book, "Wish me luck, I haven't spoken to my eldest daughter in about a hundred years —literally."

With a smirk from Steve, Vincent turned to face the window and pressed send, hoping with all his will, he'd be able to actually talk.

"Hi mom!" Adrienne said cheerfully on the other end of the phone, "You okay?"

Silence.

"Mom? Did you butt dial me?" Adrienne laughed.

Vincent told himself silently to just talk, "Adrienne."

Silence.

"Adrienne, it's your father." Vincent's voice was low, even and controlled something that Adrienne could barely remember.

"Dad?" Her voice was curious, cautious and frightened, "Why do you have mom's phone? Are you with her?"

Vincent nodded, "Yes. We're in New York; of course we're in New York. There's a little bit of a problem."

"What kind of problem?" she asked curiously, her sentences short and clipped, "Why are you there? Where's mom?"

"Well," Vincent replied, running his free hand through his shaggy black hair, "Your mother has a bit of amnesia and can't seem to remember me. I'm hoping that you, your brother and your sister would be able to trigger something."

Adrienne sighed and Vincent heard her flick her tongue against her teeth, "Let me call them. I'll call you right back."

"Thank you, sweetheart," Vincent said with a smile, "I can't wait to…" He pulled the phone from his ear looked at it and then up at Steve, "She hung up on me."

Steve smirked and sat back down on the black leather couch, "Can you blame her? You've been a pretty selfish bastard over the last hundred years or so. You not only left your wife, but you left your kids too."

"Stop being so insightful okay?" Vincent replied quickly, knowing Steve was right. Suddenly, the phone began to buzz and he opened it, "What'd they say?"

"Text me directions," Adrienne replied, her voice calm and her words clipped, "We'll meet you there as soon as we can. It might take an hour or so, Audrey is coming from Long Island."

Vincent smiled, "Where are you coming from?"

"I'm in the city today with André," she says quickly, "he's not too keen on seeing you by the way."

Vincent's eyes closed slowly, guilt hitting him in the gut so hard he didn't think he'd be able to breathe again, "Adrienne, I'm so sorry."

"Stop," she replied and he could only imagine her holding up her hand as well, "It's not me you have to apologize to. I've come terms with the fact you left us, but we are all adults and we can handle this. We just have to focus on mom."

Vincent nodded as if she could see him, "I'll text you the directions. See you soon."

"Bye."

"Bye."

Vincent ended the call and quickly sent the address to Adrienne. With a sigh, he closed the phone and looks up at Steve, "Now we wait. They'll be here soon."

"Awesome," Steve replied sarcastically, "Your wife and your kids all in one day —and all immortal."

Vincent stood and tossed the phone against the chair near the piano, "Look Steve, I didn't ask you to stay, I didn't ask you to be a part of this. If it's just too much for you then there is the door."

Steve shook his head, "Nope, you're stuck with me. And you did ask me to be a part of this by the way. The day you and I came here you asked me to be a part of this. Sure, I'm not one hundred percent keen on the situations, but I'm here with you till the end."

"Thank you, Steve," Vincent said quietly and began to stare out the window as he watched the sun dip low in the evening sky, "Why don't you get some rest. It'll be an hour or so before the kids get here. You're going to need your strength, my daughters are spitfires; or at least they used to be."

About an hour and a half later, a knock at the door woke Steve, causing him to fall off the couch and onto the floor. Shaking his head, Vincent stepped over him, "Get up, you have drool on your face."

Steve laughed and sat back on the couch, "Are they here?"

Vincent nodded and with his hand on the door, opened it. On the other side, standing in the hallway were his three children. His eyes drifted over each of them; Adrienne wore a knee length brocaded coat with a pair of dark wash jeans and black boots. Her long raven black hair was brushed away from her porcelain face and piercing blue eyes and was held together in a ponytail at the nape of her neck. Audrey stood beside her sister, standing an inch or two shorter, with short, cropped strawberry blonde hair. She wore brown leggings and a green corduroy skirt and a matching jacket on her long lean form. André, his youngest and most wild of the bunch, wore baggy jeans and a black leather jacket. His dark raven black hair was brushed away from his face with a few loose tendrils teasing the long lashes that framed his mother's green eyes.

A smile tugged at the corners of his lips and he laughed out loud when he saw a black eye forming around André's left eye, "Is that the encouragement your sister gave you?"

André rolled his eyes and pulled up the collar to his black leather coat, "Whatever, where's mom?"

"Oh good to see you've acclimated yourself to modern teenage life, André," Vincent replied sarcastically, allowing them to enter the apartment, "Everyone this is my friend Steve. Steve, this is André,

Adrienne and Audrey. And before you ask, yes he knows all about us."

Adrienne quickly snapped her gaze to her father, "Is he mortal?"

"Yes I'm mortal," Steve answered, stretching out his arms on the back of the couch, "Problem?"

She shook her head, "No, just not like our father to go spreading around how old he is or us for that matter." She bent down and offered Steve her right hand, "I'm Adrienne."

Steve shook Adrienne's hand and smiled, "Nice to meet you."

Vincent closed the door and moved towards the couch. He was frustrated at the amount of people in his apartment; he never let this many people into his home, let alone his life. His silence must have been noticed for his children were standing side by side by side, all their arms folded across their chests staring at him. "Well that's intimidating. You're probably wondering where your mother is."

Audrey nodded, "You think?"

"You don't have to be rude, Audrey," Vincent answered, "I'm trying to do this the right way. I know I've screwed up in the past, but this is important."

Audrey rolled her eyes and turned to her sister, "Did he tell you what happened?"

Adrienne shook her head and set her piercing gaze on their father, "What did happen, Vincent?"

Vincent cringed when his daughter called him by his first name and not father. To not let them see his frustration, he motioned for everyone to follow him to the bedroom, "Long story short, your mother's mentor, André returned, told her that he was her father and offered her to become a goddess." He smirked when his children gasped and continued, "She refused and chose me instead. So he took her memory away and sent us back."

"Back?" André asked, taking off his jacket to reveal a death metal t-shirt, "Where were you?"

Vincent leaned against the doorframe, his gaze on his slumbering wife, "The Otherworld."

"Oh," André whispers.

Adrienne moved to stand in front of her father, "So why is she sleeping? How did you get her to calm down if she doesn't know who you are?"

"He sedated her," Steve replied from the back of the crowd. Everyone turned to face him, "Don't ask me how he got her to take it, but she did. She's been out like a light for about seven hours."

"A mild sedative," Vincent corrected, bringing their attention back, "she's all right. She cried most of the morning, telling me she wanted to remember who I was. I calmed her down, fed her and she took the pill. The affects should wear off any time now."

Audrey moved to sit on the edge of the bed, placing her hand on her mother's shoulder. Glancing up to her father, she smiled, "She looks different. Her glow is gone."

"I know," Vincent answered, "I noticed that too after she fell asleep. When André took the power out of her she seemed less bright. To hear her scream like that, as if her heart were being ripped out is a sound I never want to hear again."

"You shouldn't have to."

Everyone turned around quickly at the sound of André's voice. André stood in the frame of the front door, his brown robes blowing softly from an unforeseen wind. Closing the door, he stepped in and glared at Vincent. Without a second thought, Vincent lunged at him, fully intent on knocking him to the ground. André extended his hand out and stopped Vincent, freezing him in mid-air.

Growling, Vincent shouted at André, "Let me down you bastard!"

André rolled his eyes and closed his fist, sending Vincent to the ground with a thud. Adrienne rushed to her father's side and placed her hand on his head, "Are you all right?"

"Yes, it's just a bump," Vincent replied, rubbing his head. Standing with the help of his daughter, Vincent glared at André, "What are you doing here?"

André let a sly grin form on his aged face and he began to pace around the immaculately clean apartment. His gaze fell onto everyone in the room; Adrienne and Audrey, André and Steve. Stopping at

Steve, he tilted his head to one side and smirked, "Good to see you again."

"Excuse me?" Steve asked, "I've never met you before."

André laughed and patted Steve on the shoulder; "We've known each other for centuries."

"You've known me for centuries?" Steve asked with a slightly frightened huff. He masked his fear with his sarcastic remark, "Dude, I'm only thirty two years old."

André smirked at the idea of someone calling him a 'dude' and shook his head, "In this form you might only be thirty two, but your spirit is much, much older."

Vincent glared at Steve and put himself between his best friend and André. Growling, he pushed André away and repeated his question, "What are you doing here?"

André laughed and winked at Steve before turning his attention back to Vincent, "Well as much as I love watching you attempt to hurt me and fail miserably every time, I've come to strike you a deal."

Vincent folded his arms across his chest and raised a sleek black eyebrow, "A deal? What kind of deal?"

André looked around the room, his gaze falling on each of his grandchildren and he smiled, "It's so good to finally meet all of you. Your father must have told you by now who I am."

Adrienne rolled her eyes, "Yes, he told us. And we'll have to side with our parents on this one. I agree with Vincent and call you a bastard as well." She growled and pointed to her mother lying motionless on the bed, "How dare you do this to your own child!"

"How dare I?" André calmly asked, "Well Adrienne, I am a god and my child defied me. She deserved the punishment given. Yell at me again and I shall do the same to you as well."

Vincent stepped in between his daughter and André. Glaring at Adrienne, he shook his head and then turned to face André, "Just say what you've come here to say and go. We don't want you here."

"Well that's obvious," André replied with a smirk and stopped pacing, "I've come across a bit of a problem in The Otherworld; a problem that Vivienne could help solve."

Vincent clenched his jaw tight as he watched André, "What kind of problem?"

"Renée has taken Vivienne's power," André stated matter-of-factly, "So now, here's my deal."

Chapter Twelve
Power

I don't like my dreams.

My dreams are frightening me and making me feel as if I can't escape my own head. I feel as if I am a prisoner in my own thoughts and it disturbs me to not know who I am. My name is Vivienne, which I know, but other than that my life is a complete blur. How old am I? Where do I live? Why do I keep having visions of places I've never seen and glimpses of faces I can't place? Why do I feel as if there is a fire in my blood —an unspoken power that I can't quell?

Slowly, I feel my mind coming back to my body and telling me to wake up. It feels as if I was forced to leave myself for a time and I can't figure out why. In the distance I can hear voices —three men and two women —I think I should know them. I can hear someone saying my name over and over again. They're talking about me, discussing my life as if I don't have a say in it.

"Wait, dad," I hear one of the girls say, "I think I hear her." I look over at the door and see a tall girl with long raven black hair peek into the doorway. She smiles at me and turns back to the others in the hallway. "She's awake."

Fear is overwhelming me as I lay on this plush mattress beneath me, and I pull the blanket up to my chin. Watching the girl with the dark hair smile at me, I whisper, "Who are you?"

The girl moves toward me slowly, a look of utter bewilderment on her face. As she moves closer to me I can see that she is more a woman than young girl, "It's me, Adrienne, your daughter."

I shake my head at this woman claiming to be my child when she looks just as old as me, "My daughter? How is that possible?"

Adrienne lets out a frustrated huff and turns to the man claiming to be my husband. I sit up in the bed, watching them intently, and barely hear Adrienne speak to him, "She doesn't even know me, Vincent. What the hell happened?"

He rolls his eyes, catches my gaze and then looks back at her, "You know what happened, but for right now we have to take this slow. We have to tell her about us as calmly as possible. We have to make sure she understands our lives."

"Please stop talking about me within earshot," I blurt out angrily, "Stop telling her what you have to and don't have to do when it comes to me. I don't even know who you people are, except for the fact you keep telling me you are family. Mais je ne vous connais pas!"

Adrienne blinks at me, astonishment filling her eyes when I yell, "What did you just say?"

I shake my head and blink at her, "Was, was that French? How do I know French?"

"She said she doesn't know us," Vincent says softly, his eyes filling with a mixture of concern and anger. With a sigh, he turns to look down the hallway and motions to someone.

A moment later, two more people stand in the doorway, over-whelming me even further. Now standing with Vincent and Adrienne is another young woman who looks remarkably like Adrienne except for her short strawberry blonde hair. Their bone structure is almost exactly alike. They even have the same shade of cobalt blue eyes that pierce directly into the soul of whoever they are looking at. Beside the other woman is a young man, perhaps a teenager, who looks like an exact copy of Vincent. As I look closer to the young man I could see a scar above his right eye that seems to turn white as he scowls at me.

I smirk at this parade of people before me and lean back against the headboard of the large bed, "And who are you two?"

The young man moves into the room quickly and sits beside me on the bed. His hand is warm and his touch is gentle as he takes my hand in his, "Come on, mother. Snap out of this. I know dad's a bastard, but you don't have to do this to yourself and us just to get us all together."

I pull my hand from his hesitantly and slide out of the bed, "Another child?" I close my eyes and drop my head. My bare feet are cold against the hardwood floor and I feel a shiver creep up my spine. I pull the long silk robe around my body in an attempt to warm myself and my gaze travels across the strange faces watching me from across the room, "Will someone please explain to me how any of this is possible? You three, even if it were possible, could not be my children. I'm not old enough to have three grown kids. And you," I point to Vincent, my voice accusing, "you can't keep me here. I don't know any of you and I want to leave. I want to go home."

"Where is home to you, Vivienne?" Vincent asks me, his arms folding across his chest, "Where would you go if you left here?"

My eyes widen at his outburst and I drop my arms at my sides, "My bookstore! I have an apartment there."

Vincent's face sobers instantly as if I have just kicked him in the gut. With a laugh of defeat he shakes his head, "You remember your bookstore. Of course, you remember that but not your family, not the people that love you more than anything in the world."

I watch Vincent as he begins to pace and I growl in frustration, "I don't know what you want me to say. I don't know what you want from me. All I know is that I need to leave."

Vincent holds my gaze for a moment and as a tear slides down his cheek, he steps to the side and extends his arm out in a gesture to leave, "Then by all means, go. If you think that is what you truly need. But we can help you; we have the love and patience to help you bring your memory back."

Slipping past him, I move into the large living room area with chrome and glass details and black leather furniture. Pulling the thin silk robe around my body I fight back the urge to cry and fall to the cold wooden floor in defeat. As I reach for the door, my hand just resting on the cool metal handle, I hear a voice coming from behind me that sounds familiar. "This is my fault."

The cool metal handle slips from my hand and I whip around to face the disembodied voice, seeing the man attached to it. Before me is an older man, old enough to be my father, with gray hair falling to grace strong shoulders. His eyes—warm and honey colored—pierce into mine and seem to silently plead with me not to leave, "Who are you?"

The man smirks at me, a tug of thin lips hidden behind a short growth of silver whiskers, "My name is André."

"And how do you fit into all of this madness?" My voice shakes and I can feel myself on the verge of a nervous breakdown if I don't get some fresh air soon, "How do you know this is your fault?"

His gaze softens and he begins to move towards me, slowly, as if stalking me in the narrow hallway, "I know this is my fault because I made you this way. You have no memory because of me. That's why you don't know them," he gestures behind him without looking, "It's because of me."

I feel an anger rising in me that I don't think I've ever felt before; an anger that heats my blood and causes sparks to shoot from my fingertips. Breathing heavily, my gaze pierces into his, "This is because of you?! It is all your fault that I have no idea who these people are?"

Throwing my hands up in the air, a ball of fire thrust from my fingertips, hitting the wall directly behind Vincent at the end of the hallway. A scream rips from the throat of both girls and the teenage boy claiming to be my son stares at me with wide green eyes. As soon as the fire hits the wall, André extends his arm out and flips the long white drapes with an unseen wind, knocking the small fire out before the alarms even have a chance to go off. Immediately I drop my arms and fall to my knees in front of the door. Fear is so intense in the room I can feel it thrumming on my skin with a soft sound that only my ears can hear.

Cowering and rocking back and forth, I look up at them through a flood of tears streaming down my face, "How did I just do that?"

André kneels down beside me and takes my chin in his hand and tilts my head up to face him. With a smile he kisses my forehead and wipes away the tears drying on my cheeks, "It's all right, love. I'll explain everything." Helping me stand up, he turns to the girls, "Can we find her some clothes other than the robes from The Otherworld?"

The girls nod and Adrienne grabs her jacket, "I have some laundry in my car. I'll be right back."

A silence fills the room after Adrienne leaves. My eyes hold Vincent's, his gaze piercing into mine, silently telling me something that I don't understand. I don't like the look on his face either; his dark eyes hold a mixture of sadness and fear as he watches me. It's as if he's hoping I'll suddenly remember everyone in the room. But I don't remember anyone in the room. All I remember is my bookstore and sitting at the window looking out at the busy New York City streets, wishing for...wishing for...something. I don't know what I wish for. All I know is that I would sit at the window and hope that something would happen to make my life more interesting and exciting. I smirk to myself at that thought, exciting. Well this was defiantly interesting, but scarier than anything else I've ever come across.

As my mind begins to wander, I hear the door open behind me and I turn to see Adrienne with a mesh laundry bag full of clothes. She smiles at me and shows me the clothes, "I don't know what will fit you, but we can go into the bedroom and try stuff on. Do you want me to help you?"

I nod and silently follow her into the bedroom I had awoken in only hours before. Closing the long floor to ceiling black drapes, she turns on a lamp to illuminate the darkening room as midnight creeps over the city.

"Skirts," I whisper, keeping my gaze on her hands busily working to open the knotted drawstring, "I like skirts."

She lifts her head and smiles at me, her blue eyes almost twinkling in the lamplight, "I like skirts too." She keeps the soft grin at her lips as I watch her go back to the laundry bag. Dumping the contents out on the large bed, still rumpled from sleep, she sorts through, "You always have liked skirts. I think it's because you wish you could have the gowns you wore when you were in France."

"France?" I ask her, walking slowly over to where she is, "I don't remember France. Was I born there?"

She holds up a black knee length skirt with a red belt and holds it up to my waist, "Both you and father were born there. Audrey, André and I were born there as well."

I eye her curiously as she finds a red shirt and holds it up to my torso, "Really? You have no accent."

She grins again and points to the robe, "Take off the robe." She hands me a pair of panties, a bra and stockings, "We don't have accents because we haven't lived there in years. Every once in a while the accent comes out, especially when I'm mad or when I say something in French. But, we left France in 1955 and traveled the world over before that."

I don the undergarments and slip the skirt on, "I still don't understand any of this. How is it that we aren't old if we left France in 1955? How is it that I'm only twenty-five and have grown children?"

Adrienne bends down and pulls her purse onto the bed. Opening it, she pulls out a small vile filled with a blue-ish green liquid, "This is our fountain of youth. Father found it when he was young and passed it along to us when we felt we were ready for it. You are almost eight hundred years old." She looks to the dainty watch on her left wrist and smiles, "Actually, you'll be eight hundred in about fifteen minutes."

Pulling the red sweater over my head, I adjust the mock turtle neck and just stare at her and choke, "I'll be how old?"

Adrienne smiles and places her delicate hands on my shoulders, spins me around and pulls a brush through my tangled tresses, "It is all right mother. We'll get your memory back, you and father will be together again and we can all be safe." She turns me around to look me in the eye, "You won't have to worry about anything, mother. You're in safe hands."

I pull away from her slightly. I'm afraid of what she is telling me, afraid of knowing things that I don't know, feeling things that I don't know how to feel. She talks of safety and a worry free life, but I have that now. I have a life that is simple; they are the ones bringing me trouble. I feel tears welling up in my eyes as I stand there and stare at Adrienne. This woman before me is strong and beautiful and very sure of what will happen in my life.

"You're too sweet," I don't know what else to say to her; "I wish I could remember you. I think I'd like you."

Adrienne places a soft kiss on my forehead, "Well that's okay mother, I remember enough for the two of us." She pulls away from me and studies me for a moment before reaching into her pocket, pulling out a silver Fleur di Lis ring that she hands to me, "This is yours. I took it from dad when he wasn't looking. He never notices when I take things." She laughs as I place the ring on my right hand and she shakes her head, "No, it's your wedding ring."

I swallow hard and watch as she switches the ring to my left hand. I study the ring, watching as the tiny diamonds in the design glisten in the lamplight. A memory flashes before my eyes and I can't help but smile as I recall what I can only assume is an important moment in my life. Suddenly I am remembering when this ring was first put on my finger. The light hit it differently then, it wasn't modern light, it was candles. Hundreds of them lit up the small room that I stood in with…Vincent.

With a gasp, I raise my head and my eyes meet Adrienne's, "I remember when I first saw this ring."

"You do?" She is grinning at me, her eyes lighting up in the dim room. "What do you remember?"

With a shake of my head, my smile fades as the memory fades. It's as if the memory was taken from me the moment it was given to me by some cruel twist of fate. With a sigh, I drop my head and feel a tear fall down my cheek, "I don't remember. It's gone now."

Adrienne sighs and places her hand under my chin, brining me to face her, "It is all right mom. It's in there. We'll get it back someday."

"Yes we will, no matter what it takes."

I look over to the doorway to see Vincent standing there, a smug grin on his full lips and his arms folded across his chest. As my gaze sweeps over him, I notice the bags under his eyes and the lines around his lips have deepened. He looks worn, weary and ready to crash at any moment. Sadness fills me for a moment at the thought of him being out of my sight for even a moment more than he has been already.

"What do you think?" I ask him, opening my arms and showing him the outfit Adrienne had picked out for me. "Is this better than the robe?"

Vincent smiles and walks over to me, his gaze never leaving mine, "I'd take you covered in mud and still love you, Vivienne. It doesn't matter what you wear as long as you are with me."

I blush and hide my face, "Did you say things like this to me when you first met me?"

"Yes," he replies with a smirk. He reaches down and gently picks up my left hand, "Adrienne found this?" Adrienne nods toward her father and smiles as she picks up the scattered clothes, "Good. I'm glad."

I pull away from him slightly, not understanding the feelings coursing through me; "Adrienne tells me it's my birthday tonight?"

Vincent widens his eyes as if he had been struck by lightning. Looking to the watch on his left wrist he smiles and lifts his gaze back up to mine, "Looks like it. You'll be eight hundred at midnight."

I give him a fake smile. I still don't quite understand how I can be so old yet look so young. I don't understand how I threw fire from my hands and I don't understand at all the fire I feel in my blood. I really feel as if I need to go, need to go to the bookstore and get away from these people that frighten me.

Several silent moments pass as I stand staring at Vincent from across the room. Adrienne has left the room, taking with her the mesh laundry bag. Vincent and I are alone and I am scared beyond belief and don't know what to say to this man. He claims to be my husband, to be the man that has loved me since before he could remember. But that's the problem —I don't remember him. I don't know if I love him.

"What are you thinking?" His voice is barely an audible whisper. I have to move closer to him to understand what was said.

Shaking my head, I rub my upper arms with the palms of my hands, "A lot of things. Mostly how I don't understand any of this."

Vincent sighs and places his hands on my upper arms. I feel the heat from his palms and close my eyes at how wonderfully comfortable his touch makes me feel. When I open my eyes I see his gaze piercing into mine; that's when I realize that his eyes are almost the color of onyx.

"I know you are confused and that you would rather curl up in the corner and be left alone than do what I'm about to ask," he begins, his voice wavering, "but I need you to come to the living room and do something for me."

I shake my head, as if doing so will clear the cobwebs and make an easy answer burst from my lips. With a hard swallow and speak on a breathless whisper, "Okay."

Taking my hand, Vincent leads me out of the bedroom and down the hallway. Walking past the people claiming to be my children, my eyes hold Andre's gaze. André is standing in the living room, his brown robes still draping his tall, lean frame, causing him to look more menacing than I'm sure is intended. The look on his face is stern, his eyes hard and unmerciful as he stares at me. Gripping Vincent's hand harder, I feel a mixture of fear and heat in my blood.

"I'll just come out with it," André states bluntly, "I can offer you a piece of your memory back if you do what I ask of you."

I stare at him blankly, my eyes blinking at him, "Do what you ask? What are you asking of me?"

André walks over to me, taking my hand from Vincent's a little too violently and pulls me away from him. This act seems to be filled more with jealousy than with wanting control of the situation. I turn my head to stare at Vincent as André pulls me away, wishing for a moment that Vincent will take me back in his arms. Instead, he stands still, watching as I walk away from him with a look of painful longing in his onyx eyes. Walking over to the large floor to ceiling windows, he opens the sliding door to step out onto the balcony, pulling me along with him the entire way in silence.

"What are you doing? It's cold out here." I sound like a whining child, but I can't help but feel as if he might push me off the edge if I don't comply with his demands.

Pointing to the large clock on the church nearby, he grins, "Look at the time. It's almost midnight on the evening when you become eight hundred years old."

Nodding, my frightened gaze follows his hand to the clock. Suddenly, the chime in the clock starts ringing, signaling midnight. The fire I feel in my blood starts to course stronger and warmer through my body as the clock continues to chime. My breathing becomes labored and I feel as if I've lost my balance on the balcony. I hear shouting coming from behind me; it's Vincent and the girls telling me to come back inside, but I am unable to move from the spot André has me glued to. My eyes swell up with tears as I feel myself being dragged away from the balcony on a strong wind —swirling in vibrant colors of orange, red and green —lifting me from the concrete floor. André closes and locks the sliding glass door with nothing but a flick of his wrist and a mischievous grin forming on his thinning lips.

"Stop!"

I yell, as if doing so will help me from the power I feel coursing through my body. Closing my eyes, my head begins to throb with an unspeakable pain, causing me to scream out. From my fingertips I feel fire sparking and setting the plants on the balcony ablaze. The heat is unbearable, both inside and outside of my body. Memories start to flood back into my head as I fall to my knees on the concrete. My long fingers pull at my flame red hair and I almost feel as if my nails are drawing blood from my scalp.

Opening my eyes, tears clouding my vision, I look up to André who is standing over me like an ominous statue. Opening up the brown robe, he kneels down and envelops me from everyone's view. I let out one last gut-wrenching scream as I feel myself slipping away from the conscious world and into the arms of André —my father.

My memory is coming back like a flood. Images of a life I feel I had never wanted is pouring back into my head. I am longing for the time when I knew nothing of this magic, power or of immortal gods. All I want is to live a simple, normal life with…with…

***

I hurt beyond anything I have ever felt before. Every part of my body hums loudly with a painful cry only I can hear. Keeping my eyes closed, I rub them with the heels of my hands, hoping that the headache will go away if I apply enough pressure. A flood of memories comes upon me quickly as I suddenly realize what had just happened. Afraid to open my eyes, I inhale deeply and try to figure out where I am by scent alone. All I smell is a sweet scent of cherries blooming in a giant orchard.

Sitting up quickly, I press the palms of my hands into the plush mattress beneath me. My eyes dart around the room quickly, scanning the area only to find an unfamiliar room filled with familiar scents. The round room is sparsely decorated, the only furniture being the narrow bed I rested on and around bedside table with a white pitcher of water atop it. At the opposite end of the room is a small rounded door with a brass handle. Sighing, I slide off the narrow bed and rest my bare feet on the cool stone floor. Looking down at myself, I notice I am still wearing the clothes Adrienne had given me, for that I am grateful —I was getting sick of all the silk robes.

From beyond the door I can hear the soft murmur of muted voices. I can't make out who is speaking, but the voices sound male. For a moment I smile, but I don't know why I am smiling. Who am I smiling for? Who am I expecting to be on the other side of the door? Stepping lightly, I place my hand on the brass handle and turn it slowly, hoping that the voices I hear don't notice the door opening. Peeking through the open crack in the door, I spy two men sitting with their backs to me and a roaring fire before them in a round pit in the center of the stone floor.

"She doesn't have the strength to defeat her," I hear the younger man say. From the back, all I see is black hair with hints of blue. For some reason this man is familiar to me, but I don't know how.

Beside him, I hear the older man reply to the younger man's statement, "Yes she does. You just have to trust me."

"You know I do father," he replies softly. I must have made a noise, because the younger man turns around quickly, his dark gaze holding mine for a mere second, but it felt like an eternity. He stands, a blue silk robe falling about his tall lean form. With a soft smile and a twinkle in his eyes, he extends his right hand out toward me, "Vivienne, you're awake."

I nod at him and slip through the doorway, ducking low so I don't hit my head on the low doorframe. The moment his gaze meets mine I know exactly who he is —Knowledge. He is the god that originally came to me in the bookstore with the punk girl, telling me of the emerald —the emerald. Oh my goodness, my emerald pendant. Why hadn't I thought of that sooner? That must be what this is all about —but whom are they talking about? Who must I defeat?

"Do you remember me?" he asks his gaze soft as he stares at me.

Nodding, I swallow back the urge to cry in fear, "You are Knowledge."

"Aeron," he replies quickly, cutting off my words as I say them. With a smirk he takes my hand in his, "Come sit with us. You remember André —our father."

Casting my gaze to the older man, I realize that he hadn't turned around when I emerged from the small bedchamber. He is sitting with his knees wide and his elbows resting on them. His head is cast downward. Though I cannot see his face, I feel as if he is smiling at the fact I am simply standing in the room with him. While looking at him, I can't help but feel this odd sensation that I should hate this man —but I can't seem to figure out why. While a sense of hatred fills me, this anguish and longing for him fills every fiber of my being and I don't want to fight the urge to run to him.

"Vivienne?"

Turning towards Aeron again, I shake my head to clear it, "Sorry. I was…"

"Daydreaming." I finish along with the older man.

I quickly cast my gaze upon him. His voice is lower than I think it should be. Kneeling in front of him, I force him to look at me, "You are my father?"

"Yes," he admits softly, as if doing so kills him to say so, "Funny how saying it so many times in a matter of a few days makes it easier after lifetimes of not being able to say it."

I look at him strangely, "You talk in riddles."

"I know."

Aeron kneels beside me, breaking my gaze with André and places his hand on my shoulder, "I hate to rush you Vivienne, but we are pressed for time."

"Aeron," André accuses, his voice harsh and demanding, "Not yet."

Aeron stands up, anger filling every fiber of his being from what I can tell. Walking over to the window, he pulls back the curtain to reveal a blood red sky and a wild, whipping wind that could pull the heaviest tree from its berth, "Not yet?! André, we are losing precious time every moment we don't act. Vivienne has to get out there and take back her power before Renée destroys her realm as well!"

"Who is Renée?" I rip my gaze from the blood red sky and settle it upon the man claiming to be my brother.

Aeron helps me to my feet and I let go of André's hand. With a sigh, he answers me, "Renée is our sister and she is not at all nice. She has taken a power that is yours and we need to get it back to you before she destroys the world. That much power in Fate's hands is not good."

Another flood of memories pours into my head and I close my eyes in defense. Pulling away from Aeron, I step closer to the window and with a barely audible voice ask him why I have to help, "Why? Why can't I just go back to my world and live a simple life?"

"Because that's not how things work, Vivienne!" Aeron roars at me, the anger in his voice filling every corner of the room. Aeron turns to André then, his gaze begging our father to help him. With a growl of frustration, Aeron yells at André, "Are you just going to sit there and let this happen?! Come on old man, do something!"

André stands up suddenly, his hot gaze piercing and dripping with anger, "Vivienne! You can't just sit idly by and let Renée do this! You are the only one that has the strength and knowledge to defeat her."

"How?" My voice is soft and I can barely hear it. I don't understand why André is so angry, "How do I defeat Fate when I am but a mortal woman?"

"But haven't always been a mortal, Vivienne," Aeron bluntly states.

André whips his gaze to Aeron and glares at him as if he shouldn't have said that, "Aeron. No."

My gaze shifts between them, my eyes wide and curious, "What is going on? What aren't you two telling me?"

André sighs and takes my hand, "It's a long story, but though you are a mortal now, you are still the only one that is able to defeat Renée and restore balance to the realms. Without your fire and passion, Vivienne, Fate is running around both this realm and yours without a care in the world but for her own agenda. You are the only one that can stop her and take away the power she has stolen. The power Renée stole is yours by birthright —a power that was given to you by both your mother and I."

Birthright —I don't know what my birthright is. I don't even know what I'm supposed to be doing let alone what my birthright is. With a growl low in my throat and a roll of my eyes, I move my gaze to André, "So let's say I do defeat Fate and restore balance. What happens to me?"

Aeron and André exchange worried glances. I growl again when neither of them answer me. Aeron nods and gently takes my hand, a gesture that makes me feel awkward, "If you take on Renée without accepting your full goddess power from André, then you will die. No mortal has ever taken on a god and lived to tell about it. Renée is a special case. She is Fate and Fate cannot be killed. But she can be controlled. It is your job to control her and take back your power."

"But how can I take back my power if I don't have any god-like abilities to speak of now?" I am so confused right now that all I want to do is cower in the corner and rock back and forth until this nightmare falls away from this world. That way I can open my eyes and see nothing but...

André takes my hand from Aeron, breaking my trance and leads me to the door. Stepping outside I smell the sweet scent of cherries again mixing with the ripening apples in the orchard only ten feet from me. There is beauty all around me on the summer island; the only thing out of place was the blood red sky menacingly staring down at us as if to swallow us whole if we don't do her bidding. Caring for me as if this were going to be the last time he'd ever see me, André led me to the orchard where a circle of buttercups blossom as I step onto the lush green grass.

"I have offered you power before," he begins, "I have offered you immortality and the chance to live a better life with us here than in the mortal realm. I can give you a piece of that power so you can defeat Renée. That way, when your power, the power Renée took, is returned, you won't suffer the same pain you would if you were to take it as a mortal."

"So basically I won't die if I take this offered power right?" I am offended by his audacity and pull away from him. Walking through the perfect circle of buttercups, I turn back around and glare at André, "Why didn't I take the power the first time? If you offered me something that was this special, why did I turn you down?"

André growls at me. He then throws his hand up in the air in what I can only assume is frustration, "Bless the spirits for my patience Vivienne! We don't have time for your questions and your endless need for my explanations! Either you accept what I am offering now or you face death if you don't!"

Frustrated, I storm away from André. I feel a fire in my blood fueling my anger and heating my skin. I can't believe that I was starting to feel as if I could have a home here. I didn't feel as if I belonged in the other realm and I sure as well don't feel I belong here. With a huff, I look over my shoulder to see André still statuesque in the circle of buttercups with a look of defeat on his strong features. Shaking my head, I turn back around and collide with a strong sturdy body.

I fall to the soft summer grass and my gaze moves up slowly. Hovering just above the ground are bare feet, connected to a pair of long, lean tapered legs with a crimson robe hanging in elegant shreds and an onyx-encrusted belt at the smallest part of an already tiny waist. The robe parts to a deep V across a robust chest, the robe ties off at a pair of strong squared shoulders. Hanging around her neck is the emerald —*my emerald*—glowing brightly and pulsing with a powerful energy. Surrounded by raven black hair, her long slim, bare arms are adorned by a pair of golden snakes winding down, the head coming to rest upon the tops of her hands. Finally, my gaze lands on the porcelain face of a goddess with vibrant green eyes filled with power and rage.

"Going somewhere?" Her voice is filled with a mixture of sarcasm and arrogance. I hate that.

With a huff, I stand up on the cool grass. Brushing off the earth that cushions my fall, I glare at the woman with the god like glow in front of me, "You must be Renée."

A smirk crosses her face as she begins to pace in front of me. As she moves, I can see an emerald green aura move about her like a mist clinging to the last moments of dawn. The emerald is almost stark against both the blood red of the sky and the crimson of her silk robe. As she continues to pace, her piercing green gaze never leaves mine, "Good to know you remember me. No, wait; you don't remember me do you?" She laughs and looks to André, "Thank you for that father. Makes taking your favorite daughter from you so much easier."

My eyes widen in fear, "Take me away? As in kill me?" When Renée only nods, my face hardens and I shake my head as if doing so would stop her, "What did I ever do to you that would make you want to kill me?"

Laughing she stops pacing and glares at me, "What did you do? That's funny." She pauses for a moment as if to contemplate how to answer me. Finally, she sighs, "Okay, I'll indulge you and jog your memory. Think back Vivienne; think back to a time when you were younger and being taught all these wonderful things about magic." I don't like her tone. "Think back to how selfish you were and how you were always being indulged by our father. You were always being told that you were special!"

"I didn't know he was my father!" I yell back.

I shake my head as I suddenly recall that memory. I remember a small cottage tucked in a circle of tall trees. I remember learning magic and to hone a natural ability that laid dormant inside me waiting to come out again.

My eyes must have lit up, because Renée smirks, "Well, well, well. That was a nice little trip down memory lane, wasn't it? Are you ready to try and take your power back yet?"

I hesitate for a moment and shift my gaze to André who is still standing in the circle of buttercups. He looks afraid to move, afraid to come close to me and Renée; afraid of what would happen if he were to interfere and help me and not her. Shaking my head, I look back to Renée and take a deep breath. Raising my hands up, I summon the fire that I feel surging in my blood and with the memory of almost setting Vincent's apartment on fire, I let a ball of roaring hot fire loose from my hands and hit Renée square in the chest.

She seems to be flying backwards in slow motion. Renée finally lands at the base of a large willow tree near the water surrounding the summer island. Placing her hand on the scorched edges of her robe and black marks on her exposed skin, she stands slowly.

"Well," she begins as her voice becomes less arrogant than before, "that was unexpected."

I'll probably regret it, but I smirk arrogantly and place my hands on my hips, squaring off my feet and shoulders, "I guess I pack more of a punch than you thought I would."

Renée shifts her gaze over me slowly, I guess trying to figure out what I would do next. Smirking, she looks to André and points to me, "Get a load of her, father. Did you give her that little boost of power?"

André shakes his head, his warm honey brown eyes never leaving me, "No, I didn't. Vivienne's power will never truly go away Renée. What she showed you is in her blood and her blood alone. No amount of the emerald's power or mine courses through her."

Renée grins, her perfect white teeth gleaming maniacally in the shifting light of the afternoon, "Well then that means your precious Vivienne is mortal. And that also allows me to do this." She appears next to me in an instant, almost flying towards me against the soft summer breeze. Taking my arm, she twists it behind me and pulls until I feel the pop of my shoulder coming out of the socket.

"No!" I scream at the top of my lungs in pain. Tears pool in my eyes and stream down my face. She pulls on my arm again and I scream louder, my cries bouncing off the trees and echoing across the other islands.

I can hear Renée's teeth grinding in my ear as she twists my arm and laughs as my painful cries rip from my burning lungs. With her teeth clenched, she rubs her cheek against mine and breaths heavily, "This is nothing compared to what I will do to you if you blast me again with another fire ball."

She pushes me to the ground and I grab my arm, pressing my face into the dirt. Tears are still streaming down my face and I kick my bare feet against the path beneath me. Rolling onto my side, I watch as Aeron rushes towards Renée and topples her to the dirt path beneath her. Climbing on top of her, he starts punching her face. Blow after blow against the face and Renée continues to laugh as blood starts to come out her nose and her eye swells. I watch as she places her long talon like fingers into the soft earth beneath her and with a push of energy, vines and roots thrust from the earth and rip Aeron off his sister.

Struggling against his confines, he glares at Renée, "You bitch!"

Renée stands slowly, her hand rubbing her face. When her hand falls once again back to her side, she is as perfect as she was before Aeron had tackled her to the ground. With a roll of her eyes, she walks over to Aeron and shakes her head, "Tsk tsk, brother. I told you before, choose her side and suffer my wrath. Well, this is my wrath."

"Having a tree hold me captive is what I'm supposed to fear, Renée?" Aeron smirks as he continues to struggle against the tight hold of the vines, "For some strange reason I thought that your wrath would be a little bit more painful."

Renée tilts her head to one side like a curious child. A slow sly smile tugs at the corners of her crimson lips and she opens both hands, palms wide and the vines begin to stretch, pulling on Aeron's limbs, "You want painful, Aeron? I can give you painful."

"Stop!"

I stand up slowly, holding my arm. With long deep breaths, I slowly make my way over to Aeron and Renée and shake my head, "Stop this. You two are acting as if this is life or death. This power struggle between the two of you is childish and selfish."

Renée turns to me and places her hand on my dislocated shoulder and pushes hard, "This is a matter of life or death, Vivienne; yours."

I roar in pain, my face red from straining. I pull my head back and spit in her face, the action causing her to pull back from me, taking the pressure off my shoulder. Taking the time given, I struggle backward holding onto my bad arm.

"All you're doing Renée is upsetting me," I blurt out, hoping that she'll not see through my bluff. This way I can try to keep her at bay for even a moment so I can give myself time to push my arm back in the socket. "André always said my power lies in my temper."

Renée rolls her eyes as she wipes off my spit, "I'm sorry to burst your bubble Vivienne, but André is a fool. All he's ever wanted was to bring you here to live with us and to make you one of us. You have no other purpose in this world other than to be at our father's beck and call. He didn't need you here; he just thought that he did. André should have stayed in the mortal realm he created and leave us be! It's entirely your fault that we even had to go look for you. It's your fault that André vanished in the first place! So now we are here in this realm, are you trying to fight for your place in our world or in yours? Ha! You are nothing but a weakling, sister —nothing but a cowering mortal that has no knowledge of what she is getting herself into."

From behind Renée, Aeron pulls himself loose from his confines now that I have Renée's attention. I try to keep my gaze on Renée as Aeron moves behind her, but I can tell Renée knows what's going on. Turning quickly, she takes our brother by the neck and lifts him off the ground, "What do you think you are doing, Aeron?"

He smirks as he is suspended in the air. He struggles against her grasp and smiles, "You said something rather interesting a moment ago." He peels Renée's hand away from his neck and lands on the ground softly, "You just said that Vivienne has no knowledge of what she is getting herself into."

"So?" She replies, her shoulder shrugging as if his statement has no meaning to her.

Aeron smirks and pushes Renée out of the way, shoving her to the ground. Jumping over her in one leap, he grabs me, pops my shoulder back into place and rests his hands on my head. Suddenly, a green light surrounds me and I scream out in pain as more memories flood my mind. My eyes open and my gaze blurs as I stare up at Aeron. His eyes are usually a cool and collected blue, but they are now pitch black as his power rises out of him and shift into my body. My breathing becomes labored and I am fighting the urge to push him away, to stop this onslaught of pain and power. As the urge rises stronger inside me, Aeron rips himself from me and I scream loudly and thrust my head back and spread my arms wide.

I feel a strong power inside of me, pulsing as if it were my own blood. I lower my head so it is almost resting on my chest. My arms are now at my sides and I feel myself floating just off the dirt path.

"What in the name of the spirits did you just do Aeron?" Renée demands, stalking her way over to where he lay on the ground. Picking him up off the dirt path with one hand as if he were a rag doll, she lets out a low growl, "You are a stupid, stupid god! No, you're not even a god anymore." She throws him back to the earth, his head hitting the dirt and blood comes from his nose, "You are a mortal now."

Aeron sits up and stares at his sister. With a shake of his head and a smirk, he points to me, "She has knowledge now —all knowledge."

"I am all knowing."

My voice doesn't sound like me. I hear an echo in my head as I speak; it's almost as if I am no longer in control —Knowledge now has control of me. "We are the beginning. We are the end. Fate is at our fingertips and we will make her suffer the wrath of Knowledge."

Extending my hand out, palm facing Renée, I send a bombardment of fireballs at her. Scorching every flimsy piece of fabric dangling off her strong form, I slowly step forward. Renée grabs my shoulders, fully intent on causing me more pain, but I am healed and feel nothing but the power coursing through my body.

"You can't hold onto knowledge for very long Vivienne," she sneers at me, "you weren't built to withstand all of the world's intelligence."

I shake my head at her, "No, we are not built to withstand the power of Knowledge, but you are not built to withstand the power of the emerald. The emerald is more powerful than the earth itself. It is the heartbeat of both realms and with its power coursing through your veins, you are killing the world."

André comes between us, pushing us apart. Glaring at Renée, he shakes his head and turns to me, "You can't keep Aeron's power. It isn't fair."

Without even giving me a chance to answer, he rips the power from me without even placing his hand fully on my forehead. His left hand extends out to Aeron who still lays motionless on the dirt path at our feet. He convulses as his mortal frame once again glows green with his god-like aura.

I fall to my knees, as I am once again powerless against my sister's seamlessly never ending threats. I don't know what to do —I am once again mortal. Renée lets out a sinister laugh as she pushes André out of the way and lifts me off the ground. I lay limp in her hands, feeling defeated and broken in her arms.

"Awe, are we giving up Vivienne?" Her voice is mocking me. I have no energy to care how she is speaking to me. "You are making this too easy, sister. You are tired and sore and in way over your head. Even with knowledge you were too weak to take me on. No one can defeat Fate. I am forever!"

Forever.

Fate may be forever, but it is not the end all, be all. Fate is always there, yes, but she can only take you so far before you have to take matters into your own hands. Lowering my gaze, I see the emerald hanging around her neck on a thick silver link chain. I smirk and shake my head at her, causing her to tilt her head at me in confusion.

"What are you smiling about?"

I smirk and wink at her, "This."

I kick my feet, struggling against her grasp. She lets go as I squirm hard against her hands. As I slide down, I grab hold of the emerald and pull it from around her neck, and hear her scream in response, "This stone is something you'll never understand! Only I can understand what it means to be the carrier of its magic. And you, my dear sister, are nothing more than a selfish god that needs to pick on the weak to make yourself feel more powerful. Fate may be what you are, but free will is where we are set apart. And it is free will that sets me free!"

Taking the stone, I violently send it smashing to the ground.

"No! Don't do it Vivienne!" She is pleading with me. How nice.

I grin at her and shake my head as my foot comes down hard against the stone. Breaking apart beneath my bare foot, I feel the stone cutting into my skin, my blood mixing with the jagged pieces of the stone I have spent my entire life searching for. A wild wind swirls around me as a pulsing green energy fills my body, causing me to convulse and writhe against the air as I am lifted off the ground. I feel myself becoming suspended in the air, rising up into the sky on a green cloud of power swirling around me and fighting its way into every pore of my body. My mortal clothes are torn away as the power surges through me, leaving me bare. A scream is torn from my throat and my lungs feel as if they are on fire. Sparks shoot off my fingertips and a sweaty sheen appears on my skin. The power is so loud it is drowning out all other noises. I think I can hear Vincent. I try to focus my eyes on where he is coming from, but the energy swirling around me is too great and making my vision hazy. I think he is shouting at me —no —he is shouting at André. Vincent is begging him to stop this so he can bring me home.

Home.

A lazy, contented smile slides across my lips and I am suddenly feeling a peace I have never felt before. I want to go home and the thought of France brings me down to the ground slowly.

"What's wrong with Vivienne?" It's Vincent. His voice I would recognize anywhere and it sounds more scared than I have ever heard it before.

I slowly open my eyes; it's a struggle as my body feels sluggish. But through my lethargy, I feel a smile cross my lips, "Vincent, you're here. Oh I'm so happy."

"Yes, Vivienne, I am here." Though my eyes are open, I can't see anything but a red hue that surrounds me. Maybe it's still the sky I see, but something in my head tells me it's me, not the sky. "Vivienne, you are glowing red. What is happening to you?"

I smile, another lazy smile that makes me feel at peace, "I'm moving on. Death isn't so scary, you know. I don't know why we have feared it." I let out a small laugh at my thought. "Vincent I can see it. It's red and it glows brilliantly. There is a wild wind here. I want to ride it home."

"Home, yes," he replies, I can tell in his voice that he doesn't know what I am talking about, "Let's go home. I'll have André heal you and we can go home."

I shake my head or at least I think I shake my head, "I am home Vincent." I take his hand and place it on my stomach, "Come home with me. We can raise her together."

His hand splays wide on my bare stomach and I hear a hitch in his voice as he chokes back a sob, "Raise who?"

I laugh; it's a shallow sound that I can barely hear. The heat in my blood is rising again and I feel fire boiling beneath my skin still heated from the surge of power. I am going home. I smell ashes and smoke —it's coming from me.

I let out one final scream as the fire of rebirth overtakes me.

Conquering Fate was only the beginning —Understanding Knowledge is the key to the end